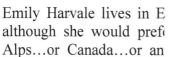

Emily Harvale lives in E
although she would prefe
Alps…or Canada…or an
months of snow. Emily loves snow almost as much
as she loves Christmas.

Having worked in the City (London) for several years, Emily returned to her home town of Hastings where she spends her days writing. And wondering if it will snow.

You can contact her via her website, Twitter, Facebook or Instagram.

There is also a Facebook group where fans can chat with Emily about her books, her writing day and life in general. Details are on the 'For You' page of Emily's website.

Author contacts:
www.emilyharvale.com
www.twitter.com/emilyharvale
www.facebook.com/emilyharvalewriter
www.instagram.com/emilyharvale

***

Scan the code above to see all Emily's books on Amazon

Also by this author:

Highland Fling
Lizzie Marshall's Wedding
The Golf Widows' Club
Sailing Solo
Carole Singer's Christmas
Christmas Wishes – Two short stories
A Slippery Slope
The Perfect Christmas Plan – A novella
Be Mine – A novella
***

The Goldebury Bay series:
Book One – Ninety Days of Summer
Book Two – Ninety Steps to Summerhill
Book Three – Ninety Days to Christmas
***

The Hideaway Down series:
Book One – A Christmas Hideaway
Book Two – Catch A Falling Star
Book Three – Walking on Sunshine
Book Four – Dancing in the Rain
***

Hall's Cross series
Deck the Halls
The Starlight Ball
***

Michaelmas Bay series
Christmas Secrets in Snowflake Cove
Blame it on the Moonlight

The Cottage

on

Lily Pond Lane

Emily Harvale

ISBN 978-1-909917-34-7

Published by Crescent Gate Publishing

Print edition published worldwide 2018
E-edition published worldwide 2018

Editor Christina Harkness

Cover design by JR, Luke Brabants and Emily
Harvale

This book is dedicated to David Cleworth.
Thank you for always being there.

Acknowledgements

My grateful thanks go to the following:

Christina Harkness for her patience and care in editing this book.
My webmaster, David Cleworth who does so much more than website stuff.
My cover design team, JR.
Luke Brabants. Luke is a talented artist and can be found at: www.lukebrabants.com
My wonderful friends for their friendship and love. You know I love you all.
All the fabulous members of my Readers' Club. You help and support me in so many ways and I am truly grateful for your ongoing friendship. I wouldn't be where I am today without you.
My Twitter and Facebook friends, and fans of my Facebook author page. It's great to chat with you. You help to keep me (relatively) sane!
Thank you for buying this book.

The Cottage on

Lily Pond Lane

Part One:

New beginnings

Chapter One

Mia Ward tugged on the handbrake of her newly-purchased, second-hand 4X4 and breathed a sigh of relief that she had made it. At least as far as the outskirts of Little Pondale. She stared at the signpost to her right, still unable to fully take in the fact that she, a city-girl to the core, was moving to a thatched cottage in this tiny and remote seaside village – a village she didn't know existed until seven weeks ago.

It was all so unbelievable. A fairy tale come true, some might say. Although Mia wasn't convinced this one would have a happy ending. Muddy fields, trampled by a variety of animals ranging from horses, cows and sheep, to ducks, geese and chickens, not to mention the field full of Llamas, yes Llamas, she had passed five minutes ago, might appeal to some, but not one of the creatures was on Mia's list of favourite things. Neither were seagulls, which had been bombarding her vehicle with foul-smelling bombs of bird poo since the moment she had turned onto Seaside

Road. She felt about as welcome to the south coast of England as the German Luftwaffe had been in the Second World War.

Despite her apprehension and a niggling worry that she may be trampled to death by large, unpleasant farm creatures the minute she got out of her vehicle, she had to admit she was excited. She couldn't wait to see the cottage.

Sunbeam Cottage on Lily Pond Lane.

Even the name sounded jolly, bright and optimistic. And she could do with some of that.

Seven weeks ago she had been struggling to pay her rent after losing both her job and her boyfriend in rapid succession. Although in truth neither was a great loss. Whitley, Smythe and Black might be one of the top five accountancy firms in London but the pay was dismal and the working conditions weren't much better. The partners had plush, gleaming white offices so large that it took a good two minutes to walk across the dove-grey carpet from the doorway, to the floor to ceiling window of each overlooking the traffic-jammed streets below. Mia and the other admin staff were squeezed into row upon row of miniscule, soul-less 'pods'; the only light beamed down on them from halogen bulbs, like mini UFOs, embedded in white, false ceilings. Several times, Mia had wished that one of them would 'beam her up'. The air conditioning was so cold the staff all had to wear cardigans or jumpers even when it was 80 degrees outside with steam rising from the roads. Scrooge himself, might have had qualms.

Mia was definitely better off without her rat of a boyfriend. One week after losing her job he dumped her because, he said, she wasn't spontaneous enough for his liking. The irony of that wasn't lost on her considering the reason she had been fired was due to her spontaneity. Admittedly on that occasion it was probably more to do with the copious amounts of alcohol she had consumed, but even so. She had been spontaneous. So much so that she and 'the rat' had been caught, almost having sex on her boss's desk at the annual, end-of-the-financial-year office party. They didn't actually get as far as doing the deed, but far enough for her boss to nearly have an apoplexy on the spot when he opened the door and found them. A few days later, Mia no longer had a job. Some things, it seemed, were unforgivable in the eyes of Whitley, Smythe and Black, but over-billing clients and acting for several rather shady characters was apparently fine. Not that Mia was bitter or anything.

She could have fought her dismissal. But this wasn't her first warning. She had also received a warning last Christmas, for asking one of the firm's 'celebrity' clients whether it was really necessary to wear a real fur coat in this day and age and explaining just how abhorrent that was to most people. Another act of spontaneity on Mia's part, as she had reminded the rat when he dumped her.

It was okay for him. He could afford to be spontaneous. He lived on a trust fund and had a life-long career at his dad's law firm. Mia had a student loan she was still trying to repay – and her dad died two weeks after she left university. That was how she had come to work at Whitley, Smythe and Black. A friend of a friend of her mum's had offered her a temporary job at the firm to "help take her mind off the tragedy". That was nearly twelve years ago. Mia had been stuck in a soul-less pod at Whitley, Smythe and Black ever since.

Perhaps the rat did have a point after all.

The only downside of being fired was that Mia hadn't realised just how hard it would be to find a new job. Particularly without a glowing reference. The rat, she soon discovered, she could easily live without. Money was another matter. And she couldn't ask her mum for a loan. Not again. At least not until her miniscule savings ran out. Lori Ward would willingly hand over the cash, but it would be accompanied by a lengthy but well-meaning lecture on her only daughter's choices, and endless concerned questions about where, exactly, Mia was heading in life. And Mia wasn't ready for that, especially as she appeared to be heading nowhere.

But her dad's two favourite sayings of 'time changes everything' and 'when one door closes, somewhere a window opens' seemed to be true.

Time had definitely changed everything, and it wasn't merely a window that had opened. It was the door to an entire cottage. Someone called Matilda Ward had died, at the ripe old age of ninety-nine from natural causes, and left her great-niece, Mia Ward, a substantial legacy.

Seven weeks ago, Mia had not known that she had a great-aunt Matilda, let alone that she would be a beneficiary in Matilda's will. Now Mia had inherited Sunbeam Cottage and all its contents, on Lily Pond Lane in the seaside village of Little Pondale. There was just one condition. She had to live in the cottage for one entire year, after which, it was Mia's to do with as she pleased. There was an additional bequest of ten thousand pounds which was to be paid to Mia immediately and was hers, regardless.

Mia may not have heard of Matilda Ward but Matilda clearly knew about Mia. And that was a bit of a mystery. A mystery Mia was now determined to solve.

Mia glanced at her best friend Ella, who was snoring softly beside her in the passenger seat, before checking the rear-view mirror to ensure that Ella's brother, Garrick, was still following behind in his van. In a moment, she would take the turning three metres ahead on the right and after another four metres, she would reach her destination. A fact the Satnav had now informed her for the third time as she waited for the tractor in front of her to move. She had no idea why it had stopped in the middle of the narrow lane. It appeared from a field, without warning, a mile or so back and trundled along at a pace even a snail would find tedious before suddenly coming to a halt. Now it seemed to be turning, although the driver gave no indication of quite what he was intending to do. He shunted back and forth and Mia craned her neck to try to see where he could possibly be going. Was he trying to turn around and go back the way he'd come? She suddenly spotted a small gap between the hedge. He appeared to be manoeuvring to reverse through the gap. If he managed that, she'd applaud him although why he didn't simply drive straight in was beyond her comprehension.

Ella let out a yawn and stretched as Mia turned off the Satnav midway through its fourth pronouncement.

'Did I nod off? Sorry. Are we there yet?'

Mia grinned at her. 'Yes to both. We're on what is laughingly called Seaside Road. As you can see it's no more than a lane. According to the signpost,' she said, pointing to it, 'we're now in Little Pondale and the Satnav informed me several times that we're only seven metres or so from our destination. We've got to take the next turning on the right and that should take us directly into Lily Pond Lane. But unless this guy gets a spurt on, we may not get there until after dark.'

Ella sat upright, shook her mop of blonde curls and, yawning again, peered through the windscreen.

'So where's the sea?'

Mia shrugged. 'I caught a glimpse of it a couple of miles back but the minute we turned onto Seaside Road it disappeared behind a wall of green stuff.'

'What's this guy doing?' Ella nodded at the tractor.

'Trying to perform a small miracle. He seems to be attempting to get that large tractor into that tiny opening.'

Ella grinned. 'Said the tart to the vicar.' She winked and leant forward as Mia tutted loudly. Since Ella had spent Easter at her elderly uncle Bert's, she had picked up his favourite quip – and used it every chance she got, no matter how stupid or inappropriate it was. 'Now what's he doing?'

Ella and Mia exchanged glances as the hunky looking driver got out of the tractor and vanished into the hedge. A moment later he reappeared. With a brief wave of his hand, he doffed his flat cap, smiled, got back in and reversed the tractor out of sight in a matter of seconds.

Ella gasped. 'Bloody Nora! Did you see that?'

Bloody Nora was another little gem from Ella's uncle Bert's repertoire. Mia loved her best friend to bits, but sometimes she wished Ella wasn't quite so easily influenced.

Mia nodded. 'It was incredible. He's a better driver than I thought.'

'Driver? I meant him, Mia. Did you see *him*?'

'Of course I saw him.'

'Then why aren't you having palpitations? Unless my eyes are deceiving me, that guy puts the yum into yummy. He looked gorgeous.'

Mia frowned. 'I didn't notice his looks but he did seem rather hunky.' She was clearly more pre-occupied than she realised. 'Where would he be on the list?'

The list was a non-existent document containing the attributes required by men for Ella and Mia to consider them 'the perfect man'. The more attributes each man had, the higher up the list they went. *The rat* had made it halfway up. The list needed revising, in Mia's opinion. As far as 'the perfect man' was concerned, the rat had been a long way off.

'Pretty close to the top, from what I could see.' Ella fanned herself with her phone. 'Damn. I should've taken his picture.'

A toot of a horn made them both jump.

Mia glanced in the rear-view mirror. 'Garrick's clearly getting impatient.'

Now that the tractor was out of the way, she let the handbrake off and pressed her foot gently down on the accelerator. As they neared the gap in the hedge at a crawl, both she and Ella turned their heads to the left. The tractor driver had got out again and was closing a gate. He glanced up, took off his flat cap, shook his lustrous hair which was the colour of midnight, winked and smiled at them as they drove past.

Ella was right. He would definitely be near the top of the list. Mia was so busy taking stock of his visual attributes, she had to swerve to avoid driving into the hedge.

Chapter Two

'This is Lily Pond Lane,' Mia announced, driving slowly into the lane after turning off Seaside Road.

The first thing Mia spotted was the large pond to her left, its glass-like blue-grey surface shimmering in the afternoon sunlight. Brightly coloured ducks swam serenely between huge Lily leaves and pink Lily buds, whilst a conga-like trail of fluffy ducklings paddled feverishly behind their mother, bumping into the leaves, and each other, in their haste, like tiny dodgem cars. It was the picture of tranquillity, even to a city-girl like her. The pond was surrounded by meadow-grass with clumps of tulips and wild, spring flowers and one ancient-looking tree, dressed in pink blossom. A cherry tree perhaps. Mia's knowledge of trees extended to the fact that each one had a trunk, branches and leaves and one or two had blossoms of varying colours. That was about it. Which made this move even more bizarre. As her mum, Lori had reminded her when Mia said she intended to move to the cottage she had inherited.

Ella fidgeted in her seat. 'Bloody Nora, Mia! I'm sure I've seen this place on a box of chocolates.' She glanced at Mia and the grin turned to a look of concern. 'Is this it? Is this Little Pondale? Just this lane, that pond, that sort of village green, the church at the end, that hill and a couple of rows of cottages?'

Mia shook her head and a strand of golden-brown hair that had worked its way free from her ponytail, flopped into her eyes. She pushed it behind her ear and looked Ella in the eye.

'It seemed bigger on Google maps. I think there's another lane of cottages behind the church because I can see some rooftops.' She tipped her head towards the church directly ahead and the lane snaking up the hill behind it, dotted with cottages and then pointed to the other side of the pond and village green. 'And another leading from the church, heading in the opposite direction but that's about it.'

'No Starbucks? No pizzeria? No shops? There must at least be a pub! Please tell me there's a pub.' Ella grabbed Mia's forearm, harder than she had possibly intended, causing Mia to swerve slightly to the left.

'Don't panic or we'll end up in that pond. I'm sure there was a pub. Yes look! There it is. Right beside the church. The Frog and Lily, I think the sign says.'

Mia slammed on the brakes and even though she hadn't been driving at more than fifteen miles per hour, the screech of tyres behind told her that Garrick's van had almost hit her 4x4. Ella's hands shot to the dashboard in a dramatic fashion as if to stop her careering forward.

'Jesus, Mia! I almost went through the windscreen.'

'Don't exaggerate. Sorry, but I just realised, if I can see the pub then I might've passed the cottage. I remember it being about halfway up the lane, according to the map. She turned in her seat to look behind her down the lane. 'Oh my God!' She almost jumped out of her skin as Garrick's face appeared at her window. He didn't look pleased.

'I nearly rear-ended you. Why the hell did you swerve then stop like that? And earlier, you almost drove into a hedge. Or did that have something to do with the pair of you ogling that farmer?' He frowned at Mia and ran a hand through his mop of sandy-brown hair. 'I know you've only had this car for two days and you're still getting used to it, but please be careful. God alone knows where the nearest garage is. Or the hospital. Let's at least get you moved in before we need to find either one.' He let out a sigh and rested one tanned forearm on the open window, appearing more relaxed as he glanced over his shoulder. 'Is this it?'

Mia shrugged an apology. 'Sorry. I don't know. I just know it was halfway up.'

'Said the vicar to the tart,' Ella quipped. 'Why don't these cottages have numbers? At least then we'd have some idea.'

'They have names instead,' Mia pointed out.

'Then they should be in alphabetical order. Go and look, Garrick. What's that one called?'

Garrick frowned at his twin sister but crossed the lane and looked for the name of the thatched cottage opposite while Ella rummaged in her bag for something and Mia tried, yet again, to get this whole thing to sink in.

'I still can't really believe this. Seven weeks ago I was having Sunday lunch with Mum and Vernon and now I'm here in Little Pondale.'

Vernon Brett, the family solicitor and life-long family friend, had been the one to give Mia the news of her inheritance. He had been contacted by great-aunt Matilda's solicitor who had been told to get in touch with Vernon in the event of Matilda's death. Matilda's solicitor had written to Vernon with details of the will and informed him that the keys to Sunbeam Cottage, together with the sum of ten thousand pounds would be handed over once Mia had signed various documents. It all happened so fast that Mia half-expected to wake up and discover it had all been a rather wonderful but mysterious dream. Yet here she was, seven weeks later, scanning a row of thatched cottages to find Sunbeam Cottage – her new home.

Ella pulled a scrunchie band from her bag and used it to tie back her hair. 'I know. It's weird how quickly things can change. One minute you think the world's coming to an end. The next you've inherited a cottage and you're about to embark on an entirely new life. It's a lot to take in.'

'You're telling me.' Mia nodded.

Her mum had been as stunned as Mia, by the news. The only thing Lori Ward said she knew about Matilda Ward was that Matilda was a blood relative of Mia's dad, Ernest. He had mentioned Matilda on only one occasion, saying that he had an aunt who was an outcast from the family and that "Trouble was Aunt Matilda's middle name." Lori said that she had coaxed him to say more at the time but he knew little of the woman. Matilda had been ostracised when Ernest was a very young boy and her name had never been mentioned again. There were no photos, letters or any papers relating to her in his belongings when he passed away. Ernest was an only child and his parents, who had Ernest late in their lives, died long before him. No other relative at his funeral knew anything of Matilda Ward, although Lori hadn't asked about her other than to enquire if Matilda had been notified. That was only because an ethereal figure, dressed in an elegant, ankle-length, black gown and wearing a large-brimmed black hat had stood at the back of the church during the service, and in the distance at the graveside. It had been Mia who had pointed out the seemingly ghostly figure and the woman had disappeared before anyone had a chance to speak to her. No one knew who she was.

When Vernon broke the news of the inheritance to Mia and Lori, both of them remembered the woman dressed in black, and wondered if that woman could have been Matilda.

'It's a shame Mum's not here,' Mia added. 'I can't wait to see what she thinks of this village.'

Lori would have been with Mia, had it not been for the fact that she was on her annual six-week cruise with her book club. A cruise she would have tried to cancel had Mia not persuaded her there was no need. When Lori learnt that Ella and Garrick would be helping her daughter to settle in and would be staying with her for a week or two, she was more at ease, but she assured her daughter that the minute she returned, she would be paying an extended visit to Mia and Sunbeam Cottage.

'Knowing Lori,' Ella said, grinning, 'the first thing she'll do when she arrives is start a book club.'

'Tumblewell,' Garrick yelled, making both Mia and Ella jump. He walked back down the lane a few paces to the next nearest cottage. 'And this one's called Duckdown. What's your one called again?'

'Sunbeam Cottage,' Mia shouted, leaning her head out the window. 'Hold on. I'll check out Google maps again to see exactly where it is. According to the Satnav, it should be somewhere here.'

'No you won't.' Ella waved her phone in the air. 'There's no signal. Where the hell are we? Fairy tale land? Don't they have mobile phones here?'

Mia checked hers anyway. 'You're right.' She waved her phone in front of Ella. 'Nothing. Not even one little bar.'

Ella leant across Mia and yelled at her brother. 'Check that big yellow one out.' She pointed at the next cottage up the lane.

'It won't be that one,' Mia said, shoving Ella off her in a friendly manner. 'That one's huge compared to the rest of the cottages we've passed.'

Ella pulled a face. 'Not one of them can be described as huge, Mia. They're all so twee I half expect a beautiful princess, together with seven vertically challenged men, singing songs and carrying pickaxes, to march down the York stone paths. But it's yellow, and your cottage is called Sunbeam.'

Mia grinned at her. Ella was right. The cottages were idyllic. Each had a thatched roof, although some of them looked as if they needed a haircut, and each had its façade painted a bright colour, with a matching chimney and a complementary-coloured front door. Some window boxes filled with vivid blooms; one had a white picket fence bordering the lane and each one had a long front garden brimming over with colourful flowers and plants.

'It's the big one,' Garrick shouted, pointing to the yellow cottage just ahead as he made his way back to them.

'You see,' Ella threw Mia a smug smile. 'Told you so.'

Garrick stopped beside Mia's window and bent down to eye level. 'It's got a driveway to the side so we can get the vehicles off the road. That's a godsend seeing how narrow this lane is. You go first and I'll follow you in.' He gave a mischievous grin. 'But try not to slam on your brakes again. Okay?'

Chapter Three

Mia edged onto the driveway and made sure she positioned her vehicle as close to the cottage as she could, leaving plenty of space for Garrick and his van.

'Wow.' Ella shoved open the door and stepped out. 'Forget chocolate box. This place is the cherry in the brandy, as Uncle Bert would say. What d'you think, Garrick? Could you live here?'

Garrick's face flushed the colour of a cherry as he walked towards her, his gaze darting to Mia then the cottage and back to Ella. 'What? Yeah. Why not? There's a pub at the end of the lane. If it serves food, I could probably live here, and if it has a large screen TV and sports channels, definitely.'

'At least there're street lights,' Mia said, surprised by the fact. 'I was a bit concerned there might not be.'

Garrick nodded followed by a grin. 'I'm surprised at that. But they have electricity even in the back of beyond. Gas may be a different matter. Some places have electric storage heaters, and places like this often have oil for central heating, assuming it has central heating.'

Ella paled. 'Please tell me it does.' She stared at Mia. 'I can't live without central heating. I know it's May and it's supposed to be spring but it's still cold in the evenings and I can't get up in the morning unless it's a balmy 20 degrees. You know that.'

Mia was equally concerned. 'It hadn't even occurred to me to ask. I assumed it would.'

'I'm sure it'll have a fireplace,' Garrick said. 'Or possibly a wood burning stove, so you two won't freeze to death.' He must have seen the bemused looks they exchanged because he laughed. 'Don't worry. I know how to make a fire and I can chop wood.'

'But how do you know there's any wood to chop?' Mia asked. 'Or anything to chop it with.'

'The clue is in the trees I can see from here in your garden. If there isn't a wood store somewhere, I can lop a few branches off one of those. I know we haven't seen much of each other for the last five years, but surely you remember what I do for a living?'

'Of course I remember.' Mia rolled her eyes. 'I just didn't link the beautiful furniture you make, with chopping down trees. I assumed you had the wood shipped in.'

'I often do. But sometimes I like to find my own. I have saws, and an axe oddly enough, in the van. There's nothing quite as exhilarating as seeing a tree in its natural environment and picturing all the things I can do with it.'

'I feel that way about men,' Ella joked.

Mia laughed. 'And I can think of several things far more exhilarating than staring at a tree.' She pulled a face at Garrick. 'Don't you feel guilty when you cut them down? Trees have feelings too, you know.'

'Yeah right. The closest you've ever been to a tree is sitting on a wooden chair. Do you think it made itself?' he teased.

Mia stuck out her tongue. 'Just don't chop off your own leg or something.'

'Don't worry about him,' Ella said. 'He's a jack-of-all-trades when it comes to wood, and he's pretty good at other stuff too. He's even improved over the last few years since he moved up North, but he's still the same old Garrick. And I don't mean old in age, of course. Just in attitude and aptitude.'

'Thanks.' Garrick threw Ella a sarcastic look before returning his attention to Mia. 'And just when I decide to move back down to London, you decide to move out here, so I'm not sure we'll be seeing much more of each other in the future.' He let out a lengthy sigh, as if that thought disappointed him. 'Anyway, let's get inside and see what's what. If I need to get some wood, I'll do that first before we unload and before it starts to get dark.'

Mia edged her way past a prickly hedge with lots of orange berries and stepped onto a narrow wooden walkway which led from the driveway to the front door. The boards creaked beneath her feet and she glanced down, hoping they wouldn't give way. The last thing she needed was a broken ankle or to get her foot stuck in a hole the moment she arrived. Worse still, her leg could be grabbed by some creature lurking beneath the boards.

'You won't fall through,' Garrick said, as if reading her mind. 'They're pretty solid. They're simply creaking because wood expands and shrinks. Nothing to worry about.'

Reassured, Mia walked to the door, put the key in the lock, glanced at Ella and Garrick and took a deep breath. 'Here goes. I'm telling you now, if the place is full of cobwebs I'm not going in.'

'I'll deal with any cobwebs,' Garrick said. 'And any spiders. Do you want me to go first?'

Mia shook her head. 'Thanks, but I need to do this. I'm excited to see what I've inherited. I'm merely a little anxious, that's all.' She turned the wrought-iron knob and with hardly any effort on her part, the door flew open and thumped against the wall of the hallway. 'I wasn't expecting that.' She grinned at Ella and Garrick. 'I thought it would creak and groan like the walkway.'

'The hinges could do with tightening,' Garrick said. 'And a doorstop inside may be a good idea.' He followed Mia and Ella into the hall. 'Not a cobweb in sight.'

Mia gasped as she took in her surroundings. The walls were the colour of a summer sky interspersed with pale oak beams. The wooden floor was a shade or two darker than the walls, with a French-navy runner covering most of it. Paintings of the sea hung along the length of the hall like a row of bunting and a small, soft-white, wooden bench-seat sat beside a matching table bearing a vase of cerise tulips.

Mia turned in a circle and beamed at her friends. 'It's beautiful. I'd expected something dark, dusty and trapped in the Edwardian era, for some reason. This is almost … modern.'

'This is just the hall,' Ella said, the note of sarcasm evident as she grinned at Mia. 'Let's wait until we've seen the rest of the place before we pass judgement. But I'll admit it's a hundred times better than I thought it'd be. There's a coastal vibe about it. Which I suppose is apt as we're right by the sea.'

Mia shuddered. 'Don't remind me.' She had been afraid of water since she almost drowned at the age of six and for years she was too terrified to even look at the sea. But she had come a long way in attempting to beat her fear and she could now walk along the shore, provided not a drop of the water touched her. Not that she often went to the seaside. Probably once or twice a year, and beach holidays were a definite no-no. Which was possibly why it was taking so many years to overcome her phobia. The truth was, she wasn't really trying.

Garrick pointed to a radiator.

'Heating!' Ella yelled. She ran her hand along the top of the radiator as if she were stroking a cat then held up her palm. 'And not a speck of dust. When did you say Matilda died? Because my place is covered in dust after a week or so and this place is spotless.'

'Nine weeks ago. She was buried before the solicitors contacted Vernon. Perhaps they got someone in to clean up the place for my arrival.'

'Coo-ey!' A voice called out, and Mia, Ella and Garrick turned to see a well-rounded, elderly woman beaming at them via the open front door. 'I thought I saw you arrive, my dears. Oh goodness gracious.' She stepped into the hall and shuffled towards Mia. 'You must be Mia. You look just like dear Matilda did as a youngster. Not that I knew Matilda when she was young, of course. Oh deary me, no. She'd only recently moved here, but we became friends immediately and I saw a photograph once of her as a girl. Well, when I say 'friends', I mean friendly neighbours. But we're all friends in Little Pondale, unless some of us choose to keep themselves to themselves and have their little secrets. Oh deary me. I'm talking ten chickens at a time, aren't I? I'm Hettie. Hettie Burnstall. I live in Duckdown Cottage, two doors away down the lane. I clean for Matilda. Well, did clean for her. If you want me to clean for you, deary, I'd be more than happy to. It gives me something to do and puts a few pennies in my pocket. Well, how are you settling in?' She clasped her hands in front of her ample bosom and tipped her mane of grey curls to one side, a broad but inquisitive smile on her rosy lips.

'Hello, Hettie. Yes, I'm Mia. Pleased to meet you. Um. Did you say Matilda only moved here recently? I understood from the solicitor that she'd lived here for some time.'

Hettie shook her head and wagged her forefinger. 'Never believe a word a solicitor tells you, deary. All crooks and liars, every last one of them. Matilda only moved in twenty-five years ago this February. On Valentine's Day.'

Mia shot a look at Ella who looked as bemused as Mia felt, but when she glanced at Garrick, he was grinning from ear to ear.

'Hello Hettie,' he said, holding out his hand to greet her. 'I'm Garrick Swann, and this is my sister, Ella. We're here to help Mia settle in. It's good to meet you and thank you for the welcome. We'd love to stop and chat but as you rightly said, we've only just arrived. We need to unpack and find where everything is, so I'm sure you'll excuse us for this evening.' He placed an arm about the woman's shoulders as if to lead her out.

'Oh yes of course, my dears. But I can help with that.'

She took Garrick's hand in her fingers and did a sort of pirouette. The look of surprise on Garrick's face made Mia giggle but she hid it with a cough.

'We don't want to take up your time,' Mia said, regaining her composure. 'I'm sure we'll manage. But I would like to chat with you about my great-aunt sometime soon. I don't know much about her.'

'Happily, my dear. And I'm more than happy to help. Just Prince Gustav waiting for his tea but he can wait a while longer. Needs to lose some weight, according to Rupert. Rupert's the vet. He lives across the pond in Cherry Tree Cottage. Oh. Not 'the pond' as in the Atlantic Ocean, deary. I meant our Lily pond. And if you're wondering which came first, the Lily Pond or the name for Lily Pond Lane, no one knows. It's a mystery. Life is full of mysteries, don't you think?' She chuckled and shook her head. 'Deary me, there I go again, talking ten chickens at a time. What was I saying? Oh yes. Rupert. He takes such good care of Prince Gustav. Are you single, deary? Or is this handsome young man your beau?' She linked her arm through Garrick's and his face went as red as the cardigan Hettie was wearing.

'No,' Mia said. If the heat in her cheeks was any indication, she was blushing as much as Garrick seemed to be.

'She's single now,' Garrick said with a smile as he gently extricated himself from Hettie's arm.

'We're all single,' Ella added with a sigh.

Hettie beamed. 'He's single too. Rupert, the vet. Not Prince Gustav. Although he's also single. I'd like to find him a mate because we all need that special someone in our lives, don't we?'

'The vet?' Ella queried. 'You want to find the vet a mate?' She shot Mia a look as if to say, 'This woman is completely insane.'

Hettie chuckled and slapped Ella on the arm in a friendly manner. 'Deary me, no. I can see you're a box of trouble, aren't you, deary? I meant I'd like to find Prince Gustav a mate. Perhaps I shall one day. But yes, I'd also like dear Rupert to find a girlfriend. He's such a caring young man and he's gorgeous too. Do you like the chap who plays Poldark on TV? Of course you do, deary. Everyone does. But, now I think about it, Rupert's nothing like him, apart from the black hair. Do you have a pet? It doesn't matter if you don't. You can meet him in The Frog and Lily. He's thirty-five. That's about your age, isn't it?'

'I'm thirty-four,' Ella said, 'and so is Garrick. We're twins, even though we look nothing alike. Mia's thirty-three. Any other single young men around here?'

'Oh yes, deary. Plenty. You'll be spoilt for choice. It's when you get to my age they are few and far between. They're either dead or halfway there. Or married and too settled to have a bit of fun elsewhere, if you get my drift. Or too riddled with arthritis to move.'

Ella grinned at Mia. 'We saw a farmer backing his tractor into a field on Seaside Road. Black hair, gorgeous, built like a super hero, wears a flat cap, but we won't hold that against him. I'm sure you'll know who I mean. Is he single?'

Hettie positively glowed. 'You'll have to get in line for that one, deary. He's quite the catch, but no one's ever caught him. Or likely to, I'm afraid. His name's Jethro. Jethro Cross. But everyone calls him Jet. He's a bit of a bad boy but his eyes are so dreamy I'd forgive him anything. You'll do the same once you meet him. But I'd set my sights on one of the others unless you're looking for a broken heart. Now let me see. There's young Toby Bywater. He helps his dad run the pub. Not bad, if you like ginger tops. Franklin Grant. But he's American and only here for a few more months. He's staying at Little Pond Farm. Thomas Tyburn, the vicar, but he's a bit too straight and narrow for my liking. What's the point in having a confessional if you don't want your congregation to get up to mischief? Not that we have a confessional. We're Church of England, not Catholic, but you know what I mean. Oh and how could I forget Justin Lake? He's the local baker and his buns are the best for miles around. And I don't just mean the buns he bakes.' She winked. 'He's in one of those male stripper dance groups in his spare time. Often performs for the local W.I. He's got black hair too, like Rupert and Jet.' She leant forward conspiratorially. 'We're all fairly certain the grandmas of those three young bucks spent the night under the same blanket, if you get my drift.'

Garrick coughed and blinked several times. 'Thank you, Hettie. I think that's enough to be getting on with. Is the central heating, gas or oil, do you know?'

'Oh, deary me. It's wood. There's a Range in the kitchen that provides hot water and heating. Do you know how to cook on a Range, deary?' She smiled at Mia. 'I'll show you if you don't.' Without waiting for a response, she returned her attention to Garrick. 'You'll find a woodshed in the garden. Let me show you, deary.'

'Thanks, but I'm sure I'll find it,' Garrick said, smiling at Hettie. 'And we can manage the Range. You don't want to make Prince Gustav wait for his tea. We know where you are if we need any help.'

'Garrick's right,' Mia added. 'Please don't make Prince Gustav wait on our behalf. A prince should never be kept waiting and we'd feel terrible.'

'Yes,' Ella said. 'We'll walk out with you and start unloading the van. Now we know we have heating and a wood supply, we really should get started.'

'If you're sure, my dears.' Hettie allowed herself to be ushered outside, somewhat reluctantly but she turned on the walkway and poked a finger directly at Garrick's chest. 'And you needn't worry, you gorgeous boy. There're one or two single girls around here too. Unless of course you're also interested in the men, which is fine, but I don't think anyone in the village is gay. Although many of us think the vicar may be in the closet. He's definitely hiding something under that cassock and I'm certain his holier than thou demeanour is purely an act.'

Ella choked on a laugh. 'Well, that puts a whole new light on my vicar and tart jokes, doesn't it?'

Mia nudged her with an elbow and smiled at Hettie. 'Thank you for your help, Hettie. And for all the information. It was lovely to meet you. Say hello to Prince Gustav for us. He's a cat, I assume.'

'Oh no, my dear. What made you think that? Prince Gustav isn't a cat. He's a rat. A darling white rat. I was going to bring him with me but I wasn't sure you'd be pleased. Some folks are funny about rats, you know, deary. You must pop round and meet him once you've settled in.'

'Thanks. I'll do that,' Mia lied.

She had just been dumped by one rat. She was in no hurry to meet another.

Chapter Four

Knowing that she had inherited – or would inherit – not just Sunbeam Cottage but also its contents meant Mia didn't have to bring much of her own furniture, which was just as well, because she didn't own very much. What little she wanted to take with her had fit snugly into Garrick's van and her boxes and boxes of books, into the back of her 'new' 4x4, purchased with two of the ten thousand pounds she had inherited. It was Ella who suggested buying a car might be a good idea.

'You won't be able to hop on a tube, you know. And Mum said that lots of country villages depend on a limited bus service. They won't come along every ten minutes like they do in London, or three at a time. You'll be lucky if you see one bus a day. A car, or a bike, is a necessity if you ask me.'

'I haven't ridden a bike since I was twelve.' Transport problems hadn't even crossed Mia's mind until Ella mentioned it but her friend's comment had worried her. She was a keen walker but having to carry bags of shopping, especially bottles of wine, possibly for miles, was not a pleasant prospect. 'I can't afford a car. There must be taxis, surely?'

Ella had shrugged. 'Don't know. But you can afford a car. You've just had ten thousand pounds deposited in your bank account, remember? On second thoughts, you'll need one of those off-road thingies. A 4x4 or something. Garrick's home tomorrow. He can help you get what you'll need.'

Garrick had helped. He had also managed to get the car salesman to knock five hundred pounds off the asking price so Mia got her 'pre-loved' as the dealership called it, 4x4 for a few pounds under two thousand. It was old but it had a full-service history and Garrick said it was good for its age. It wasn't as if Mia would be travelling miles in it. Just to the shops and back. And how far could they be?

It was a stroke of luck that Garrick had decided to move back to his roots after several years living and working in Scotland. Mia knew his move had more to do with the fact that he had ended his long-term relationship with Fiona, the girl he'd moved to Scotland to be with, rather than a longing for home, but the timing couldn't have been better as far as Mia was concerned. When Ella offered Garrick's services without even asking him, Mia felt that everything was falling into place rather nicely and that perhaps this move was the start of a whole new life for her.

Once Hettie had finally left for home, Ella grinned. 'Can you believe that? The woman is mad. Do you think all those things she said were true? And did that remark of hers about the grandmas mean that the grandmas all spent the same night with one man, d'you think? Or that they each took a turn in his bed on separate nights? And why the grandmas? Surely if the guys all look alike it'd be more likely that it was their mums who did the cheating, wouldn't it? Not the grandmas.'

Garrick frowned. 'She didn't actually say the three men looked alike, merely that they all have the same colour hair, and anyway, you shouldn't listen to gossip. Just because three men in the village have black hair, it doesn't mean they have the same paternal ancestry.'

'But it's a small village,' Ella protested.

Mia lifted a box of books from the rear seat of her 4X4 and handed it to Ella. 'What I find odd is why there seems to be so many single young men in such a tiny place. Don't you think that's weird?'

Ella gasped. 'Have you got bricks in here? Garrick, take this would you? It's heavy.'

Garrick took the box. 'Leave the heavy stuff for me. You two can unload the bags of clothes and the suitcases. I'll do the rest.'

Mia tutted. 'I can manage a few boxes, Garrick, even if Ella's a weakling.' She grinned at her best friend as Garrick strode towards the cottage.

'I'm not a weakling, I'm delicate. And I don't believe in heavy lifting if there's a man about to do it for me. As for all the single guys, I suppose it is a bit strange. But I'd rather that than no young guys at all, wouldn't you? And if there's only a couple of other single girls around, that makes it even better. I know this place is miles from civilisation but I think I like Little Pondale already. I may even stay for longer than the week or two I'd planned. That's the beauty of working for ourselves. Garrick and I can move anywhere and still earn a living. You should stay too, Garrick. Just in case we need any more heavy lifting in the future.'

Ella gave a smug smile and walked to the van to grab something light to carry. Garrick turned at the door and gave Mia an odd look. It was as if he wanted to say something but then thought better of it.

'You're both welcome to stay for as long as you want,' Mia said. 'You can help me dig up everything I can about Matilda. I really want to know who she was and why no one in my family seems to know anything about her.'

'As long as we don't have to actually dig up Matilda herself, I'm in,' Ella said. 'And so is Garrick, so there's no need to ask him.'

'Thanks for organising my life, sis,' Garrick said before stepping into the hall.

'Any time,' Ella said, and as Mia joined her at the back of the van she lowered her voice and added: 'Let's face it. He needs someone to organise it, doesn't he? He's made a complete cock-up of it so far. I told him that Fiona woman wasn't the one, but would he listen?'

Mia tugged a suitcase on to the ground. 'At least he's back now. That's the important thing. Are you serious about staying on?'

Ella winked. 'I need to check out the guys first. If they make the list, you'll have to kick me out to get me to leave.'

'I'd love you to stay. Moving to the country may not be as bad as I think it's going to be but it's always good to have a friend by your side.'

'I'll always be by your side, Mia. And so will Garrick, if you want him to be.'

For some absurd reason, an image of her and Garrick popped into Mia's head. They were old and wrinkled, sitting side by side, holding hands on a sofa. It disappeared as quickly as it came but it threw Mia off balance for a moment.

Did she still have those sort of feelings for Garrick? She was certain she had got over her crush on him years ago. Shortly after he met Fiona and declared his love for the woman, Mia realised Garrick and herself had no future together. At least, not a romantic future. They'd been life-long friends and had known one another since Mia had gone to the same playgroup as Ella and Garrick, but Garrick had never shown any romantic inclinations towards Mia. Although he had once kissed her on the lips on her sixth birthday. Ella had teased him relentlessly about it for years after. But when he moved to Scotland to be with Fiona, the whole dynamic of their relationship changed. Mia had only seen him a couple of times in the last five years, mainly at Christmas and birthdays, and she hadn't felt the slightest twinge. Not after the first few times anyway. But perhaps she hadn't buried her feelings, after all.

Mia dismissed such idiotic thoughts. What she was feeling was due to the fact that she had left behind everything she had known, and come to live in a strange place, formally owned by a woman she hadn't known existed until seven weeks ago. Her life had completely altered and she was feeling vulnerable, that was all. It was only natural that she would cling to the people and things she had known and cared for all her life.

But when Garrick brushed past her on his way back to get more boxes, she couldn't deny the tingle that shot up her arm, nor the way the smile he gave her made her smile in return.

Next she'd be carving little hearts on the trees, with the linked initials of M.W. and G.S. inside, just like she did as a girl.

God forbid.

Garrick was wonderful, handsome, kind and caring and she definitely had feelings for him. Deep feelings. But some crushes have an expiration date – and rightly so. Her rat of an ex-boyfriend might have thought Mia didn't know the meaning of spontaneity but Garrick couldn't even spell it. He never did anything until he'd weighed up the pros and cons and whys and wherefores. It had taken him more than two months to ask Fiona on a date, and several years of a long-distance relationship before he finally decided to 'take a chance' and move up North. Fiona couldn't move down South and leave her sick mother, and besides, she had an exceedingly well-paid job with one of the big oil companies and she didn't want to give that up, so for the relationship to continue he really had no choice. God alone knew at what stage Garrick had realised it was a mistake, and how long it had then taken him to decide that he should move home. He was only here now because Ella had volunteered his services without his knowledge and no matter what, he would never let his beloved sister down, or a very dear friend such as Mia. Not that any of that made him less attractive. It just somehow stopped the spark from truly igniting and consuming Mia's heart.

But no one had ever done that. Mia had fallen in and out of love several times throughout her life so far, but there had never been that all-consuming passion, that undying love she knew her Mum and Dad had felt. And Mia wanted that. Mia truly believed in 'The One'.

Garrick Swann simply wasn't it. She was pretty certain of that.

No matter how much she may still fancy him.

Chapter Five

It took about three hours to unload Mia's belongings and Garrick did most of the work, although not all of that time was actually spent unloading.

Mia and Ella realised that Hettie's sudden arrival had meant they hadn't checked out the rest of the cottage, so after carrying the first lot of suitcases into the hall, they went off to explore, leaving Garrick to his own devices.

'He won't mind,' Ella said, without asking whether or not he did. 'He's happy to feel useful again. Fiona was one of those women who insisted on doing everything herself. You know the sort. They make things very awkward for girls like me who are bone idle and would rather not lift a finger unless my life depended on it.'

Ella was joking, of course. Ella was always the first to offer to help out whenever friends or family needed anything, and she was far from bone idle. Quite the opposite, in fact. Mia glanced guiltily in Garrick's direction, then followed her friend along the hall. If Garrick needed help, he'd shout for it.

'How come Fiona's a woman and you're a girl?' Mia asked as Ella pushed open a door leading to what was clearly the dining room. 'Isn't she two years younger than you?'

Ella raised her eyebrows in mock shock before grinning. 'Yeah, but somehow she seems much older than us. Garrick says it's because Fiona behaves like an adult and I still think I'm a teenager. Which I am at heart, so he's right about that. And of course as she's some hot shot in the oil industry, she's really smart. I always think smart people act older, don't you?'

Mia didn't, but she chose not to say so.

'Why did they break up? Did Garrick tell you? You only said it was his decision but you never said why.'

Ella shrugged. 'He's being decidedly weird about the whole thing. Every time I ask he tells me to leave it, or simply changes the subject. I need to get him drunk and then he'll spill the beans. Anyway. This is the dining room.'

Mia laughed. 'So I see. As Garrick would say, I think the clue is in the dining table and chairs and that rather elegant, glass-fronted cupboard filled with expensive-looking crockery.'

Ella pulled a face. 'Moving swiftly on.' She put her hands on Mia's elbows and ushered her back into the hall, towards another closed door. 'Open it.'

Mia did, and they discovered it led into a large, cream-coloured kitchen with another door at the end which clearly led into the garden. They walked towards the door and Ella opened it on to an expanse of pale-blue-painted wooden decking. A wrought iron table and matching chairs, all painted a soft white, sat to one side of the door. To the other sat an ornate, wrought iron shelf unit, also white, and packed with pots of blooms. Beside that was a wooden bench on which multi-coloured cushions were liberally scattered. The furniture sheltered beneath a glass canopy that ran the full width of the back of the cottage. Vibrant plants tumbled from pots of various shapes and sizes sitting haphazardly around the edges of the decking. Three pale-blue wooden steps led down to a long lawn which stretched for hundreds of feet and was bounded on one side by differing species of trees and shrubs. The other side had what even Mia recognised were holly bushes, and a couple of trees bearing blossom. Maybe apple, cherry or pear. Mia had no idea about that. The lawn ended at a pale-blue fence about three feet high. Beyond that were a couple of low, sand dunes, like camel's humps, and the sea, sparkling in the final rays of the setting sun.

'Bloody Nora!' Ella dragged her gaze from the view, to Mia, who couldn't find the words to speak. 'I'm never leaving. Sorry.'

'Nor am I,' Mia said, eventually. 'Although I could do with something bigger and stronger than that fence between me and the water.'

'You'll be fine. The sea's a long way off and it's got to get over those sand dunes before it smashes through your fence.'

'Thanks.' Mia threw Ella a sarcastic look. 'That's so reassuring. But at least I know one thing about my great-aunt Matilda. The woman had impeccable taste.'

'And bundles of dosh. This place must be worth a fortune. I've got to get Garrick to see this. Garrick!' Ella yelled at the top of her lungs and dashed out of the kitchen and along the hall, leaving Mia to gaze in awe at the sunset as it threw ribbons of differing shades of red, pink and violet across an expanse of baby blue sky.

Moments later Garrick stood beside her. 'Holy shit,' he said, stepping outside and dropping down onto one of the chairs. 'I could sit and look at this view all day.'

'I'll make some tea,' Ella offered. 'We can take a break and watch the sunset before we resume unloading.'

'We?' Garrick raised his eyebrows. 'I think you mean me, don't you?' He shook his head and smiled. 'I brought a couple of bottles of champagne to celebrate Mia's new home. They're in the box I just brought in.' He went to stand but Ella put a hand on his shoulder.

'I'll get them. You stay there.' Ella winked at him. 'You need to save your strength to do the rest.'

'So considerate, as always.' He nodded and turned his attention to Mia. 'Well Mia, it looks like you were right. This place is a complete dump, isn't it?'

Mia playfully slapped his arm. He was repeating what she'd said when they had started out this morning. 'Even though it looks nice on the aerial shots on Google maps, I bet the place is a complete dump,' were her exact words. She grinned at him. 'Yep. I knew it was too good to be true.'

'Absolutely. I don't know how you're going to be able to bear looking at this view every morning when you come downstairs for coffee. You'll so miss your old view of that bus stop and the busy streets filled with cars and buses spewing out fumes. It's clearly going to be very hard for you to adapt to country life. Not that this is really country life, is it? I mean look at it. There isn't a cow, sheep or duck in sight.'

Their eyes met and they both laughed until a seagull swooped down and a long line of bird poo splattered the glass canopy above them.

Ella, who was returning with the champagne and three glasses, gave a little shriek followed by a giggle.

'That was so you don't completely lose touch with reality,' she said. 'Thank heavens there's a

41

canopy or we'd all be wearing seagull poo right now.' She put the champagne and glasses on the table but held one up in her hand and it glinted in the fading light. 'Look at these glasses. I've seen diamonds with less sparkle.'

Garrick popped the champagne cork and filled the glasses, raising his in the air. 'Here's to your good fortune and your new home, Mia.'

The glasses rang out when Mia, Ella and Garrick clinked them together.

'To you, Mia,' Ella said.

Mia smiled. 'I still can't believe this all belongs to me.'

'Technically it doesn't,' Garrick reminded her. 'Not until you've lived here for an entire year.'

Ella snorted. 'That's not going to be a hardship, is it? I know we all had doubts about it and about Mia coping with life in the country, but now that we've seen the place, I think we can all agree that it'll be one long holiday. I mean, what's not to like? The cottage is everyone's dream home. The view is to die for. There's a pub just a stumble away. The village has more single men per square inch than the whole of London. And there's even a cleaner if Mia wants one. It's paradise.'

Garrick laughed. 'Today perhaps. And possibly for a few days to come. But you're forgetting something aren't you? Unless you love the sea – which Mia doesn't, or going for long rambles, there may not be much to do around here.

Personally I'd love it but you two won't last more than a week without pining for shops, theatres and restaurants. And I don't know where you'll find a Chinese or Indian takeaway, not to mention a supermarket. I didn't spot any nearby on the way here and the last town we passed through was at least fifteen miles away.'

Mia and Ella exchanged anxious looks.

'True,' Ella said, refilling their glasses. 'But Mia's got wheels. It simply means being more organised than usual. And it'll be fun. Instead of being able to nip in and out of shops whenever we want, we'll plan daytrips to the shops instead and evenings out to restaurants. Once we know where the shops and restaurants are.'

'Good luck with that.'

'I've got lots of books I want to read,' Mia said. 'And I do like walking, I just haven't done much walking in the country. I bought boots though. Proper walking boots. And wellies too.'

Garrick grinned. 'That's you sorted then.'

'And if the worst comes to the worst,' Ella said. 'There's always Netflix. I know I could easily spend a year catching up on all the boxsets and Mia loves TV as much as I do.'

'Is there?' Garrick raised his brows. 'I didn't see a TV when I took some boxes into the living room.'

'Bloody Nora!' Ella jumped to her feet. 'There must be a TV. Everyone owns a TV. I'll go and look.'

Mia jumped up too. 'I'll come with you. There must be one somewhere.'

Garrick sighed with contentment. 'I'll stay here and watch the sun set and then continue with the unloading. Let me know if you find one, but I'll bet you a pint in the pub this evening that there isn't.'

Chapter Six

Garrick was right. There was no TV. The living room consisted of two plump sofas, a couple of armchairs, a coffee table and a few side tables, one or two cupboards, several shelves of books and a sumptuous-looking rug covering the wooden floor. There were French doors leading out onto the wooden deck and a small but ornate desk sat to one side of them. The room was bright and airy but more the type of place where people came for afternoon tea than a lounge where Mia and Ella could crash out in front of a TV.

'Perhaps she had one in her bedroom,' Ella suggested. 'She was ninety-nine after all and could've been bedridden.'

'That's a cheery thought.'

The only other room downstairs was a WC so Mia and Ella headed upstairs to search the bedrooms.

'Which one was hers?'

Mia tutted. 'How am I supposed to know that?'

Ella shrugged and opened the first door they came to. 'Bathroom. Oh look! It's one of those whirlpool baths. That's pretty snazzy. And check out that shower. It's got at least three rows of jets. Can't wait to try that out.'

'Wow!' Mia opened the shower door three times just to check that it really was one of those ones that closed silently no matter in what position you left the door. 'Matilda must've had all this put in fairly recently, don't you think? She doesn't strike me as being bedridden, for some reason.'

'Come and look at this,' Ella called from another room, so she clearly hadn't heard what Mia said. 'I think I've found Matilda's room.'

Mia followed the voice along the hall and her mouth fell open as she stepped in to the most opulent bedroom she had ever seen.

The walls were the palest lavender sheen but the massive bed, luxurious bedding and matching curtains, together with a plush armchair, were deep purple. An elegant but somewhat ostentatious mirrored-glass dressing table stood in front of a large window next to which, French doors opened onto a small balcony just large enough for a bistro table and two matching chairs. Mia reasoned the balcony must have been directly above the glass canopy because the view was the same as the one they'd been admiring a few minutes earlier. There were two sleek, glossy deep purple chests of drawers but no wardrobes.

That was until Ella leant against one of the walls and shrieked, 'Bloody Nora!' A door slid silently open and she tumbled in. An entire row of wardrobes was camouflaged along the length of that wall, as Ella proved by pushing and prodding it in various places once she'd regained her composure.

'Now that's classy,' Mia said, but goose bumps prickled her arms as she glanced inside.

Row upon row of expensive and colour co-ordinated dresses, suits, blouses, skirts and cardigans hung proudly above shelves of equally expensive shoes. One section contained enough handbags to open a store. Another, hats that had obviously made a milliner rich.

'The more I see of this place,' Ella said, running her hands almost reverently over Matilda's clothes, 'the more I wish we'd met your great-aunt Matilda.'

'Me too,' said Mia. 'And the more I wonder what on earth she could have done to make her family ostracise her.'

'Perhaps she was a high-class prostitute.'

'Trust you to think of that.'

'Well, she must've got all her dosh from somewhere, mustn't she?'

'Perhaps she had an extremely well-paid job. Like Fiona does. Only in Matilda's day there wouldn't have been the same opportunities, of course.'

Ella shook her head. 'If she had a good job, the family would've been proud of her, wouldn't they? Perhaps she fell in love with someone the family didn't approve of. That sort of thing mattered when she was young. Now, no one could care less but in those days they thought marrying beneath you was as bad as committing murder.'

'But she didn't marry. She was Matilda Ward. Miss Matilda Ward.'

'Just a lover then? A married lover. A rich married lover. Oooh! Perhaps she was a gangster's moll. Perhaps she ran off with lots of his money. That's why she was hiding in the country.'

Mia laughed. 'I think it may be a good thing we don't have a TV, after all. You've clearly been watching too much of it to come up with a story like that. And she wasn't exactly hiding, was she? No one could hide with Hettie Burnstall living two doors away and coming in to do the cleaning.'

Ella shrugged. 'Well, she must've got her money from somewhere and let's face it, your family may be comfortably off but your mum couldn't afford a place like this, could she?'

Mia shook her head. 'Nope. But if she didn't go on so many cruises with her book club she might be able to,' she joked.

'Doesn't anyone in your family know anything about Matilda?'

'No. I told you. Mum said that Dad only mentioned her once saying that he had an aunt whose middle name was trouble, or something like that. Not literally, of course. Her middle name was actually Anastasia according to the documents I saw at the solicitor's.'

'Anastasia! That's it then. She was a Russian princess in hiding.'

They both giggled at that.

'Of course she was,' Mia said. 'She was old, but not that old. Dad couldn't even tell Mum why Matilda was ostracised from the family because he was very young when it happened and no one was allowed to mention her name afterwards. The only other relatives on Dad's side have all died now.'

'And the solicitor wouldn't tell you anything?'

'No. But he said he didn't know anything about the family history. He told me it was his dad who was really Matilda's solicitor but as he'd passed away shortly before Matilda, we couldn't even ask him.'

'Ella!' Garrick called from downstairs. 'I could do with some help, please. There're a couple of things that need two people to carry them.'

'One of those will be your rowing machine,' Ella said to Mia, rolling her eyes. 'Why you brought that with you is beyond me. You never even use the thing.'

'I've used it once or twice.' Mia followed Ella out of Matilda's bedroom and closed the door behind her. 'I'm not sure where I'm going to put it though. I definitely can't put it in there. It would be almost sacrilegious.'

Ella pointed to a room next to the bathroom. 'That one didn't have much in it. I haven't looked at the other two rooms yet.'

Mia quickly poked her head in as they walked towards the stairs. It was rather ordinary compared to Matilda's room but still beautiful by most people's standards. It had a bed with pretty floral bedding and matching curtains and wallpaper, a wooden wardrobe, chest of drawers and a small dressing table. There was definitely space for the rowing machine. But as this room also had that incredible view, it seemed a shame to turn it into what may possibly become a 'junk' room.

'I'll just pop back and take a peek at the other two,' Mia said, turning in her tracks. 'I'll catch you up.'

'Okay. But don't be long. Carrying your rowing machine may be the only exercise you'll get from it while it's here.'

Mia pulled a face before opening the door to her right. It faced the front of the cottage and was another unexpectedly large room, but it had a more masculine look to it. Plain blue walls, and bedding in a darker blue. The wooden furnishings were darker too. This was perfect for Garrick.

She opened the door to the next room, also facing the front. It had pale lemon walls and the bedding and curtains were a bird and butterfly pattern. The furniture in here was a soft white.

The final door was at the end of the hall. It would be a very small room judging by the layout of the cottage but when Mia tried the handle, the door wouldn't budge. She tried it again. It was clearly locked.

The bunch of keys the solicitor had given her was downstairs. From memory there were eight keys on it. The only one marked was the front door key. One of the others must unlock this door. But why was this door locked when none of the other doors had been? And come to think of it, why weren't the French doors to the garden, and the kitchen door locked?

Hettie Burnstall, no doubt. The solicitor must have told her when Mia was planning to arrive. Hettie had come in to clean and had opened all the doors, locking only the front door when she left.

But that meant that Hettie had keys to the cottage.

For some reason, that wasn't a comforting thought.

Chapter Seven

All thoughts of the locked door were quickly forgotten once Mia was downstairs. She did not think she had a great many belongings but now the hall had become a narrow passage with boxes and cases piled to one side and still more to come.

'I didn't know where you wanted them,' Garrick said, as he and Ella manhandled the rowing machine through the front doorway. 'This can go in the dining room for now, can't it? There's a table in the kitchen so we can eat in there until we sort all this stuff out.'

'Good thinking,' Ella said, puffing and panting. 'This is heavier than it looks. I'm not carrying it upstairs, no matter what.'

They managed to squeeze past the boxes and Mia stepped into the living room to give them space to pass, almost falling over more boxes as she did so. Garrick may be a jack-of-all-trades when it came to wood, but home removal and unloading was clearly not on his list of skills.

Using a great deal of strength, Mia shoved the boxes against one wall before starting on the hall.

She had meant to write on each box the name of the room she wanted it to go in, but in all the rush, she had forgotten to do so. That meant each one had to be unsealed to see what it contained and Mia had used several rolls of parcel tape to secure every one.

If only she could remember where she had packed the scissors.

Garrick gave her an odd look as he headed back outside and she tried to unpick the tape on one box with her nails.

'Don't look at me like that. I haven't got any scissors.'

Garrick rolled his eyes and shook his head. 'The cottage is fully furnished and equipped. You'll probably find some scissors in the kitchen. That's where most people keep them.'

Damn. Why hadn't she thought of that?

'Oh yeah? How can you be so sure? Most people have a TV but Matilda didn't.'

'A TV isn't a necessity. Scissors are. She'll have scissors, believe me.'

'Some people would say a TV is a necessity,' Mia threw at him as she squeezed past him in the hall. His musky scent filled her nostrils and as her arm brushed against the T-shirt covering his hard chest, she averted her eyes.

'I would be one of them,' Ella said, rubbing her forehead with her hand. 'A TV will be at the top of our list when we go on our first shopping daytrip. I would kill right now to be sitting in front of a TV and eating a pizza. Bloody Nora. I wish I hadn't said that. It's made me realise I'm starving.'

'Me too,' Mia agreed.

'I could definitely eat something,' Garrick said. 'There're only a few more boxes to come in. I know all these boxes make this place look a bit of a tip right now but there's plenty of time to unpack. Your suitcases with your clothes and personal stuff, and mine and Ella's cases are the ones nearest the stairs. Why don't we get the last lot in, then have a quick wash and change and go to the pub to see if they serve food? Unless one of you fancies finding the box with the groceries and is willing to cook a meal, because I know I'm not.'

'There's no way I'm going to figure out how to use that Range tonight,' Mia said. 'Even if we can find the food.'

'Don't look at me.' Ella held up both her hands. 'The pub gets my vote. And if they don't serve food, someone will know where the nearest restaurant or takeaway is.'

'And I believe you two owe me a pint,' Garrick remarked, grinning over his shoulder as he went back outside. 'I told you there wouldn't be a TV.'

'Smart arse,' Mia said, watching him go.

Heat burned her cheeks as he turned again and caught her looking at his bottom.

But he did have a really good bottom, especially in the jeans he was wearing.

Ella raised her arms and smelt her armpits then pushed one in front of Mia's nose.

'Do I smell? I'm too tired and hungry to have a shower. A quick wash and a change of top is all I need, unless you say I stink.'

Mia shoved Ella's arm away, pinched her own nose and pretended to reel backwards.

'Oh God. I can't breathe. I've never smelt anything so awful in my life.' She grinned when Ella frowned. 'I'm joking. You smell fine. But aren't you forgetting the pub may be full of single men? It is a Saturday night, after all.'

Ella's eyes shot wide open. 'I'd forgotten the men. And there's a sentence I never thought would escape from my lips. Bloody Nora. That means a shower, shave my legs and pits, full make-up, and at least three hours taming my hair.' Her shoulders slumped. 'You know what? I really don't care. We're in the country. They're probably used to seeing women covered in mud and pig shit. A girl with a bit of dust in her hair will be nothing to them.'

'And you always look gorgeous anyway, so a bit of lippy and a dab of mascara will do the trick. Your hair looks great. I know you prefer it straight but the curls make you look really cute.'

'Cute? I want to look sexy.'

'You always look sexy. Now you look cute *and* sexy. What country bumpkin isn't going to find that a hot combination?'

Ella brightened. 'True. And let's not forget we're dealing with men who wear flat caps. That's not a good look on anyone. Not even Royalty. Although that gorgeous hunk with the tractor did manage to look sexy in his. Where did you say you'd put my stuff?' Ella asked Garrick as he returned with more boxes. 'I need to go and get changed.'

Garrick dumped the boxes in the space Mia had made in the living room and Mia tutted at him.

'I've just cleared that space.'

He grinned at her. 'Thanks. I needed somewhere to put them.' He frowned at Ella. 'So I guess I'm finishing the unloading alone then?'

Ella leant forward and pinched his cheek. 'That's one of the things we love about you, Garrick. You're so smart. And so helpful too. We'd love you even more if you carried our cases upstairs. Too much to ask?' she added as his frown deepened.

'What was it you said? Oh yes. "You need a break, Garrick. Come to the country with us. Mia's only got a couple of boxes to move. It'll be relaxing. A week or so of doing nothing but breathing in the country air. I've already told Mia you'll come." So when does the relaxing part start, that's what I'd like to know?'

Ella laughed. 'As soon as you've finished unloading. And once you've taken all our stuff upstairs. And locked all the doors. We don't want

Hettie Burnstall popping in and rummaging through our stuff when we're in the pub, do we?'

'Hettie must have keys,' Mia said, 'because she came to clean, remember? And all the back doors were unlocked. So you'd better hide whatever you don't want her to see. Oh! That reminds me.' Mia remembered the locked door. 'There's a locked door upstairs.'

'Well, it can stay locked until I've eaten,' Garrick snapped. 'Sorry. I definitely need some food.'

'But I'm dying to know what's behind it.'

'Fine. You go and look. I'll get the last lot of boxes.'

He marched outside and Mia looked at Ella. 'Come with me. I know it's silly but it was the only locked door in the cottage and I'd rather have someone with me when I open it.'

'Now who's been watching too much TV?'

Mia grinned and grabbed the keys from the small table where she'd left them. She picked up her suitcase as she passed it at the foot of the stairs and Ella followed her up, grabbing not just her own case but also Garrick's.

'Jesus! What's he got in this? It's heavier than mine.'

'There's a blue bedroom at the front of the house that I think is perfect for Garrick,' Mia said. 'Which room do you want?'

'I'm tempted to say Matilda's but you'll obviously be having that.'

Mia glanced over her shoulder and saw that Ella was grinning.

'Actually, I'm not sure I will. The thought of sleeping in her bed makes me feel a little uneasy.'

'I've seen the bed in there. Once your head hits the pillow you'll be out like a light. Besides, it must be the best bedroom in the place, and we know Hettie will have washed the sheets. You've got to sleep in it. And after a glass or two of wine at the pub, you won't be feeling anything other than half-sloshed.'

'That's true.'

Ella was right. It was the best bedroom. If Mia was going to live here for at least a year she may as well get used to it.

'I'll take the other room at the front,' Ella said.

'Don't you want the other room that overlooks the garden and the sea?'

'Maybe later. I think I need the traffic noise from the front until I get used to not being in London. I've had blaring horns, speeding cars and rowdy drunkards outside my bedroom window for more years than I care to remember. It'll take me a while to get used to the quiet. It's bad enough when I go somewhere peaceful on holiday and I've never been anywhere as peaceful as this. I haven't heard one car, or come to that, one person, other than Hettie, since we arrived.'

'I hadn't noticed.'

Ella rolled her eyes. 'You're already settling in to being a country bumpkin. So where's this door?' She dumped Garrick's case outside the blue room and her own suitcase in the doorway of the room she was having and rested her hands on her hips.

Mia put her suitcase in her new bedroom and pointed to the door at the end of the hall. They walked towards it, grinning at one another. The fading twilight outside cast the hall into shadow but neither of them looked for a light switch. A cold draught met Mia and she shivered as she stood in front of the door, which was odd as it was a warm day. Mia tried several keys before one eventually clicked into place and with a final glance at Ella, she turned the key.

This time the door did creak and Ella and Mia shot a look at each other and sniggered.

The door didn't lead to a small room; it led to a flight of steep and narrow stairs. A flight of stairs covered in dust and cobwebs. There was a wooden banister on one side of an off-white wall and it looked as if it hadn't seen a duster for a while. From where they stood they had to lean in to see the top of the stairs but neither of them wanted to. Mia spotted a light switch and that did look as if it came out of the Edwardian era. She gingerly flicked the tarnished brass knob but nothing happened.

'It doesn't work.'

Ella linked her arm through Mia's. 'I can see that. Have you got a torch?'

Mia shook her head and then remembered what Garrick had said. 'Matilda probably did. It may be in the kitchen.'

'Well, I'm not going up there without one. I've seen too many horror films to not know how this will end if we do.'

'What's that?'

Garrick's voice made Mia and Ella scream before they looked at one another and laughed.

'You nearly gave us both a heart attack,' Ella said, one hand on her chest, the other still linked with Mia's. Have you got a torch?'

'Not on me, no. Isn't there a light?'

Mia nodded. 'Yes. But it doesn't work. There's a flight of narrow stairs leading somewhere.'

'Probably to an attic,' Garrick said, with a hint of sarcasm. 'Thanks for bringing my case up. Is this the room I'm having?'

Mia nodded again. 'Unless you want the one next to mine. It's got the view of the garden and the sea. Ella needs the road noise so she doesn't want it.'

'Road noise? Here? Good luck with that, sis. I'd love the room with the view, if that's okay with you.'

'Of course. If we find a torch, will you come upstairs with us? It looks pretty creepy and it's really dark. So dark that we can't even see the top of the stairs.'

He frowned. 'I'll happily go up there, but can't it wait until the morning? Not because I'm scared, before you make any sarky remarks. Just because I'm tired and hungry. Besides, it may be easier to see up there in the daylight and it'll give me time to find a replacement bulb for the light.'

'But … what if something's up there?' That sounded ridiculous even to Mia and she wished she hadn't said it.

'If something's up there, and I think we all know there isn't, it's been locked in. Lock the door again and it'll stay there.'

'Garrick's right,' Ella said. 'Lock the door and we'll look tomorrow.'

Mia took a final peek at the stairs and quickly locked the door, shivering slightly as she did so. Whatever was up there could wait until morning. Although she wasn't sure she'd get much sleep.

Chapter Eight

It was almost dark by the time they strolled up Lily Pond Lane to The Frog and Lily pub and a light drizzle started a few seconds after they left the front door of Sunbeam Cottage. It had been a very warm, spring day and they hadn't got a jacket between them.

'It's only a shower,' Ella said, as they cooed at the ducks and ducklings on the pond.

'You always say that and then it pours hard,' Mia reminded her.

'It's less than a three-minute walk,' Garrick pointed out. 'We'll be there in as much time as it'd take to go back. Once we're inside, it'll probably stop. Sod's law I think they call it. Come on. We can look at the ducks tomorrow.'

They quickened their pace but by the time they reached the front door of the pub, they were running and it was bucketing down.

'Only a shower,' Mia said, not bothering to hide her sarcasm as Garrick pushed open the door and held it for her and Ella to pass.

Ella shook her curls and grinned as she stepped inside. 'A heavy shower.'

The three of them stopped just inside the doorway and looked at one another. The Frog and Lily not only appeared to be heaving at the seams, it appeared that everyone in there had suddenly stopped talking and was staring at them.

Garrick was the first to speak. 'Hello. It's chucking it down out there.'

No one said a word.

'We've only just arrived,' Mia said. 'Well, we arrived earlier today but what I meant was, we're new to the village.'

Still not a word.

'Do you serve food?' Ella asked. 'We're starving.'

'Aye. We do.' A voice that sounded as if it would be more at home in the Highlands of Scotland than in a remote village on the English South coast, piped up. 'But not the scran you're used to, I'd as like.'

'Scran?' Mia whispered, looking at Garrick. He'd lived in Scotland for five years. He'd know what the gruff-looking man pulling a pint behind the bar was talking about.

'Food,' Garrick said, in a low voice.

'As I said, we're starving,' Ella repeated. 'I could eat a horse right now.'

'No horse here,' a woman said, jovially. She appeared from nowhere and was wearing an apron with the words: A Scottish Moon, emblazoned

63

across the front above an illustration of a man wearing a kilt, bending over and showing his bum. Her accent was definitely English though and her smile was warm and welcoming. 'We don't have a large menu but the food we serve is good and wholesome. There's a free table over there.' She pointed to a table near a crackling log fire. 'Take a seat and I'll bring the menu over. What can Alec get you to drink? Alec's my husband. I'm Freda. Say hello to these lovely young people, Alec.'

The gruff man looked up and thumped the glass of beer he'd poured, down on to the bar.

'Hello,' he said. And he suddenly smiled.

'And what are you lot staring at?' Freda continued, casting a beaming smile around the pub. 'Mia will think she and her friends aren't welcome.'

As if awoken from a trance, the throng of people smiled and nodded at Mia, Ella and Garrick, then instantly broke into animated chatter.

'You know my name?' Mia said to Freda.

'Aye,' Alec answered.

Freda smiled. 'Hettie was in earlier. She didn't think you'd be popping in tonight. She said you had a lot of unpacking to do.'

'Oh did she?' Garrick said.

'And you're Garrick. You're just as handsome as Hettie said you were. And single, I understand? The girls round here will soon try to do something about that. I'd try myself if I didn't have my darling Alec.'

Mia grinned. Garrick looked flustered and Ella burst out laughing.

'And you're Ella,' Freda continued. 'Hettie said you'd be a box of trouble. But don't take any offence at that.'

'I won't,' Ella said. 'I like the idea of being trouble.' She grinned and glanced around the pub. 'Speaking of trouble. Where are all the single young guys tonight?'

Freda laughed heartily. 'Rugby. Not the place, the sport. All mad about it, they are. There's a rugby pitch off Seaside Road. You probably passed it when you arrived today. They'll all be there throwing their balls all over the place.'

Ella looked excited. 'Throwing their balls all over the place? I like the sound of that.'

'Rugby balls. They're doing a training session tonight. They should all be in soon. It's almost dark. The rugby pitch isn't as grand as it sounds. It's really a field with a few benches but it does have a couple of floodlights, but they're only brought in during game nights. We play other villages throughout the season, which is almost at an end. The final game is next Saturday. Come along and watch.'

'Hunky men in tight shorts,' Ella said. 'I'll definitely be there. And so will Garrick. But not for the men in the shorts. He's a bit of a rugby fanatic too.'

Freda shook her head. 'Most men are. I can't see the appeal, myself. But all to our own. Now, have you decided what you're drinking?'

'A pint of your best bitter, please,' Garrick said. 'And two glasses of wine. Chilled white wine. Pouilly Fumé, if you have it.'

'And what about you girls?' Freda quipped. 'Apologies. Just my sense of humour. I'm afraid we don't have any posh wine. Just basic Sauvignon Blanc, which is the grape the posh stuff's made from anyway. I don't know much about wine but I do know that.'

'That's absolutely fine, thanks,' Mia said.

'Sit then, and I'll bring the menu.' Freda walked towards the bar but she stopped to chat to at least three people on the way.

'I don't think Pouilly Fumé's posh,' Ella said, taking a seat beside the fire and pulling out the chair beside her so that Mia could sit by the fire too, for which Mia was grateful. The soaking from the shower had chilled her to the bone.

'Are you cold?' she asked Garrick.

'No. I'll be fine over here.'

He sat down opposite the fire and Mia saw the glow from the flames dancing in his eyes. At least she thought it was the flames, but he seemed to be staring at something above her head. She turned in her seat and noticed a large painting of a beautiful redheaded girl, about the same age as them.

What was it with him and redheads? Fiona was a redhead too. And so was his girlfriend before Fiona. Mia had even dyed her own hair red once, just to see if she could get him interested, but it was a complete disaster. It ended up the colour of a bright red post box. It was her own fault. She shouldn't have told the friend of a friend who was training to be a hairdresser and had offered to do it for free, that she wanted bright red hair. Especially as the hairdresser's own hair was a vivid lime green. Mia should've said mahogany, or Titian, or something less striking. She was so pleased when it finally grew out and she was back to her natural golden brown. Not that Garrick even seemed to notice at the time.

'That's a lovely painting,' Garrick said to Freda when she returned with the drinks and the menu.

Freda looked as proud as a peacock. 'That's our daughter, Alexia. She's a real stunner. I don't know where she gets it from. It certainly isn't from me or her dad.'

'I would say she looks just like you.' Garrick laid on the charm. 'Does she live here?'

Freda gave him a playful shove. 'Get away with you. I never looked as good as that when I was her age and I know I don't look like that now. But thank you for the compliment. Alexia lives with us and so does our son, Toby. They'll both be here later, after rugby.'

Garrick took a sip of his pint and looked thoughtful.

'Is she watching her brother training?' Mia asked.

Freda chuckled. 'Watch? Not our Alexia. She'll be in the scrum with the rest of them.'

Garrick choked on his beer and Ella slapped him on the back.

'I think my brother's fallen in love,' she said.

Why did that statement send a chill through Mia? It wasn't as if it mattered to her who Garrick fell in love with.

Rowdy laughter and a cacophony of male voices made Mia and Ella glance towards the door and Garrick swivel in his seat. Perhaps that's what had sent the chill through Mia; the pub door was flung open as a crowd of people barrelled in.

Freda placed her hands on her hips and beamed. 'The boys are back.' She tapped Garrick on the shoulder. 'And so is Alexia.'

Mia, Ella and Garrick looked to where Freda was pointing and Mia gave a little sigh. The painting of Alexia was beautiful – but it was nothing compared to Alexia in the flesh. And there was a lot of flesh to be seen. Perfect breasts were crammed into what was possibly the tightest, low-cut T-shirt in living history. Tanned, gleaming arms and hands pushed the thickest, richest-red hair on the planet from an angelic, porcelain face. And bronzed legs, longer and shapelier than a super model's, sashayed the dream body towards the table where Mia, Ella and Garrick sat.

'Bloody Nora,' Ella said. 'I think I'm half in love with her myself.'

'Hi, Mum,' the goddess Alexia said, leaning forward and kissing Freda on the cheek. 'Need any help?'

'Hello angel. You can tell Mia, Ella and Garrick about our specials if you like, while I help Alec behind the bar. Those boys will all want drinks, and food of course.' She winked at Garrick. 'You'd better decide what you fancy fairly quickly, or those boys will leave nothing for you.'

Mia wasn't sure if Freda was talking about Alexia, or the food, but when Freda smiled and walked away, Alexia gave Mia and the others the friendliest smile.

'Mum's right. You'd better get your food order in because that lot will eat everything on the menu and still want more. I'm Alexia, by the way. Which one of you is Mia? Oh wait. It must be you. I can see the resemblance to Mattie.'

'Mattie?' Mia queried.

'Your great-aunt,' Alexia said, still smiling but looking perplexed.

'You called her Mattie?'

Alexia nodded. 'Didn't everyone?' She glanced from Mia to Ella to Garrick, who seemed to be having trouble closing his mouth, or moving his love-struck gaze from Alexia's face.

'I don't know,' Mia said. 'I never met her.'

'Oh.' Alexia frowned, but even frowning, the girl looked gorgeous. Life really wasn't fair sometimes. 'I didn't know that. How peculiar. She talked about you all the time.'

Chapter Nine

Mia couldn't believe it. Had Alexia just said that great-aunt Matilda not only knew about Mia but talked about her to this goddess – and possibly, the rest of the villagers?

'Talked about me? Are you sure?'

Alexia grinned. 'Unless she had another great-niece also called Mia, yes I'm sure. She even showed us a photo of you once, I think. Many years ago. I was only young at the time but I'm sure she said it was you and that you were about the same age as me.'

'How old are you?' Garrick finally found his voice.

'Thirty-one.'

Alexia winked at him and his mouth fell open again. Mia was tempted to give him a good slap. He was behaving like a ten-year-old seeing his first pin-up girl.

'I'm thirty-three,' Mia said.

Ella joined in. 'I'm thirty-four, and so is he.' She nodded towards Garrick. 'And if I don't eat soon I won't live to be thirty-five. I'm starving.

Can we order please, Mia and carry on this conversation afterwards?'

'Yes. Sorry.' Mia briefly glanced at the menu. 'Scampi and chips for me, please.' She handed it to Ella.

'I'll have the same,' Ella said, without looking at it and before she could pass it to Garrick, he nodded.

'Me too.'

Alexia smiled. 'Three scampi and chips coming right up. Would you like more drinks?'

'Absolutely,' Ella said. 'But I'll come to the bar and get them, to save you a trip. Come and help me, Mia.'

'I'm happy to bring them over,' Alexia said.

Garrick rolled his eyes. 'I think my sister wants to check out the rest of the rugby team.'

Alexia glanced over her shoulder and grinned at Ella. 'I'm not sure tonight is the best time to meet them. They're a pretty rowdy bunch and you know what guys are like when there's a group of them and they've been playing rugby. So much testosterone in the air you won't be able to breathe. But it's up to you. I'm happy to introduce you if you like. If you'll take my advice though, you're better off waiting until tomorrow. They'll all be in here at some stage around lunchtime. A couple of them always stay for lunch. Mum and Dad do a mean Sunday roast. The guys will be a lot calmer and quieter then. Mum won't take any nonsense on a Sunday.'

72

Ella hesitated for a second but sat down the minute some of the men broke into song.

'Tomorrow's fine by me.'

Alexia nodded and headed towards the bar.

'That's a first,' Mia said. 'But I'm glad. Frankly, I'm not sure I could handle a rugby team tonight. It's been a long day and we've had one surprise after another. I think I need an early night.'

'Sorry I interrupted your chat about Matilda,' Ella said. 'Or should we call her Mattie now? That was weird, wasn't it? She said everyone called your great-aunt, Mattie, but Hettie Burnstall didn't, did she? She called her Matilda.'

Mia nodded. 'That's true. Perhaps that was out of respect.'

'I'm not sure Hettie is the type of woman who worries about respect,' Garrick said, still looking at Alexia, until she disappeared from view. He turned his attention back to Mia and Ella. 'Perhaps Matilda was a snob. Maybe she felt the paid help shouldn't get too friendly. Didn't Hettie say something along those lines? Something about being friends and then she changed it to friendly neighbours.'

'She did,' Ella said, craning her neck to look at three men standing at the bar, who seemed to have suddenly noticed the strangers amongst them. Ella gave them her best – and sexiest – smile.

'Don't do that,' Mia said. 'Oh god. They're coming over.'

She was wrong. They walked right past and headed for the dart board several feet away, although they did smile and say 'Hello' as they did so. One of them had a distinct American accent, blond hair and was built like a mountain. Was he Franklin Grant? One had ginger hair but looked so much like Alexia that he must have been her brother, Toby. The other one Mia recognised. It was the sexy, tractor driver. He looked even sexier now. His damp hair was still the colour of midnight but his light blue eyes held the promise of dawn. His lips proffered a 'come to bed with me,' smile and merely the sight of his body, this close at hand made Mia want to scream. In a good way. A very, very good way. She wanted to reach out and touch him. The problem was, he gave the same smile and the same look to Ella. He even smiled at Garrick, though in a much more matey and not remotely sexy way, thankfully.

'That was the tractor guy,' Ella said, almost bursting with excitement.

'Uh-huh.' Mia nodded, still ogling him. He was equally sexy from the back. 'Jet Cross.'

'Did you see his eyes?'

'I couldn't miss them. I've never seen eyes like them. I think Hettie told the truth about him. One look in to those eyes and I'd forgive him anything. Even if it did mean I'd end up with a broken heart.'

Ella let out a sigh. 'I'd definitely risk a broken heart for a night with him.'

Garrick tutted. 'I don't know. One good-looking guy and you two go to mush.'

Ella punched him on the arm. 'Says the guy who couldn't take his eyes off Alexia.'

Garrick ran a hand through his hair and gave a long low whistle.

'You've got to admit. She is absolutely gorgeous.'

'I bet she's broken a few hearts in her time too,' Mia said.

'Even I'd risk a broken heart to spend the night with her.'

Did Garrick mean that? If he did, it would be the most spontaneous thing he'd ever done.

Mia wasn't sure if she was pleased about that or not, and when Alexia brought more drinks and then the food, smiling and flirting with Garrick on both occasions, Mia wondered whether spontaneity was all it was cracked up to be.

'Alexia,' Mia said, spooning lashings of tartare sauce on her scampi and chips, along with sprinkling ample quantities of vinegar. 'Is there a problem with mobile phone reception in the village? I've been trying to call my mum on and off all day but there doesn't seem to be a signal. I can't even send a text.'

Alexia shook her head. 'It's sporadic and seems to depend on the weather but generally you won't get a signal. You have to go to Frog Hill and about halfway up, just past Frog's Hollow, you'll get one. That's the hill behind the church. Or at the top of the church steeple, if you fancy climbing three hundred circular stone steps. There's a landline in Mattie's cottage though. Couldn't you call your mum on that? Most of us rely on old fashioned communication methods in Little Pondale. Landline. Postal service. Face to face conversation. You'll soon get used to it.'

'I'm not sure I will,' Ella said. 'My business relies on my mobile. It's how people contact me, other than via the internet.'

'I'm an idiot,' Alexia said, tutting. 'Mattie's got WiFi. We don't have fibre optic here and the broadband reception's very slow to what you're probably used to, but you can make mobile calls and send texts via WiFi, assuming your phone's compatible. Most recent smartphones are. I'm not with it when it comes to technology so you'll have to ask my brother Toby, but I know it's possible because he often does it.'

'Matilda had WiFi?' Ella looked incredulous. 'She didn't have a TV but she had the internet?'

Alexia nodded. 'Yes. She had a laptop. I often saw her using it.'

'I didn't see a laptop in the cottage,' Mia said. 'Did you?' She looked at Ella and Garrick who both shook their heads.

'Well, she definitely had one. Perhaps the solicitor took it for safe keeping. Or Hettie. She may know Mattie's WiFi password although I wouldn't count on that.'

'Do you have WiFi here?' Garrick asked. 'For public use I mean.'

Alexia nodded. 'Yes. The password is FrogandLily. All one word. Capital L for Lily.'

Garrick smiled at Mia. 'In that case you can send your mum a message via Facebook. She's bound to be checking that and posting photos of her cruise, knowing Lori.'

'Your mum's on a cruise?' Alexia looked wistful. 'I'd die to go on a cruise. Especially to somewhere romantic, like Italy, for example. But just being on a cruise ship looks romantic, doesn't it? Of course, I suppose it depends who you're with. Has your mum gone with anyone special? Sorry. I suppose that's none of my business. But that's another thing you'll have to get used to. No one minds their own business in Little Pondale. Everyone knows everything about everybody.'

'I'm beginning to realise that,' Ella replied.

Mia shrugged. 'It's okay. Mum's gone with her book club. There's been no one special in her life since Dad died, and that was many years ago now.'

'Apart from you,' Alexia said, with a sincere smile. 'I'm sorry about your dad. I think Mattie loved him dearly but she didn't talk about him much. Just about you. But I'd better get on. And you'd better finish your meal before it gets stone cold. See you later.'

Chapter Ten

The scampi and chips were delicious and the tartare sauce, the best Mia had ever tasted. But the evening at the pub had also given Mia food for thought. The more she was hearing about great-aunt Matilda the more confused she was becoming. Or Mattie, as she must now get used to calling her because it sounded so much more 'friendly', and Mattie was clearly friendly, at least to some people.

What was the most confusing was the fact that Alexia had said, not only that Mattie loved Mia's dad, but also that she often talked about Mia. Yet Alexia had seemed genuinely surprised that Mia had never met Mattie. Surely Mattie had made it clear that she wasn't in touch with her relatives? Or had she pretended that everything was fine and that she simply didn't see them often? It was all such a mystery. As was the fact that Mia, Ella and Garrick hadn't spotted Mattie's laptop. But then again none of them had seen the telephone, so they clearly hadn't been very observant. Perhaps Mattie did in fact have a TV and they were all too blind to see it. Perhaps it was camouflaged in some way, like the wardrobes were in Mattie's bedroom. Mia smiled at the thought. If she mentioned that to Ella, she'd probably tear the place apart looking for one.

'Who gets the cottage if you decide not to live here for the year?' Garrick asked out of the blue as the three of them walked back to Sunbeam Cottage.

The rain had stopped and a full moon hung over the thatched roofs, giving them a silvery glow. In the distance an owl hooted. At least Mia assumed it was an owl. It sounded, owly, if there was such a word.

Mia shook her head. 'No idea. The solicitor said Matilda … I mean Mattie, had drawn up a codicil to the will, with his father. It was in a sealed envelope and only to be opened if I choose not to stay. He said that he didn't know what it contained but the instructions were clear and precise. If I leave, he'll open it and the cottage will be dealt with according to the instructions in the codicil. If I stay for the entire year, the cottage will be transferred to me and the codicil destroyed. I can dispose of the cottage as I see fit after that and leave it to whoever I want in my will, or sell it, or do anything I want to do with it.'

'So no one knows?'

'No.' Mia had already told him and Ella that the solicitor who drew up the will was now deceased and that the son, with whom Mia had dealt, had little knowledge of Matilda Ward, other than that his firm held her will and several other documents, including the deeds to the cottage. 'The only other beneficiary in the main will was given a specific bequest. Like me, they were to be given the sum of ten thousand pounds immediately. It was the local animal sanctuary. I asked if he thought they might also get the cottage if I decided not to live there, but for some reason he seemed fairly certain they didn't. He said that he believed if it were that straightforward, the will would simply have declared that. Something along the lines of, 'if she doesn't want it then the charity gets it', only in legal speak, of course.'

'He believes someone else will inherit it then? Not that it will simply be sold off and form part of Mattie's estate? Who gets that? The residual estate, I mean? Or did she only own the cottage and twenty thousand pounds? And if so, who is paying her legal fees?'

'I have no idea. This whole thing happened so fast and was such a shock I'm not sure I asked enough questions. Or the right questions. All I wanted to know was who was great-aunt Matilda and why she had left me her home, together with ten thousand pounds? I didn't really ask much else about the will and he didn't offer to tell me anything other than about the animal sanctuary also getting ten thousand pounds, from what I remember. Perhaps he'll be billing me. I hadn't even thought of that.'

'I think he would've told you that at the start. He probably has to by law, if you're the one paying his bill. Mattie must've made a separate provision for costs.'

'Why all the questions?' Ella asked. 'You're giving me a headache.'

Garrick pulled a face. 'I think the four large glasses of wine are what're giving you the headache, not to mention the champagne we drank earlier.'

'Oh bugger. I'd forgotten that.' Ella jumped onto the grass and stared at the pond. 'It's so bloody quiet here, isn't it? It's ten-thirty on a Saturday night and there isn't a sound, is there?'

'Apart from the wildlife,' Mia said. 'And I don't mean the rugby team.' She grinned.

Ella grinned back. 'Even they weren't that rowdy, were they? In London there would've been at least one punch-up when that lot started singing. I'm already looking forward to Sunday lunch, aren't you?'

'I know I am,' Garrick said.

'I'm looking forward to going to bed,' Mia said, and hastily added, 'I mean tonight. On my own. I'm shattered. And tomorrow's going to be busy. We've got to start unpacking.'

'And looking for Mattie's internet password,' Garrick said.

'And her laptop,' Mia added.

'What about the locked door?' Ella asked, turning from the pond and continuing towards

Sunbeam Cottage. 'We were going to check that out in the morning, weren't we? Perhaps that's where Mattie kept her laptop. You know, away from a certain someone's prying eyes.' She nodded her head towards Duckdown Cottage, Hettie Burnstall's home. 'Bloody Nora! I swear I just saw her lace curtains twitch.'

Mia saw that too but she was busy thinking about the locked door again now.

'Thanks for reminding me about the door. I'll be wondering about it all night and probably won't sleep a wink.'

Garrick grinned. 'I bet you'll sleep fine. Perhaps we'll find a TV up there too.'

Ella tutted. 'Now I'll be wondering about that all night and I won't get a wink of sleep either.'

'You'll be snoring the minute your head hits the pillow,' Garrick said.

'I don't snore!' Ella was indignant.

'You do,' Mia said. 'Especially after four large glasses of wine.'

Garrick laughed. 'Don't sleep with your window open. You'll scare the wildlife.'

Ella thumped him on the arm and he let out a little yelp but it was drowned out by a horrific scream, like someone was being brutally murdered.

Ella and Mia grabbed one another's hands and they both grabbed Garrick.

'What the bloody hell was that?' Ella croaked.

'That was a vixen,' Garrick said, prising himself free from their grasp. 'Surely you've heard a fox call before? There are urban foxes in London.'

Mia shook her head and so did Ella.

'I've never heard anything like that in my life. Are you sure it's a fox? It definitely sounded like a human screaming for their life.'

'I'm certain,' Garrick said. 'And besides, this is Little Pondale. Do you honestly think someone would be murdering somebody in a tiny village like this?'

'It happens in *Midsomer Murders*,' Ella said. 'And in those *Miss Marple* mysteries.'

'Fiction,' Garrick pointed out. 'In real life, you probably have more chance of winning the Lottery jackpot than you do of being murdered in a village like this.'

'I hope you're right,' Mia said, seeing the curtains of Duckdown Cottage twitch once more as she turned towards the path of Sunbeam Cottage.

For some strange reason, she had a very uneasy feeling about that cottage, and its owner, Hettie Burnstall.

Chapter Eleven

'Morning sleepyhead. Wakey wakey. I've made coffee.'

Mia stirred on her cloud. At least it felt like a cloud. Was she dreaming? That was clearly Garrick's voice she could hear and she could definitely smell coffee. Tentatively, she opened her eyes, trying to remember where she was because she was sure this wasn't her bed. Her mattress was never this comfortable, even when it was brand new, although that was many years ago.

'It's eight a.m.' Garrick said. 'The sun is shining. The birds are singing. It's a beautiful day.'

'What?' Mia sat bolt upright, nearly knocking the coffee mug from Garrick's outstretched hand. 'Eight? It can't be.'

She stared at him in disbelief. Not only was he washed and dressed in jeans and a T-shirt that clung to him in all the right places, his aftershave smelt divine. Or maybe that was the coffee. He was smiling down at her and it struck her again just how handsome he was.

He and Ella weren't identical twins, in fact, they barely looked alike, although they both had a dimple in their chins. It looked ruggedly roguish on Garrick; cute and sexy on Ella.

They had similar hair, although Garrick's was more a light, sandy brown; Ella's was dark blonde. Curls on Ella, which she tamed flat with a hair straightener. Waves on Garrick, which either he did absolutely nothing with, or he spent hours with a heated brush getting them to fall in perfect symmetry. Mia doubted that Garrick would ever be seen dead with a hot brush in his hand. A hot woman, maybe; a hair beautifier, never. It simply wasn't his style. His waves must have tumbled naturally over the tips of his ears and just kissing his collar when he wore a shirt. Now, in this T-shirt, the waves danced around his firm, tanned neck.

'Stop daydreaming and take this coffee,' he demanded. 'Breakfast will be ready in ten minutes. And I'm not bringing that up to you.'

'Okay, Grumpy.' Mia puffed up her pillows with her fists, wriggled into a comfy position and took the mug from him. 'Is Ella awake?'

'Not only awake but already in the shower. The heating's on and there's plenty of hot water. I've got more wood from the woodshed and the Range is frying bacon and eggs as we speak. So get up and at 'em, madam.' He turned and walked towards the door. 'Oh, and by the way, I slept like a log and so did Ella, much to her amazement. How about you?'

'I don't think I slept a wink,' she lied.

'Really?'

She shook her head and her ponytail swished to and fro. 'Nah uh. I lied. You were right. I fell asleep the second I closed my eyes and I was still asleep when you brought me this coffee. This bed is unbelievably comfortable. You should spend a night in it and see.'

He raised his eyebrows and a devilish grin crept across his lips. 'Is that an offer, Mia Ward?'

'What? No! I didn't mean … What I meant was, alone. On your own.'

'I was kidding, Mia. I know what you meant.' He turned to walk away, stopped and glanced back. 'But if you ever change your mind.' He smiled the sexiest smile she'd ever seen on him. Then he winked.

'Yeah right. Is that before or after you jump into bed with Miss Frog and Lily, the goddess of the village?'

He tipped his head to one side and a wave of hair tumbled over his brow. Mia wanted to go to him and push it back in place.

What was the matter with her this morning?

He rubbed his chin between his thumb and forefinger as if he were deep in thought.

'That's a tricky one. After, I think. Or maybe before. Perhaps both. Or is that pushing it too far?'

Mia threw a pillow at him but he laughed and ducked out of the way of the missile. When he looked back at her, he had a strange expression on his face.

'Does that give you a hint?' she asked.

'It does,' he said, with a catch in his voice. 'And I hope you won't mind me saying this, but so does that nightdress. I think you may want to tie it a bit tighter.' He abruptly walked away and closed the door behind him.

Mia looked down at her nightdress and gasped. She had forgotten that it was quite so sheer but not only that, that it had a loose, off-the shoulder neckline with a row of ribbon that could be tightened or undone. It was incredibly sexy and she'd driven her ex-boyfriend, the rat, wild with passion on more than one occasion by standing in front of him and with just one finger, untying the ribbon and letting the nightdress slip to the floor like a gossamer veil. The problem was, it had come undone of its own accord when she'd thrown the pillow and now the left side of it sat just below her left breast, giving Garrick an eyeful.

'Bloody Nora,' she groaned, mimicking Ella as she yanked the nightdress back in place. 'I only, bloody well flashed my boob at my best friend's brother. What a fabulous start to my day.'

She put the coffee mug down and clambered out of bed. Ella had finished in the shower because Mia could hear her singing and it was coming from Ella's room. Not that it mattered, because Mia had discovered another thing last night before she had gone to bed. Mattie had an en-suite bathroom. It was camouflaged, just as the wardrobes had been and she'd found it when she rested her hand against the wall on which the chest of drawers sat, opposite the wardrobes, to take off her socks. After the champagne and the wine, she had felt a bit unsteady.

She dashed in there now and turned on the shower. She closed her eyes and let the water wash over her. Suddenly, she imagined Garrick's hands on her and her eyes shot open because the feeling was so intense that for a split second, she actually wondered if he'd returned to her room, seen her in the shower, and done something incredibly spontaneous.

But he hadn't. She wasn't sure whether she was disappointed, or just annoyed that, yet again, she was having inappropriate thoughts about Garrick Swann.

Anyone would think she still had a crush on him.

Which she didn't.

She definitely *did not*.

She fancied him, but that was different. She fancied a lot of men but it didn't mean she'd jump into the shower with them the first chance she got. Garrick was good to look at. He was a lovely person. He was reliable and kind.

But he definitely wasn't the man for her.

He definitely wasn't the one.

Absolutely not.

Chapter Twelve

Garrick seemed to be avoiding her. Or at least, he was avoiding looking at her.

From the moment she appeared in the kitchen, he looked away.

She was wearing her skinny jeans and a T-shirt that was almost a second skin, it was so tight, but he didn't even seem to notice. Well, perhaps he did but he quickly turned away. The bacon and eggs he was cooking seemed to demand his undivided attention because he stared at the pan the entire time she talked.

'I've discovered an en-suite in Mattie's room. It's hidden, like the wardrobes were. This place continues to amaze me. Something new and exciting keeps popping up in front of me.'

Garrick made a strange coughing slash choking sound but he didn't say a word.

Even when Ella came charging in, he didn't look up.

'Morning,' Ella beamed. 'I've just been down to the shore and the sea is like a mirror of diamonds this morning. It's so beautiful I had to take photos. Then I remembered that we don't know the WiFi password so I can't upload them to social media. We must see if we can find it today. What's up with you two?'

'Nothing,' Mia said, a little too quickly.

'I'm cooking,' Garrick said, still staring into the pan.

'Hmmm.' Ella sat at the table and poured herself some coffee from the jug. 'You haven't had a row, have you?'

'No,' they replied in unison.

'Then why the serious faces? Didn't you sleep well?' She directed the question to Mia.

'I slept very well, thanks. I hear you did too.'

'Yep. God. Listen to us. Next we'll be discussing the weather. We sound like three old fogies. So what's the plan for today? Apart from going to the pub for lunch and meeting all the single guys. Are we tackling the locked door first? Or hunting for the password?'

'We're having breakfast,' Garrick said, and put plates of bacon, egg and tomatoes in front of Ella and Mia. He put his plate as far away from Mia as it was possible to get without it falling off the table.

'We should eat outside,' Ella said. 'It's a gorgeous day. Bloody Nora! Listen to me. I've really taken to this country living, haven't I? I think I may marry a farmer. Jet Cross is a farmer, isn't he? Or did I misunderstand Hettie? Oh for

God's sake you two. Snap out of it. You're like extras in *The Walking Dead.*'

Chapter Thirteen

Thirty minutes later, Mia, Ella and Garrick stood in front of the locked door. After Ella's comment about *The Walking Dead*, Garrick had soon returned to his usual self, much to Mia's relief, although he still wouldn't meet her eye.

'Are we taking bets on what's up there?' Ella asked, as Mia turned the key.

'We'll probably find it's simply an attic filled with junk,' Garrick said. The door creaked open and he shone the beam of the torch he'd found in one of the kitchen cupboards, up the steep, narrow stairs. 'D'you want me to go first?'

Mia nodded and stepped aside. 'Yes, please. There seem to be even more cobwebs than yesterday.'

'Make way for my duster-on-a-stick-thingy,' Ella said, holding up the mop-like duster Garrick had also found while searching for the torch. She handed it back to Garrick. 'You're going first, so you'll need this.'

'Not quite a knight in shining armour,' Mia quipped, as he held the torch in one hand and the duster in the other, 'but pretty close.'

'I'm going in,' he said, in a deeply serious voice but the grin on his face belied him.

The stairs creaked twice as loudly as the door had done and with Mia following closely behind Garrick and Ella immediately behind Mia, their footfalls played out an eerie tune.

Ella gave a nervous laugh. 'I know this is silly and the sun is blaring down outside, but this still feels really creepy.'

'I can see a beam of light,' Garrick said. Then he let out a strangled shriek.

Mia screamed and Ella echoed it as they reached out for one another before realising that Garrick was laughing.

'That wasn't funny,' Ella snapped. 'I almost fell down the stairs when Mia screamed and turned around.'

'I almost had a heart attack,' Mia croaked, trying to stop shaking.

'Sorry,' Garrick said. 'I couldn't resist it. The roof's been boarded, so at least you won't need to worry about spiders, birds or mice falling on your head.' He stepped inside and flicked a switch on a wall. 'And then there was light.'

Mia followed him in and glanced around. The beam of light now blended with the ceiling light but Mia spotted two circular windows at each end of the attic room and one larger square window in the eaves, looking towards the sea. It had a padded seat beneath, piled high with cushions and a book lay open on a small wooden table beside it, as if someone had just left and would return at any moment. The roof boards had been painted white between dark wood rafters, as had the floor boards and the room had an ambience unlike anything Mia had ever experienced.

'Wow!' Ella said, once again linking her arm through Mia's. 'What a beautiful room. It's like a little sanctuary. I bet Mattie came up here when Hettie was doing the cleaning.'

They grinned at one another. 'I definitely wasn't expecting this,' Mia said, letting out a long sigh. 'I really wish I'd met her.'

'It sort of feels as if she's still here,' Ella remarked. 'But not in a creepy way. There's a mellow, chilled-out kind of vibe up here, don't you think?'

Mia nodded. 'It feels like a happy place. The rest of the cottage feels like a home even though some of it looks like it came straight from a magazine. You were right when you said this feels like a sanctuary. There's something very personal about this room.'

'There's hardly anything in it,' Garrick said, glancing around him. 'This would make a great bedroom. Or a games room. Or an artist's studio. But it faces the wrong way for that, I suppose. Artists prefer light to come from the north, I believe.'

'I think it's perfect just the way it is.' Mia strolled to the square window, knelt on the window seat and looked out. The sea glistened turquoise in the morning sun and as she took in the scene, a solitary couple strolled along the shore with a dog dashing in and out of the flat-calm water. Even the seagulls looked serene as they dipped and soared across a cloudless baby blue sky.

She had a sudden urge to grab a paint brush herself — which was odd because the last time she had held a paint brush was probably at infants' school and even then, art wasn't her favourite pastime.

'It's unbelievably strange,' she continued, taking a deep breath of salty, sea air once she'd eased the window ajar. 'I thought I was allergic to the countryside and wouldn't dream of living near a beach, and if you'd told me seven weeks ago that I'd be saying this after only one day of being here, I'd have said you were mad, but I feel at home here.' She turned from the window and looked at her friends. 'It's as if I belong in this cottage. As if it's been sitting here waiting for me. That sounds crazy, doesn't it?'

'Coming from you, yes,' Ella said.

Garrick looked doubtful. 'I hate to say this, but as you said, it's only been one day. I think you may be romanticising the place. Don't shout at me.'

Mia opened her mouth and closed it again as Garrick continued:

'You were half expecting a hovel in the middle of nowhere and instead you found a beautiful cottage with an incredible view, in what appears to be a picturesque village filled with warm and welcoming people.'

'And Hettie Burnstall,' Ella said sarcastically.

'She was warm and welcoming,' Mia added in her defence.

'She was nosey, a dreadful gossip and dare I say it? A bit of a bitch. Especially about the vicar.'

Mia nodded. 'Fair enough.'

'As I was saying ...' Garrick shook his head. '... This is a wonderful place. A true idyll. Even not being able to get mobile phone reception doesn't seem to matter that much. But give it a few months and you may feel differently. A few weeks, even. At the moment, this is an adventure. And a bit of a mystery to get your teeth into. Plus Ella and I are here. Will you still feel so at home when you're alone in an empty cottage? Especially when the nights draw in and the wind howls through the thatched roof. Things might not seem so perfect then.'

'Well, you're a real party pooper this morning, aren't you?' Ella threw him a look of reprimand.

'I'm simply being practical.'

Mia nodded. 'You're right, Garrick. I suppose it is too soon to tell. But I can't help the way I'm feeling. And right now, I feel as if this is where I belong. Besides, Alexia said there's a landline, so not having phone reception actually doesn't matter that much. As for being alone, I'll have to wait and see. I lived alone in London and it didn't bother me. I've got a car, so it's not as if I'm trapped here or anything. And as Ella said, I can buy a TV if I want one. I've got eight thousand of Mattie's money left, so it's not as if I'm destitute either. And I can always get a job. That'll provide both an income and some company.'

'Where and doing what?' Garrick asked.

'Oh. Well, I haven't had time to think about that, have I? But when I popped to the loo in the pub last night, I did ask Freda where the nearest town was, and it's only fifteen miles away, along the coast. That's not far at all.'

Garrick nodded. 'True. But weren't you struggling to find another job in London? Ella said you were.'

'Don't glare at me,' Ella said. 'It's true. You were. And you know I tell my brother everything. Well, almost everything. So I don't know why you're surprised.'

'If you couldn't get a job in a massive place like London,' Garrick reasoned, 'what makes you so sure you can get a job down here?'

Mia tutted. 'I hate it when you make sense. Okay, so I may not be able to get a job, but at least I'll have people in this village to talk to. Everyone's been very friendly so far.'

'I'm sure you won't want for friends,' Garrick said. 'Or boyfriends come to that. I just think that, knowing you as I do, the appeal of this place may soon wear off.'

Mia crossed her arms in front of her chest. 'Perhaps you don't know me as well as you seem to think you do, Garrick Swann. You've only seen me a few times over the last five years. People change you know.'

Mia waited for him to respond but he merely looked her up and down, as if he was trying to decide if she had changed. At least on the outside. Ella didn't say a word. Which was very unlike her.

Eventually, Garrick nodded. 'People do change. You're right about that.' He looked away and glanced around the room once more. 'Anyway, I don't think there's anything else to see up here. And definitely no laptop. It must be somewhere else.'

'Oh, I'd forgotten about the laptop,' Mia said, pleased for the change of subject. 'I wonder where it could be? It's definitely not in her bedroom because I looked for it last night before I got into bed. Unless there's another hidden door. Although I don't think there is. After I found the bathroom last night, I banged and pushed all the remaining wall space and nothing else popped open.'

'Perhaps there's a hidden safe,' Ella suggested. 'You know, behind one of the paintings or something. There were several in the hall, a couple in the living room and quite a few in the dining room. None in the bedrooms though from what I could see.'

Mia nodded. 'That's a possibility.'

'Not many homes have safes, I would have thought,' Garrick said. 'But it's worth a try.'

'I've got a safe,' Ella added.

Garrick tutted. 'You've got a biscuit tin in a cupboard.'

'But I hide my savings in it. And the jewellery Gran left me. So it is a safe. It just doesn't have a lock.'

'And it isn't hidden or impenetrable,' Garrick pointed out. 'Not that all safes are hidden of course, but most have some way to stop or at the very least, deter burglars and thieves.'

'Burglars and thieves are the same thing,' Ella said.

Garrick sighed. 'No they're not. A burglar breaks in, or sneaks in through an open window or door, with the intent of committing a crime. A thief could be living in the property or staying as a guest. A thief can be someone you know and trust. Or someone who comes to your home on a regular basis.'

'Like a cleaner?' A sudden thought popped into Mia's head.

Garrick nodded. 'Yes. A cleaner could be a thief. Oh, are you wondering if Hettie Burnstall could've taken Mattie's laptop?'

'That's exactly what I'm thinking. I know it's a horrible thing to say, but she does have keys and she said herself that she'd been in to clean. There was something about her that made me feel a bit uneasy.'

'You know something else that's odd,' Ella said. 'I've got jewellery I've bought or been given, plus the jewellery Gran left me. You've got jewellery. Your mum's got jewellery. Our mum's got jewellery.'

'Okay,' Garrick said. 'I think we've established everyone's got jewellery. What's your point?'

'My point is, where's Mattie's jewellery? With her expensive clothes, shoes and bags, she would definitely have had expensive jewellery.'

'You're right!' Mia shrieked. 'But there wasn't a jewellery box on her dressing table and no special drawer in those built-in wardrobes. So where is it?'

'I see,' Garrick said. 'Well then, there must be a safe. And now we're not just looking for a laptop. We're also looking for Mattie's jewellery.'

Chapter Fourteen

'Perhaps we should've started by asking Hettie Burnstall,' Ella suggested, as they sat in the warm spring sunshine at one of the bench sets outside The Frog and Lily, three hours later.

After leaving the attic room they searched the cottage from top to bottom, moving all the pictures and mirrors hanging on the walls and banging all the walls in case there were more hidden doors, but they found nothing. By the time the church clock struck twelve they were thirsty and disheartened – until Ella suggested it was time they retreated to the pub for a glass or two of wine and Freda's purportedly delicious Sunday lunch.

Garrick shook his head and lowered his voice. 'You can't go around accusing people of stealing.'

Ella pulled a face. 'I wasn't planning to. I was merely saying that, if there is a safe, and we now believe there must be even though we can't find it, she may know where it is.' She grinned. 'But if she goes bright red and looks all flustered, then we'll know she's stolen the lot and we'll force a confession out of her.'

Mia grinned. 'She's such a gossip, she'll probably blurt it out anyway.'

'Perhaps it's all a front,' Ella said. 'Perhaps she's an international, jewellery and laptop thief hiding here in the village and doing people's cleaning to cover her tracks.'

'My word,' Garrick said, a slight grin lightening his serious expression. 'This village is a den of iniquity. First Mattie was a gangster's moll, then she'd stolen all her lover's money and was hiding in the village. Now Hettie's on Interpol's most wanted list. I wonder what Alexia and the others are hiding!'

'Alexia's hiding very little from what I've seen,' Mia said, perhaps a little bitchily. 'I'm sure the shorts and T-shirt she's wearing today are even skimpier than yesterday. There should be a dress code for a Sunday. Especially as the pub's right opposite the church.'

Garrick smiled. 'I didn't have you down as a frump. Besides, I like what she's wearing.'

Mia glared at him. 'Why doesn't that surprise me? Is that why it took you so long to get a few drinks and order three roasts dinners? Ella and I wondered if we should send out a search party.'

'Don't be a bitch,' Ella said, playfully slapping Mia's arm. 'If I had a body like hers, I'd be wearing even less. And so would you.'

'True.' Mia sighed. 'I'm just jealous.'

'Why?' Garrick asked. 'You've got a great body. Um. You both have. You simply don't flaunt yours. And, not that it matters, but I wasn't talking to Alexia. Freda took the order and I was chatting to Toby about the rugby team. If I'm going to be visiting here on a fairly regular basis, I thought I might be able to play a few games, or at least join in with some of the training sessions. You know how much I love rugby.'

'Who says you'll be invited for regular visits?' Ella queried, but with a grin.

Garrick winked. 'Alexia. At least she did in my dreams. I'm only joking. You're right. I shouldn't have assumed I'll be invited.' He cast Mia a puppy-dog look and she laughed.

'You're welcome anytime, Garrick, you know that. And so is your lovely sister.'

Ella tutted. 'I told you last night, I may never leave. And I was only half joking.'

'Look who's coming our way,' Garrick said. 'Better call Interpol quick.'

'Coo-ey!' The cheery tones of Hettie Burnstall rang out from the direction of the church and within a matter of minutes she was standing at their table, puffing slightly in her haste to get there. 'I thought it was you, my dears. How are you settling in? I hear you came to the pub last night. Did you manage to get all your unpacking done?'

'Hello Hettie,' Mia said, forcing a friendly smile. 'Um, no. We've still got some to do.'

'Well, if I can be of any help you only have to ask.'

'Actually, you may be. Alexia told us last night that Mattie had a laptop but we can't find it anywhere. We've been looking for it all morning. Do you happen to know where it is?'

'And her jewellery?' Ella added. 'We can't find that either and we know she would've had some.'

Hettie's face turned a pale shade of beetroot and she loosened the white collar of her high-necked blouse. She gave a little cough and then the cheery smile returned.

'Wasn't the laptop in the attic room? That's where she kept it. I don't have a key for that because dear Matilda said that was her 'special' room and she didn't want anything disturbed. I understood of course. We all have our special places, don't we? She kept it locked at all times, even when she was in there, and she wore the key around her neck. I was always curious as to what was quite so special about it, but I believe in giving people their privacy and I wouldn't dream of asking. You've been in there you say?'

Mia struggled to prevent her mouth from falling open. Could Hettie actually hear herself? Did she honestly believe she gave people their privacy? The woman was clearly delusional.

'Yes,' Mia replied. 'This morning. It *is* a very special room. I think I'm going to keep it locked, just like Mattie did, in honour of her memory.'

'Oh, I see. Well of course, deary. I understand.'

'And the jewellery?' Ella persisted, while Garrick remained surprisingly quiet and sipped his beer.

Again Hettie coughed. 'I believe she kept her jewellery up there too. Family heirlooms, she once said, and the jewellery I saw her in was certainly old and expensive-looking, not that she wore it often. But once or twice, and at Christmas and birthdays, that sort of thing. I'm not one for adornments, myself, but if others choose to wear their little trinkets and keep them hidden away, who am I to judge them? My wedding ring is all I need.'

Hettie twisted the simple gold band on her left hand and Mia stared at it. She hadn't noticed it yesterday and hadn't thought to ask if Hettie was married. From the things Hettie had said, Mia had assumed she wasn't. And the fact that Hettie had mentioned that only Prince Gustav, her pet rat, was waiting for his tea, made it obvious that if there had once been a Mr Burnstall, he was no longer around.

'But your husband's no longer with you?' Mia asked. That hadn't sounded quite as tactful as she'd hoped, and Hettie looked shocked by the question.

'Hector? Of course he's with me. Where else would he be?'

'Oh! Um. I'm so sorry. It's just that yesterday you said it was only your rat waiting for his tea. I mean, Prince Gustav. I assumed it was just you

106

and Prince Gustav in your cottage.' Mia fumbled an apology.

'It is,' Hettie said, clasping one hand over the other and resting them an inch or so beneath her ample bosom. 'Hector died years ago, but just because he's dead, it doesn't mean he's not with me. Even the vicar knows that. Although he doesn't hold with my talking to him. Talking to Hector, I mean. Not the vicar. Reverend Thomas Tyburn doesn't believe we can converse with the spirits, but we can. Matilda agreed with me about that. The dead are always with us, deary. Whether we want them there or not.'

Garrick finally spoke: 'Has anyone else been in the cottage since Mattie's death? Any relatives or friends?'

Hettie shook her head. 'Only me, deary. And I certainly hope you're not suggesting that I would help myself to Matilda's belongings because if you are, I'd take offence at that. Besides, as I told you, she kept those sort of things in her special room and I don't have a key to that, and clearly won't have in the future, so it can't be me who took them, can it?'

'I'm not suggesting anything of the sort,' Garrick replied calmly. 'We're simply trying to find out where the laptop and jewellery are and who has had access to them since Mattie's death. You're the only person, other than Mia, with keys so anyone wanting access would come to you, I assume?'

Hettie pursed her lips. 'They would. But no one's been near other than that solicitor and I let him in myself because Matilda didn't answer the door. We found her together. Dead as a doornail, she was.'

'What?' Mia didn't believe her ears. 'Are you saying that Matilda ... Mattie died in the cottage?'

'Of course she did, deary. I thought you knew that. Right outside the door to her special room. Whether she was going in or coming out is anyone's guess but the door was locked and the key hung around her neck. She just dropped down dead on the spot. It was awful, deary. The police came. They do that you know if someone dies in such a fashion. A massive heart attack, the doctor said. No doubt about it. Natural causes. As if it could have been from unnatural causes? Dear Matilda was ninety-nine. We all have to go sometime, don't we, deary? It was just her time, that's all. But now I think about it, that solicitor took Matilda's keys. I didn't pay much attention. Talking ten chickens at a time, I was, because it was such a terrible shock. I mean, I've seen a few dead bodies in my days but not like that. All alone and lying there just waiting for someone to find her.'

'Bloody Nora,' Ella said. 'Had she been dead long?'

Hettie shook her head. 'No deary, bless you. The doctor said it happened just a few short hours before we found her. Good thing the solicitor turned up when he did I suppose because it was a Friday afternoon and I wasn't due to clean until the Monday, so she'd have been there for a few days, if not for that. Mondays and Thursdays were my days and she was as fit as a fiddle on the Thursday. We chatted about the weather, and I told her old Mrs Dupont's arthritis was playing up again. Matilda was alive and well when I left her, I can assure you of that.'

'I'm sure she was,' Garrick said. 'Oh well, let's not dwell on such an upsetting topic. Thank you, anyway. We'll speak to the solicitor and see if he can shed any light on the mystery of the laptop and jewellery.'

'Hello, Hettie.' Alexia appeared, balancing three plates piled high with Freda's Sunday roast and deftly placed them on the table, taking three sets of cutlery, each wrapped in a napkin, from the pocket of her skimpy apron. 'You coming in for Sunday lunch?'

'No, deary. Not today. I'm watching my waistline and my pennies. Now that dear Matilda's gone I'm down by twenty pounds a week and these healthy young dears don't need me to clean for them. Twenty pounds is probably not much to you, Alexia dear, but when you've only got a pittance of a pension, it makes a big difference, I can tell you. Oh. Not that I'm blaming you, my dear.' She tapped Mia on the shoulder. 'When I was your age I couldn't afford a cleaner either.'

Hettie couldn't have made Mia feel more guilty if she'd tried.

'Twenty pounds?' Mia glanced at Ella and took a deep breath. She would probably regret this, in fact she was sure she would, but before she could stop herself the words tumbled out of her mouth. 'I can stretch to twenty pounds, and Ella and I hate cleaning at the best of times. Why don't you come and clean for me, at least for a while anyway, and we'll see how things go?'

Ella gasped and Garrick groaned but tried to muffle it by taking a gulp of his beer. Even Alexia made a strange little choking sound and stared at Mia as if in disbelief. If Hettie noticed, she pretended not to because she beamed at all of them and bent down and gave Mia a big hug.

'Oh, you're an angel, just like your dear sweet great-aunt Matilda. You've made an old woman very happy. I'll be round first thing on Monday. Nine o'clock sharp. And Alexia?' She straightened up and smiled at her. 'I will be having Sunday lunch. This calls for a little celebration. I'll have my usual table if it's free. See you later, dears.'

Without another word, Hettie hurried into The Frog and Lily, and Mia wondered what on earth had made her employ Hettie Burnstall to be her cleaner. She wasn't at all sure she liked the woman, let alone trusted her.

Alexia smiled and shook her head. 'Enjoy your meals. And good luck with Hettie, Mia.'

'Bloody Nora,' Ella said. 'What in God's name made you do that?'

'I was about to ask the same thing,' said Garrick.

Mia tutted. 'She made me feel guilty. I couldn't sit here eating Sunday lunch, knowing that, because of me, Hettie Burnstall couldn't afford to do the same. I know what it's like to struggle financially and besides, when all is said and done, twenty pounds a week for me to never have to do housework again, seems like a bit of a bargain.'

'That's true,' Ella agreed. 'And you can always lock yourself in Mattie's special room while Hettie does the cleaning. I bet you that's what Mattie did.'

'Isn't it awful about Mattie dying outside that door?' Mia shivered in a dramatic fashion. 'I didn't mention this, but yesterday I felt a little chill when we were standing on that spot. I wonder why the solicitor didn't tell me?'

Garrick rolled his eyes. 'For the very reason you've just stated. He probably thought there was a chance you'd start imagining you were seeing ghosts or something.'

'I didn't say I saw a ghost. I said I felt a chill.'

'Probably a draught because the front door was open. Anyway, I didn't want to say this when Hettie was here, but perhaps the solicitor took the laptop and jewellery for safe keeping after he and Hettie found Mattie dead.'

111

Mia shivered again. 'The very thought of finding a dead person is enough to give me nightmares. Poor Hettie.'

Ella shrugged. 'I don't think it would bother me. I wonder why the solicitor was visiting Mattie that day.'

'No idea. He didn't mention that either.' Mia looked at Garrick. 'Surely, if he had removed anything he would've given it to me when he handed over the keys? Or at the very least, he would've told me he'd taken them. Wouldn't he?'

Garrick nodded. 'Good point. I'm sure he would've done that. We should give him a call tomorrow just to check. Although he didn't tell you he found her dead, so perhaps he only tells you what he believes you need to know. And what we don't know, is whether there is a residual estate and if so, who gets it. If there is, perhaps the beneficiary of that also gets the laptop and the jewellery. Perhaps that's why he didn't mention them.'

'But Mattie left Mia the cottage and its contents,' Ella said. 'Surely the laptop and jewellery are contents? And they were in the cottage when she died, as far as we know.'

'I'm not a lawyer, sis, so I don't know. Maybe personal items like laptops and jewellery don't come under contents.'

Ella frowned. 'They do for insurance purposes. We should ask the solicitor.'

Mia sighed. 'This is becoming more of a mystery by the minute.'

Garrick unexpectedly reached out and squeezed her hand. 'I'm sure there's a simple explanation for all of it, but we can't do anything until tomorrow so let's eat this delicious-looking lunch before it gets too cold. We can spend the afternoon unpacking so we won't have to keep moving boxes around when we're looking for things.' He gave an encouraging smile.

'Oh,' Ella said. 'Perhaps the solicitor also knows the password for the WiFi. We should add that to the list of things to ask him. At least then we can use our own laptops, and I can do five minutes' work next week. And speaking of work. On Monday morning, at nine o'clock sharp, Hettie will clean up the mess we make unpacking today.'

Ella grinned and shoved a large roast potato in her mouth; in an attempt to brighten her mood, Mia did the same.

It was Sod's Law that Jet Cross and another gorgeous, black-haired guy chose that precise moment to appear and stop beside the table where the three sat.

Chapter Fifteen

Trying to chew and swallow a whole roast potato and look attractive at the same time was a feat Mia could not achieve. She looked down at the table and placed one hand in front of her face, pretending to rub the tip of her nose, but she wasn't fooling anyone. Ella didn't even bother. She munched away regardless and when Mia cast a glance in her direction, Ella was giving a perfect impression of a demented hamster, both cheeks puffed out and a strange twisted smile on her face. Mia almost choked with laughter and had to cough and swallow several times to ensure the potato didn't get stuck in her throat. It was as if the whole thing happened in slow motion and the expressions on Jet and his friend's face spoke volumes.

So much for making a good impression.

'Hi,' Jet said, his voice soft and lilting as he looked directly at Mia. 'I think I owe you an apology. Two apologies, in fact.'

Mia couldn't speak so she raised her brows instead.

'One for making you wait on Seaside Road yesterday while I faffed around with the tractor and the gate. And two, for the raucous behaviour of me and my mates in here last night. We're not usually that obnoxious and we didn't even say hello and welcome you and your friends to the village.'

Mia tipped her head from side to side. What on earth was she doing? This was simply making things worse. Could she look any more stupid?

A broad smile crept slowly across Jet's gorgeous face. 'Let me rectify that now. Hello, Mia. I'm Jet Cross and this is Rupert Day.'

Mia managed a smile and a nod and Rupert smiled back.

'Everyone calls me Bear,' Rupert ventured.

Garrick was the first to speak, obviously realising Mia and his sister couldn't.

'Hi. I'm Garrick and this is my sister Ella. We're staying with Mia for a while. Why do they call you Bear? Sorry. Just curious.'

Rupert smiled at him. 'Not for the reason most people think. Mum and Dad met on one of those bear watching trips in Canada, so to mark the occasion, they gave me Bear as a middle name. Rupert was my Grandfather so my name is Rupert Bear Day. I got some stick at school for that, as you can no doubt imagine. What can I say? Crazy parents, I'm afraid.'

'I think it's cute,' Ella said, in a rather odd tone. She was clearly still swallowing potato.

Finally, Mia managed, 'Hi. It's good to meet you both.'

'We'll leave you to get on with your lunch,' Jet said, still smiling. 'Just wanted to say hi and to apologise. Hopefully, we'll be seeing you in here on a regular basis. It's the only pub for miles around, so it's not as if there's a lot of choice. But it can get pretty crazy. Freda and Alec have quiz nights, darts matches, drinking contests and that's just for starters. After the bright lights of London, you won't know what's hit you.' He winked. 'See you again soon, I hope. And Garrick ...' He placed both hands on Garrick's shoulders. '... If you're interested in rugby, give us a shout.'

'I am. I was just chatting about it with Toby.'

'Good man. See you on the field then.' Jet smiled at Ella and then at Mia, but his gaze seemed to linger on Mia for a few extra seconds.

Or perhaps Mia imagined it.

'Bloody Nora,' Ella said, when Jet and Rupert disappeared inside the pub. 'They had to come along at that exact moment, didn't they? I'm not sure which one is better looking. Jet or Rupert.'

'Jet,' Mia said, without even thinking.

'He's really hot. I thought that yesterday. But now that I've seen Rupert, I think I may prefer him.' Ella grinned. 'And I like the idea of having a boyfriend called Bear. Didn't Hettie say he was a vet?'

Garrick nodded. 'And that he lives across the pond. So it must be in one of those cottages.' He pointed at the row of cottages diagonally opposite.

'Oh good. Not far to stagger home after a night of unbridled passion then.'

Garrick grinned as he cut into a juicy slice of beef. 'He might live with his mother.'

Ella pulled a face. 'Well, Alexia not only lives with her parents, she lives with her brother too. That'll cramp your style.'

'I wouldn't bet on it.' He tilted his head slightly to the left. 'And here comes one of the other guys from last night, I think.'

Ella turned to look. 'He's got black hair too. That must mean he's Justin Lake, the male stripper-cum-dancer. He's certainly got the body for it from what I can see from here. Hmmm. I may have to have a rethink about Bear.'

'How can you remember all their names from yesterday?' Garrick looked surprised. 'Hettie only mentioned them in passing.'

'It's a talent I have. One of many, I hasten to add.'

'You're telling the wrong man. I couldn't care less.'

They waited for Justin to saunter past and as he did so, he nodded and smiled in their direction but he made no effort to introduce himself.

'Hmm. I like the quiet ones,' Ella said. 'And you could learn a thing or two from Jet. Like charm, for one. It simply oozed out of him. Are you sure it was you who dumped Fiona? I'm beginning to think she may have given you the boot.'

Garrick stiffened noticeably. 'No one dumped anyone. I began to think I had made a mistake and when we discussed it, we both agreed to go our separate ways. I'd rather not talk about it, thanks.' He got to his feet abruptly. 'I need another drink. And I know without asking that you want one too.'

'That hit a nerve,' Mia said, once he was out of earshot.

'I told you he was being weird about it, didn't I? How am I ever supposed to really understand the workings of the male mind if I can't even figure out what's up with my own brother?'

'Don't ask me. You know my track record with guys as well as I do. I can never figure them out. If they weren't so bloody appealing, I swear I'd give them up.'

'They're definitely more trouble than they're worth half the time.' Ella cut a potato into small pieces and grinned at Mia. 'So which of the three guys is going on your list? Jet, Rupert or the strong, sexy, silent Justin? Or all three?'

'You're forgetting Alexia's brother Toby. He's single, so Hettie said.'

'If being single is all it takes to be on your list,' Ella said, as Mia put her wine glass to her mouth to finish off the contents, 'you could add Garrick. He's single too. And having sex with someone else may help to improve his mood.'

Mia choked on the large gulp of wine she'd taken and as she quickly clamped her hand over her mouth and turned her head to ensure she didn't spit it over the remaining food, someone in a long black and white outfit walked by. An arc of wine burst from her and sprayed the person down their left side. And to Mia's mortification, she realised it was the vicar.

Chapter Sixteen

'I am so, so sorry,' Mia said, jumping to her feet and grabbing her napkin. Hettie had not had very nice things to say about the vicar and he would no doubt give Mia a lengthy lecture on the sin of consuming too much alcohol, especially on a Sunday.

'It's okay,' he said, smiling. 'It could've been worse. At least it was white wine.'

He wasn't at all as Hettie had described him. He was actually rather good looking, although not in the league of Jet, Rupert and Justin. Or Garrick. He was of slim build, but his jaw was firm and his cheekbones pronounced. His hair was thick and golden brown, like Mia's and his eyes held a warmth and a friendliness as he held up his hands and shook his head, stepping away when Mia attempted to dab at the wine spatter.

'Please. There's really no need. It was going in the wash as soon as I got home in any event.'

Even his voice sounded friendly and when he laughed, Mia and Ella laughed too. He was the complete opposite of the sanctimonious git Mia had been expecting.

Which was odd, because until now, Hettie Burnstall's brief descriptions of the men in the village had been spot on.

'I really am sorry.'

'Don't give it another moment's thought. It's a novel way to be introduced. I'm Tom Tyburn, the vicar of St Michael and All Angels.' He leant forward and grinned. 'We're a welcoming bunch, hence the 'All Angels' bit. I don't think I saw you in church this morning.' He winked. 'Don't worry. I'm not the type to lecture you on church attendance. But we do have a choir if you're interested in that. And you must be Ella. I'm very pleased to meet you. So, Mia, how are you settling in?'

Mia smiled brightly. 'It's lovely to meet you, Reverend.'

'Please. Call me Tom.'

'Hi, Tom,' Ella said, with a strange look in her eye. 'You're not at all what we were expecting.'

His brows furrowed and he grinned. 'Ah yes. I can imagine. You've obviously met Hettie Burnstall. And this must be Garrick.' He glanced towards the door of the pub.

Garrick carried the drinks to the table and smiled when Tom introduced himself.

'Well, it's lovely to meet you all but I'll leave you in peace to finish your lunch. Choir practice is

121

Tuesday evening, if you're interested but I expect we'll bump into one another before then. Little Pondale is hardly a metropolis.'

He gave a friendly wave and marched off down the lane.

'I wonder what Hettie's got against him?' Garrick said, resuming his seat. 'He seemed a perfectly normal, friendly guy to me.'

'I was just wondering the same thing,' Mia said.

Ella remained unusually quiet, but she craned her neck to watch Tom Tyburn walk down the lane.

Chapter Seventeen

Nine o'clock on Monday morning came far too quickly for Mia's liking, especially as she and her friends all overslept. It was eight-thirty when Garrick banged on her door, popped his head in and told her to get up.

'Hettie'll be here in half an hour. I'm going down to put the coffee on while Ella's in the shower. Mia? Are you awake?'

'Ye-s. I'm awake. Go away and I'll get up.' She was wearing the same nightie as yesterday and there was no way she was risking giving Garrick a repeat performance.

He closed the door and a second later she heard him racing down the stairs. It took her five minutes to shower and another three to throw on jeans and a clean T-shirt.

They had spent the rest of yesterday unpacking and finding space for all of Mia's belongings, not that there were that many, but Mia's clothes still lay folded in her suitcases which she'd shoved into the bottom of one of Mattie's wardrobes. She didn't know what she was supposed to do with Mattie's clothes and thought she had best leave them alone until she'd spoken to the solicitor.

Garrick showered as soon as Ella went downstairs and by the time Hettie arrived at precisely nine o'clock, they had wolfed down breakfast, turned on the dishwasher and were sitting on the decking admiring the view.

'Coo-ey,' Hettie called out from the hall. 'It's only me, deary. Isn't it a beautiful morning?'

'Hello, Hettie,' they all replied in unison.

'D'you mind if I disappear for an hour?' Ella said, getting to her feet. 'I want to go to the top of Frog Hill and see if I can get phone reception. I need to check my emails and make a few calls.'

Mia frowned at her but Ella did have a business to run and she was doing Mia a huge favour by staying with her, so she smiled.

'I don't mind.' She lowered her voice. 'But I'd like you here when I call the solicitor, please. I'll do that after Hettie leaves.'

'I'll be back by ten.'

Garrick also stood and Mia glared at him. 'Don't tell me you've got calls to make too.'

He grinned and shook his head. 'No. But I was going to offer my sister a lift to the top of the hill. I won't though. I'll give her my keys instead.'

'You're looking gorgeous this morning.' Hettie joined them on the decking and poked Garrick on his chest with her finger. 'Didn't have time to dry your hair, I see. Or you, deary. Not early risers then?'

Garrick managed to hide his look of surprise rather well. Mia wasn't so sure she had.

'It's the sea and country air,' Garrick said. 'It makes me sleep like a log. And we're all used to road noise and hustle and bustle in the mornings. There's nothing here to wake us up.'

'There's birdsong.'

Garrick nodded. 'Yes. At five a.m. I heard it and went back to sleep.'

'Never do that, deary. Up with the lark, that's the saying. It's the early bird who catches the worm.'

'I'll try to remember that. Excuse me, Hettie. I need to give Ella my keys.'

'Speaking of keys ...' Mia got to her feet. '... I hope you won't mind, but I need to take the set you've got. Please don't take offence.' Hettie looked as if Mia had asked for her soul. 'It's temporary. I've only got one set, you see and with Ella and Garrick staying, that's a little inconvenient. We don't want to live in one another's pockets, so at least if we had another set, we could be a bit more relaxed about one of us always needing to be in.' She held out her hand. 'I know you'll understand.'

'Oh, I see. But couldn't they call at mine, if they need to get in?'

'We don't want to trouble you like that, and besides, we're from London. We keep late nights.'

That was a bit of an untruth, but Hettie wouldn't know that.

'Oh. Well, if you need my keys, you should have them. Only temporary, you say?'

Mia nodded. 'Uh-huh.'

Hettie handed them over but she looked as if she may burst into tears at any moment. Mia couldn't deal with that.

'Thank you, Hettie. I'll let you get on. I hope we haven't made a mess. We tried to clear up as best we could after all the unpacking.'

In truth, the place was spotless. Mia, Ella and Garrick had vacuumed and dusted from top to bottom, although none of them was sure why. They simply felt they had to. Then Mia remembered she hadn't cleaned the shower this morning.

As she dashed through the kitchen with Hettie close behind, she spotted a bag on the table with a loaf of bread sticking out.

'I've brought bread from Justin's bakery, and milk, eggs, butter and cheese from Little Pond Farm. I've left the receipt inside. You can pay me on Thursday. Matilda always paid me once a week on Thursday. Unless she asked me to get her anything special. Gave me the money right away if she did that.'

Now Mia felt really guilty. They had only been saying over breakfast that they'd have to go and get some fresh supplies today and the things

Hettie had bought included several of the things they had wanted.

'That was so thoughtful of you, Hettie. And I'll pay you now. In fact, unless you'd rather not, I think I should pay you each time you come instead of once a week. That way, I'll know that we're all square at any given time.'

Hettie appeared to give the matter a moment's thought before she nodded and smiled.

'That's perfectly fine with me, deary.'

'Good. Then today I'll pay you ten pounds plus whatever I owe you for these. The receipts are in the bag, you said?'

'Yes. Well, deary, I'll get on. I always make a cup of tea when I finish. Not one for coffee but if that's what you'd prefer that's fine by me.'

'Oh. Um. Please don't trouble about me. You can get off home as soon as you're finished and I've paid you. In fact, I'll pay you now. That way you won't need to come and find me.'

'Nonsense, deary. I always made tea for Matilda and had a chat. It brightened my day. Prince Gustav isn't very talkative and Hector never comes to me in the mornings. It's good to have the company.'

Hettie Burnstall seemed to have the ability to make Mia feel guilty every time she spoke to her.

Mia forced a smile. 'In that case, I'll have coffee. And so will Garrick,' she added as Garrick reappeared.

'So will Garrick, what?' he asked.

Mia beamed at him. 'Join Hettie and me for coffee at ten. Right, I'm going upstairs to do a few things. I'll see you both later.' She winked at him as she passed by and he returned it with a glare.

'Where's your sister off to?' Hettie asked.

Mia heard Garrick say, 'Frog Hill.' She also heard Hettie gasp, and she couldn't help but wonder why. Against her better judgement, she returned to the kitchen, making the excuse of getting the receipt so that she could bring the right money down later. She thought Hettie would explain her reaction but she didn't and Garrick was on his way out in the two seconds it took Mia to reach the doorway. She grabbed his arm and spun him round.

'I forgot the receipt,' she said. 'By the way, Ella's gone to Frog Hill but she'll be back in time for coffee.'

No gasp this time, merely a shake of her head.

'It's an odd name for a hill,' Mia added.

Hopefully that would extract the necessary information.

'It's called Frog Hill for a reason, deary, and if you know what's good for you, you won't go near Frog's Hollow on a Monday. I'd have given your friend that advice if I'd known that was where she was going.'

'Really? Why's that?'

'It's a long story, deary.'

Mia pulled out a chair. 'Well, why don't we sit and have coffee now instead of later and you can tell me and Garrick all about it.' She saw Garrick raise his brows but before he had a chance to respond, she added: 'Put the kettle on, Garrick and make some coffee. Oh, but tea for Hettie, I believe.'

Hettie thought about it for a second before pulling out another chair and sitting at the table. 'Nice and strong, for me, deary. Like my men.' She winked at Garrick whose shoulders appeared to shake slightly as he turned to the kettle.

'So why should we avoid Frog's Hollow on a Monday?' Mia asked. 'And what, exactly, is Frog's Hollow anyway?'

'Terrible place. I've not been there more than once or twice in my lifetime, but many go there deary, especially in the winter when the pond is frozen over. They skate on it! Madness, deary. Utter madness. But there's no accounting for some people, is there? And of course, Alexia and her brother, along with all the other young things, go there on Midsummer's Night and bathe in the pond. Naked, deary. Naked!'

A clatter of spoons made Mia glance at Garrick. His head had shot up and he half turned to Hettie as if he was suddenly interested in her story.

'Need some help there, deary?'

'No thanks, Hettie. I'm fine.' Garrick brought three mugs to the table and smiled. 'I'll make a pot of coffee and one of tea in case we're here awhile. What were you saying about Midsummer's Night?'

Hettie chuckled and poked a finger at his stomach. 'I thought that might get your attention, deary. Naked as the day they were born. I've seen them myself, so I know it's true. But that's the thing with witchcraft, isn't it? All naked bodies and dancing and getting up to who knows what.'

'Witchcraft?' Mia shot a look at Garrick but his mind was clearly elsewhere as he had a dreamy look in his eyes and a strange sort of smile on his face. She could guess where that was.

'Yes, deary. The tale goes that if you bathe naked in the pond at Frog's Hollow on Midsummer's Night, your loins will be fruitful and your body will forever be entwined with the one you love.'

'That doesn't sound like such a terrible place to me,' Garrick said, grinning. 'When is Midsummer's Night?'

'Next month. But it's nonsense, deary. Even the vicar agrees with me on that.'

'So what does that have to do with not going there on a Monday?' Mia asked, giving Garrick a reprimanding look. She couldn't stop the image popping into her head of him and Alexia frolicking naked in a pond though and she made a mental note to go on a strict diet right away.

'Nothing. That's another tale.'

The kettle boiled and Garrick made the tea and brought the pot, together with a pot of coffee over to the table. He took milk from the fridge, found a jug and poured it in, placing that and a sugar bowl in front of Hettie.

'Would you like a biscuit?' he asked. 'We've got chocolate digestives.' He retrieved them from one of the cupboards and offered the half empty packet to Hettie.

'Trying to sweeten me up, deary?'

'Impossible,' he replied, and winked at Mia.

Hettie chuckled. 'Just one then.'

'So, Monday?' Mia persisted.

Hettie munched on her biscuit before replying, her face suddenly serious. 'Well deary, when people moved here and built the village hundreds and hundreds of years ago, they chased all the frogs and toads from the pond opposite. The toads moved elsewhere but the frogs kept coming back, so the villagers bundled them all together and took them to a new pond they had dug, halfway up the hill. But the frogs didn't like it so back they came. The villagers weren't having that, so they captured a pack of wolves, which ran wild in England in those days, and a skulk of foxes, a kettle of hawks and a flock of wild ducks and once they'd taken all the frogs back to the new pond, they set all the predators loose. Well deary, you can imagine what happened, can't you? Wild creatures are just that, deary, so not only did they eat all the frogs, they ate one another, and then the ones that were left, turned on a couple of the villagers who were daft enough to go and watch what happened. It was a Monday and to this day, anyone who goes to Frog's Hollow on a Monday is asking for trouble.'

Mia gasped in horror, picturing the scene but Garrick sniggered.

'Are there many wolves, foxes and birds of prey in Frog's Hollow then?' he asked, somewhat sarcastically. 'And do they just gather on a Monday? How do they know it's Monday? As for the ducks, I don't think I could ever be afraid of one of those. Or even an entire flock. And, just out of interest, what happens if Midsummer's Night falls on a Monday? Is it a scene of complete carnage?'

'You may laugh, deary, but I've seen the results with my own eyes. No one gets eaten, or anything like that. Well, not so far at least. That would be ridiculous, deary. They simply get a warning by seeing a frog on their doorstep and the Monday after that, they die an unpleasant death. And the curse of Frog's Hollow only applies to the day, not the night. If you go there after dark, you're safe.'

Garrick grinned. 'Even on a Monday?'

'Even on a Monday.'

'That's rather convenient for the naked bathers, isn't it? I'm sorry, Hettie, but I simply don't believe such superstitious tales. And I don't believe in witchcraft, either. Although Midsummer's Night is a pagan celebration, isn't it? Not specifically to do with witches.'

Mia shrugged. 'Don't ask me. I have no idea. I think I agree with Garrick, Hettie. I don't see how going to a pond on a Monday can possibly lead to someone dying unpleasantly exactly one week later. And why do they get a warning by seeing a frog on their doorstep? Surely if the curse says the person will die, it wouldn't bother to give them another warning?'

'Tell that to my Hector. He went to Frog's Hollow on a Monday. Found a frog on the doorstep on the following Monday and on the Monday after that, he got hit by a car, tossed several feet in the air, and landed on his head. It was very unpleasant, let me tell you, deary.'

Chapter Eighteen

There really wasn't much either Mia or Garrick could say after Hettie's revelation about her husband's death. They merely gave her their condolences and profuse apologies for appearing to make fun of it. After Garrick somehow managed to deftly change the subject to rugby, Hettie quickly finished her tea and said she really should be getting on with her work. Mia raced upstairs as soon as she could and Garrick disappeared to somewhere in the garden.

By the time Ella showed her face, Mia had paid Hettie what she owed her and Hettie had left the cottage after saying she hoped that Ella hadn't fallen victim to the curse of Frog's Hollow and warning Mia to be on the lookout for frogs appearing on the doorstep.

When Mia told Ella all about it over coffee, Ella didn't seem the slightest bit concerned.

'I know it's all nonsense,' Mia said, 'But I must admit it did give me the shivers. Especially when she told us about Hector's death.'

'Finding a frog on the doorstep would freak me out. But that's because I don't like frogs. Anyway, I'm perfectly safe, because I didn't make it to Frog Hill, so I didn't go to Frog's Hollow.' She had a rather strange smile on her lips. 'I got side-tracked.'

'Side-tracked? How?'

Ella grinned. 'I spotted Tom outside the church so I stopped to say hello and when I told him where I was going and why, he suggested I might like to go and see his bells.' She giggled. 'What he really said was that if I fancied climbing three hundred stone steps, I could get a signal in the steeple and if I was at all interested in a tour, he would take me to the belfry and show me the Angel Bell. There're four other bells up there but the Angel Bell is special. It's cast from bronze and dates from the early 1500s and it's named after Edward Angel, some local rich guy who paid for it to be made. And get this, Mattie made a substantial donation towards the cost of having the thing cleaned, and the oak beams and bell wheels restored, shortly after she arrived here. Tom wasn't the vicar then obviously, but he can remember his gran telling him about it when he visited her here as a boy. Isn't that amazing? And the weirdest thing is, it was actually very interesting. If you'd asked me before I went out this morning if I'd be happy to spend half an hour looking at a bell, I'd have laughed in your face.'

'The vicar?' Mia was surprised Ella would be happy to spend ten minutes with a vicar, let alone more than an hour, half of which was spent looking at an old bronze bell. But knowing Mattie donated to its restoration even made Mia keen to see it.

'I know!' Ella laughed heartily. 'I'll have to think twice about my vicar and tart jokes now, won't I? 'Cos I'll be seen as the tart.'

'Are you saying you like Tom Tyburn?'

'I'm saying he's going on my list and he's nowhere near the bottom.'

'Who's going on your list?' Garrick reappeared from the garden carrying a massive bunch of tulips. 'Hope you don't mind, Mia, but I helped myself because I've no idea where the nearest florist is and I happened to hear Alexia mention yesterday that tulips were her favourite flower. I thought I might pop to the pub for coffee after we've called the solicitor.'

'Oh. Um. No. Of course I don't mind.'

'Thanks.' He smiled at Ella. 'So who's on your list?'

She grinned. 'The vicar.'

Garrick burst out laughing. 'Now I've heard everything. I thought Hettie's story was the most bizarre thing I've ever heard, but my sister fancying a vicar beats that hands down. This place is having the strangest effect on the three of us. But you may soon be needing a vicar. Did Mia tell you about the curse of Frog's Hollow?'

'Yep. But I haven't been there so I'm safe. I like the sound of the skinny dipping on Midsummer's Night. But not if the pond's full of frogs.'

'Hettie didn't mention that,' Mia said. 'But if the frogs are back, then how come there's still a curse? And wouldn't they be in the pond across the road if they had come back?'

Garrick tutted. 'Why are we talking about frogs? Let's call the solicitor and get some answers to our questions. Then I can go to the pub before these flowers wilt.'

'You should've cut them later,' Mia said. 'Put them in water and they'll be fine.'

'And if we don't get the password for the WiFi,' Ella said, 'Tom says we're all welcome to use the internet at his house. He lives in that cottage with the white picket fence. The one right opposite the pub.'

'Then why was he going down the lane yesterday?' Mia asked.

'To visit his gran. She still lives here in Corner Cottage. It's the blue one as you come into the lane. She's had a bit of a cold so she didn't go to church. Bloody Nora! Listen to me. I sound like a right country bumpkin, don't I?'

'Let's make the call,' Garrick said. He was starting to sound impatient.

'I've got the number here.' Mia took the solicitor's business card from her purse.

'I'll get the phone.'

Garrick hurried towards the living room and returned a second or two later with the hands-free phone. He handed it to Mia and she dialled the number, asking to be put through to Mr Dale when the receptionist answered.

'Clive Dale here, Miss Ward. How are you settling in to Sunbeam Cottage?'

'Very well, thank you, Mr Dale, but I've got a couple of questions if that's okay? I hope you don't mind but you're on loud speaker. I've got two friends with me and I want them to hear our conversation in case I get anything mixed up.'

'I don't have a problem with that, Miss Ward. Fire away.'

'Thank you. Well the first thing is, we've been told that Mattie, I mean, Matilda Ward had a laptop but we can't seem to find it and we believe we've looked everywhere. We also believe there should be some jewellery, but we can't find that either. We wondered if, perhaps, you had removed the laptop and the jewellery for safe-keeping, or because someone else had inherited them. It may not be any of my business of course, but we thought we should ask.'

'And rightly so, Miss Ward. Miss Matilda Ward owned a large amount of very valuable jewellery. We have a copy of an insurance appraisal on file and some of the items are worth a considerable amount. As I advised you at our meeting, you inherit the jewellery, together with all Miss Matilda Ward's chattels, but only if you stay in the cottage for one year, of course. Until then, it's all held in trust, although you have use of everything until the year is up, which means you can wear the jewellery. Then, as we discussed, if you stay, it all belongs to you. If you leave before the year is up, it all reverts to the person or persons named in the codicil.'

'And you don't know who that is?'

'No, Miss Ward. My father drew up the will and codicil, as I mentioned. But did you say you can't find the jewellery?'

'Yes. We've looked everywhere we can think of, but no jewellery, and no laptop, so far, which is why we wondered if you had them.'

'I don't, Miss Ward. None of Miss Matilda Ward's chattels have been removed. As I explained, this is a most unusual situation. I would have preferred to meet you at the cottage and go through the inventory with you, but it was Miss Matilda Ward's wish that you be allowed to move in without this requirement. That was why I expressly stipulated at our meeting that it was in your best interest to go through the inventory, item by item, as soon as possible and to let me know immediately if anything was not as described. Unless the property has been broken into, which would surprise me greatly because I am certain Mrs Hester Burnstall would have notified this office, and the police, immediately if such an event had occurred, all the items listed must be there.

Has the property been broken into, Miss Ward? Is that what you are suggesting?'

'No. Um. I don't know. I don't think so because everything was neat and tidy when we arrived. The front door was locked, but not the back. Hettie Burnstall had left that open. She had been in to clean, as per your instructions, I believe.'

'That's correct. The property should not have been left unlocked though. Is anything else missing?'

'I don't know.'

'Have you checked the inventory, Miss Ward?'

'The inventory?'

'Yes, Miss Ward. The inventory. The one we have just been discussing. The one I gave you at our meeting.'

'Um. I'm sorry, Mr Dale. I don't remember you giving me an inventory.'

Mia glanced across at Ella and Garrick, shrugged and held out her palms to indicate she hadn't got a clue what Mr Dale was talking about.

A small sigh travelled through the phone. 'It was amongst the papers I gave you, Miss Ward. You may recall when you came to collect the keys, you signed certain documents of which I gave you copies. I also gave you a large brown envelope containing papers you might need during your first year and I showed you an inventory and explained what you should do. I know it was all somewhat of a shock at the time and perhaps I should have made absolutely certain that you had fully understood the situation, but I did advise you that, other than wear and tear, everything in the cottage must remain, and that nothing could be disposed of, and that you should go through the inventory, as discussed. At the same time, I explained that all services, such as electricity, telephone, and the like would be taken care of by this firm. I asked you to forward any bills or such that you may receive in error, to me and advised you that, until you become the owner, assuming you do of course, this firm will effectively be maintaining the property and paying all related bills and costs. I said that in layman's terms, you are looking after the cottage and all its contents, for one year and by way of payment, you had received the sum of ten thousand pounds and will be living there rent free. Do you recollect that conversation, Miss Ward?'

'Um. Some of it.'

Another small sigh could be heard before Mr Dale continued:

'I also said that details of where everything was, how it all works, the telephone number of the cottage, the WiFi password and the combination to the safe, were all in amongst those papers, Miss Ward. I can arrange to have copies sent to you if you have misplaced them. If you believe items may be missing, it is imperative that you check the inventory without delay and notify me, and if necessary the authorities, immediately. I can send someone from this office to go through it with you today, if you feel things are not as they should be, Miss Ward. And we must speak to Mrs Burnstall, of course. Are you certain that the jewellery is missing?'

'Um. Well it may not be missing, exactly. It's simply that we can't find it. And we're sure we've looked everywhere. I'm so sorry, Mr Dale. I'm embarrassed to say, I thought the papers were merely copies of the documents I signed. I obviously didn't take in everything you said. I was so surprised by it all that I probably misunderstood some of it. I'm afraid I haven't looked at the envelope since the day I left your office and I admit, I had forgotten all about it. I'm really sorry.'

'Wait a minute,' Garrick said. 'I'm Garrick Swann, a friend of Mia's. Did you say, "combination to the safe", Mr Dale? Did I hear that correctly? Because if there is a safe, perhaps the jewellery, and possibly also the laptop, are in that. We looked for one but couldn't find it. Do you know where it is?'

'Hello, Mr Swann. As Miss Ward is there with you and you're a friend, I'll assume Miss Ward is asking that question. I'm sure you understand I'm not at liberty to discuss the estate of the late Miss Matilda Ward with anyone other than Miss Ward.'

'We understand,' Mia said. 'But would you call me Mia, please? This is all very confusing with two Miss Wards. And yes please, I would like to know if there's a safe. If there is, perhaps we can all stop worrying.'

'There is certainly a safe, Miss Ward. Mia. I assumed, when you said that you had looked everywhere, you had already looked in there.'

'No. Because we don't know where it is.'

'The details are in the papers I gave you. But of course, as you said, you have mislaid them. The safe is in a small room off the attic room. I assume you've been up there?'

'Yes. But we didn't see a safe. Or another room.'

'That's because it's hidden, Miss Ward. I mean, Mia. It's on the wall opposite the square window, towards the end of the room. There are a row of panels and in the second to last panel, you'll find a small keyhole. It's very close to the beam, so you may have missed it. The key is amongst the set I gave you. It's a door to the room. A very small room but that room is where Miss Matilda Ward kept her most precious possessions. The jewellery, and the laptop, should be there. I'll need to get my files to give you the combination to the safe because I can't recall it off the top of my head. I'll do that now and call you back as soon as I have it to hand. I'll also have another set of papers prepared and I shall have someone from this office bring them to you later today. I don't think we need to worry after all, Miss Ward. Sorry.

Mia. I am certain the jewellery will be there, exactly where Miss Matilda Ward left it.'

'Thank you so much, Mr Dale,' Mia said. 'I am so sorry I worried you. It's my fault entirely. I should've listened more carefully at our meeting. I don't understand all this legal stuff. I'm not really sure what I've inherited and what I haven't.'

'I must accept part of the blame, Mia. I should have taken more time explaining it all to you. In hindsight, I probably should have arranged to meet you at the cottage and go through it with you there. That way we could have avoided any problems. But strictly speaking, at this moment in time, the only thing you have inherited is the sum of ten thousand pounds and the right to live in Sunbeam Cottage for one year. If you have any other questions, please don't hesitate to ask. I shall call you back shortly.'

'Thank you. Oh! There is one last thing, Mr Dale. I don't know if I'm allowed to ask this but is there a residual estate? I mean, did my great-aunt have other money or belongings that aren't included in the cottage? You said your firm will be paying all the bills for the cottage? But who will then pay yours? Did she make arrangements for all that? Or do I need to put aside some of the money I got, so that I can pay you?'

'No, Mia. All bills will be taken care of from Miss Matilda Ward's estate, including the inheritance tax and all other fees, which I won't go into detail about right now. A full breakdown will be supplied when the estate is finally wound up. But it seems I failed to make a great number of things clear to you at our meeting. Under the terms of Miss Matilda Ward's will, Mia, whomsoever inherits the cottage, also inherits the residuary estate. Which means that, assuming you comply by staying at the cottage for one year, you will be the sole beneficiary, other than one or two small, specific bequests. If you don't, it goes to the person or persons named in the codicil. What I'm telling you, Mia, is that at the end of your year in Sunbeam Cottage, you will be a very wealthy young woman.'

'What? So are you saying my great-aunt Matilda owns other stuff apart from Sunbeam Cottage and that if I live here for a year, I get it all? Every last penny of it?'

'Yes, Mia. That is exactly what I'm saying. And it's precisely what I tried to explain to you when we met. I apologise for failing to realise that you had not grasped the facts.'

'No, no. It was my fault, Mr Dale. And if I leave, that residuary estate goes to someone else? The person in the codicil?'

'Or persons. Yes. Exactly.'

'Is it … is it a very large estate? You said I'd be a very wealthy woman.'

'I can't divulge the exact amount until the end of the year, but yes. Miss Ward's estate, bearing in mind that it will also include Sunbeam Cottage and its contents, is a very large estate indeed. Even after taking into account the substantial sum of inheritance tax payable, the world, Miss Ward, sorry, Mia, would be your oyster. As I believe they say. So I'm sure you can see that it is definitely in your interest to stay the year. Having visited the property myself, although sadly, my visit was not the happiest experience, as I told you when we met, I do not believe that your great-aunt's bequest will prove to be an undue hardship, although it is certainly an unusual one. A most unusual one indeed. It raised a few questions for me, and my father before me, about the legal implications, but I assure you, it's all in order. I'll now find those papers and call you straight back.'

'Bloody Nora,' Ella said, when Mr Dale hung up the phone.

Garrick didn't say a word and nor did Mia. She was too astonished to speak.

Chapter Nineteen

Mia couldn't recall Mr Dale mentioning his visit at their meeting, but then neither could she recall most of what he had said. She clearly had not taken in much of it all. But she was in a state of shock at the time, having recently lost her job and her boyfriend, and was struggling to pay her rent. She was also searching for a new job. So it wasn't only the sudden 'appearance' of a dead, but until then completely unknown to her, great-aunt that was on her mind. It was hardly surprising that most of Mr Dale's information and advice had gone in one ear and out the other. She should have taken someone with her, or at the very least, asked Vernon Brett, her family's solicitor and friend to explain it to her. All she heard was that she could live rent free in a cottage for one year and then decide if she wanted to stay, and on top of that, she got ten thousand pounds. If she was completely honest, once she'd heard that the ten thousand would be in her account that afternoon, she hadn't really heard a word Mr Dale said afterwards. Images of her bank account being in the black for once, sort of drowned out everything else. But it was too late to worry about that now. She merely made a mental note to pay better attention in the future.

At least now she knew that somewhere in the attic room there was a safe, and that it probably contained Mattie's jewellery and possibly her laptop, and that Mr Dale would soon be calling her with the combination.

If only she could remember where on earth she had put that brown envelope. Not that it really mattered. If Mr Dale was having copies of everything delivered to her later that day, she could read it all this evening. Ella and Garrick would help her go through the inventory and it would be a relief to know where everything was and how it all worked, although so far, they had managed to find out most things for themselves.

It would be good to have the WiFi password though. She could send her mum emails, or messages on social media without the necessity of going to the pub, the top of Frog Hill, or climbing three hundred steps in the church steeple. This was only her third day here but she had felt oddly cut off from her mum, and it wasn't because Lori Ward was on a cruise ship somewhere. It was because Mia couldn't simply ping a text to her whenever she felt like it. Until coming here, she hadn't realised quite how dependant she was on modern technology.

Until coming here, she hadn't realised how dependant she was on her best friend Ella, either. And she definitely hadn't realised that she might not be quite so over her infatuation with Garrick as she thought she was. Until coming here.

'Well that's that then,' Garrick said, getting to his feet. 'There's nothing we can do until he calls back with the details, so I'll nip to the pub now for a quick coffee and I'll be back in half an hour or so.'

'That's it?' Ella queried. 'We've just heard that Mia could inherit a not-so-small fortune and all you've got to say is that you're going to the pub?'

He shrugged. 'What do you expect me to say? It's got nothing to do with me, has it? Besides, she hasn't got it yet. She doesn't get it for a year. I'll say congratulations then. In the meantime, things will carry on the way they are.'

'He's right,' Mia said. 'There's no point in thinking about that until this time next year. At which stage I'll either be homeless, or a very wealthy woman. I'm going for the second option, obviously, but a lot can happen in a year. A lot can happen in a couple of days, come to that.'

'True,' Ella said.

'I'm hoping quite a bit can happen in half an hour,' Garrick said, grinning and heading towards the front door. 'See you later.'

Ella gave him a little wave and leant towards Mia. 'I've just realised something. You don't have to pay any rent or bills for an entire year. You've got eight thousand pounds left in your account. The shops are miles away, so you won't be tempted to buy stuff, and the pub seems to be the entertainment hub around here. Unless you go completely bonkers with online shopping once we're connected to WiFi, you'll never need to work again. Eight grand will get you through the year and after that, you'll be loaded. Bloody Nora. I wish I had a great-aunt lurking somewhere. A life of luxury really appeals to me.'

'You're right,' Mia said.

She hadn't thought of that. Eight grand in London would last about two months. Here, it could easily see her through, especially with no bills to pay. Food, clothes, petrol and entertainment would be her only expenditure. She could probably even afford to go on holiday, if she wanted. Although living here was like a holiday. And the year would be gone before she knew it, if the last seven weeks were anything to go by. They had simply flown. One minute she was sitting in the solicitor's office, the next, she was here.

'I wonder who the other person is,' Ella said, slouching across the table. 'Or persons. Didn't your mum say that all your dad's relatives were now dead?'

Mia nodded. 'Yes. But I suppose there could be other relatives we don't know about. Dad only mentioned Matilda once, as far as Mum remembers, but there could be others he didn't bother to mention at all.'

'That's hardly likely. Ostracising one family member is pretty cruel. Ostracising several would be downright evil.' She grinned at Mia. 'It could be your mum, I suppose. That would sort of keep it in the family.'

'It's possible. But I get the feeling it's more likely to be a charity or something. Don't ask me why, I just do. As far as we know, I'm Mattie's only living blood relative. Who would you leave your money to if you didn't have any family?'

'As I haven't got any money to leave, it's a moot point, but if I had, I'd probably leave it to you.'

Mia nodded. 'And if I didn't have Mum, I'd leave mine to you. I might be wrong about the charity thing. Perhaps Mattie did the same. Perhaps the person, or persons, in the codicil are friends.'

Ella laughed. 'Perhaps it's Hettie Burnstall.'

'Or maybe she has shared it equally among lots of people in the village.'

'Perhaps she had other friends who don't live around here.'

Mia grinned. 'She may have returned it to that gangster you think she stole it from.'

Ella laughed even louder. 'Or distributed it equally amongst her many ex-lovers. All young men in their prime, of course.'

'Or maybe Mr Dale gets it, for services rendered by his father.'

'Or the vicar, to keep his bells in tip-top condition.'

They were still suggesting possible, but increasingly unlikely, potential beneficiaries almost half an hour later when their general silliness was interrupted by the phone. Mia managed to stop laughing and answer it. It was Mr Dale calling back.

'I apologise for keeping you waiting,' he said, after they had exchanged the usual pleasantries of hello. 'It took me a little longer than I thought. Do you have a pen?'

'No. But I have my phone. I can make a note on that. And there's no need to apologise. If I had read the papers you gave me, I wouldn't be wasting your time in the first place. It's me who should apologise.'

'No need. I'm here to help. I'll spell the WiFi password out for you. It's ErnestaiM, capital E at the start, capital M at the end, the rest all lower case. The combination to the safe is 2671958.'

'2671958,' Mia repeated, and shot a look at Ella. 'That's my dad's date of birth! The 26th of July 1958. And the password is his name then mine backwards. Ernest Mia. Ernest aiM.'

'Golly,' Mr Dale said. 'Well, they will be easy for you to remember. Although you're free to change them if you wish, but if you do, you must ensure you let me have a note of the new ones.

152

You can put them in a sealed envelope, if you like.'

'No. I'll leave them as they are, I think. No one knows them apart from us, so it's fine.'

'That keeps things simple. Now I'm sending someone down with copies of all the papers, as we discussed earlier. He should be with you by four at the latest, but we do have to make another set of copies, which is why he won't be with you until late afternoon. In the meantime, may I please ask you to check the safe and confirm that Miss Matilda Ward's jewellery and other personal belongings are there? You won't be able to confirm everything without the inventory, but the jewellery is the most important issue right now.'

'Yes, of course. I'll do that right away. This is a hands-free phone so once I get the safe open, I can call you back and tell you what's there and you can check it against your copy, if you like.'

'That's an excellent idea. That will put both our minds at rest. Goodbye for now.'

No sooner had Mia hung up than Garrick walked in with a smile on his face as big as the sun.

Ella saw it too. 'You're looking mighty pleased with yourself. I assume the tulips did the trick.'

He nodded and gave her a thumbs up. 'Worked a treat. I've got a date for Wednesday night.'

'That's nice,' Mia said, thinking it was anything but.

'Why Wednesday?' Ella asked.

'It's Alexia's night off.'

'Oh. You've got a date with Alexia,' she joked. 'I thought it was with one of the rugby team. We all know how much you *lurve*, rugby.'

'The joke's on you. I have got a date with one of the team. It seems they believe in equality in Little Pondale. Alexia's on the team.'

'What?' Mia couldn't have heard that correctly. 'Did you say Alexia is on the team? The rugby team?'

'Yes. But they're not in the official league. They don't have enough members. They only play other local towns and villages, who also have low membership. Toby and Jet are trying to put together a full squad by pulling in members from nearby teams. They're hoping to have it set up by next season and then they'll register with the league.'

'How immensely fascinating,' Ella said, pretending to stifle a huge yawn. 'In other news, we have the WiFi password so we'll soon be back in contact with the *un*civilised world of the web, and we're just about to crack the safe. Care to join us?' She got up and headed towards him.

'I wouldn't miss it for the world.'

'We've also been trying to guess who gets the dosh if Mia can't stand living here for a year, and bails.'

'Oh. And who's the lucky person, or persons in your considered opinions?'

'We've narrowed it down to a half man, half yeti called Fred who lives in a tent in the foothills of the Himalayas. We believe Mattie ran off with him when he was brought to London by the revered explorer who found him and that's why she was ostracised from the family. But their love couldn't survive the harsh conditions, or Fred's table manners, so Mattie came home broken-hearted and shut herself off from the world. But a few years ago, he sent her a friend request on Facebook so she added a codicil to her will that he would get everything if Mia bailed. And because Fred's half yeti, he will live to be two hundred and six, so the dosh may come in useful.'

Garrick raised one eyebrow. 'My only question is, how do you know his name is Fred?'

'That's easy,' Mia said, trying hard not to grin. 'He was named after the revered explorer who found him.'

'Of course he was,' Garrick said. 'And how do you know his … No, forget it. I'm not even going to ask.'

'Spoilsport,' Ella threw at him as he turned and walked towards the stairs.

'It's called being a grown-up. You should try it sometime.'

Chapter Twenty

Much to everyone's relief, once Mia, Ella and Garrick spotted the relevant panel, searched for the keyhole, found the right key and used the combination to open the safe, Mattie's jewellery was discovered inside. It was kept in three separate jewellery boxes and judging by the contents of each, was graded by value. One box contained what appeared to their untrained eyes to be costume jewellery. One contained more expensive-looking items and the final one contained rings, necklaces, brooches, earrings and bracelets that almost blinded them when they opened the lid. They assumed that box contained the most precious items.

Mr Dale confirmed that all was as it should be as they briefly described each item to him and he checked it off his list.

'We found the laptop, too,' Mia said. 'But that also seems to be password protected.'

'I have been thinking about that,' Mr Dale informed her. 'There may be items on that, containing information and details of the estate that you are not, as yet, strictly entitled to be made aware of. I feel I should ask you to hand it to my colleague this afternoon in order for me to check. I shall hopefully be able to return it once I have ensured it contains no such information, or if it does, once I have copied and removed the same from the device. I'm sure you understand. In hindsight, I probably should have removed it prior to today.'

'Oh. Um. Of course. I'll hand it over the moment he arrives. I was simply hoping that it might shed some light on who, exactly, Mattie was and a bit about her history. As you know, Mr Dale, I wasn't even aware of her existence until seven weeks ago, and my mum knows nothing about her. I would really like to understand who she was, how she knew about me, and why she decided to make me a beneficiary in her will.'

'I understand completely. I wish I could shed some light on her story, but my father dealt with her, and I only met her once or twice. I was hoping to get to know her better on the day I came to visit to go through a few things with her. Alas, that was not to be. I shall return it to you when, and if, I can. Unless I can be of any further assistance this morning, I shall say goodbye for now.'

'Bugger,' Mia said, once she was sure he had hung up. 'I was hoping I could be nosey.'

'You'll have to wait,' Garrick said. 'Or find some other means of learning more about her. I assume you Googled her name when you first got the news?'

'Yeah. But there are quite a few Matilda Wards. I haven't even seen a photo of her so I don't know what she looks like. None of the ones I saw looked like a ninety-nine-year-old, although some did look pretty ancient. And none gave a location of Little Pondale.'

'I've just realised,' Ella said, 'that there aren't any photographs in this cottage. Not one. Unless she hid those in here too. She definitely liked hiding things away, didn't she? The wardrobes, the en-suite, this little room. Either Mattie was paranoid about privacy, or she really did have something to hide.'

'You're right,' Mia said. 'That hadn't occurred to me. The photos I mean, not the paranoia. Everyone has photos in their homes, don't they? I've got loads. And thousands on my phone.'

'Did she have a phone?' Ella asked. 'That might be in here too, if she did.'

'She had a landline,' Garrick said. 'I know she was incredibly fit for a woman of her age, but I can't see her going to the top of Frog Hill to make a call, or climbing the three hundred steps in the church steeple. She probably relied on the landline and her laptop. She may have photos on that.'

'I wish I could look.' Mia hugged the laptop to her as if it were more valuable to her than the three boxes of jewellery. 'I really want to know who she was.'

'There are other ways of finding out,' Garrick said.

'How?'

'Ask the locals. She lived here for twenty-five years and everyone called her Mattie – apart from Hettie, of course – but that means they must have known at least a few things about her. Even Hettie. In fact, Hettie probably knows more than most because even if Mattie shut herself up here whenever Hettie was around, the woman knows something about everyone. And also, in all the years Mattie lived here, she must've gone to some parties, or celebrations, or Christmas events. People always take photos at those, so if Mattie went to only one even, there may be a photo of her there. We simply need to ask around.'

'You're not just handsome, are you, brother dear? You're pretty smart too.'

'Praise indeed.' He threw Ella a sardonic look. 'I'm also starving. Can we go and make some lunch?'

'But I thought we were going to ask around about photos?' Mia queried.

Garrick sighed softly. 'You're here for a year, Mia. You don't have to do everything the minute you arrive.'

Ella grinned and gave him a shove. 'Says the man who couldn't wait to ask a certain barmaid on a date.'

Garrick grinned back, grabbed both Mia and his sister gently by their wrists and ushered them out of the little room.

'That's a different matter entirely. Alexia's gorgeous and there are too many single guys in this village for my liking. Plus I haven't had sex for months. I needed to get a date as soon as possible before Alexia got away. Mattie's dead and buried. She's not going anywhere. And finding out about her isn't going to help any of us with our sex lives.'

'Then maybe you're not as smart as I thought,' Ella said, allowing herself to be marched towards the stairs. 'Asking all the single men if they have photos of Mia's dear, departed great-aunt Mattie, or if they have any stories about her to tell, may do wonders for our sex lives. We can ask to go back to their places, and see their photo albums.'

She winked at Mia but Mia wasn't listening.

Garrick having sex with Alexia was all Mia could think about.

And it was the most unpleasant thought she'd had all day.

Since when had Garrick Swann become so spontaneous?

She preferred him the way he was before.

Chapter Twenty-One

Mr Dale's colleague, who introduced himself as David Dale, arrived at Sunbeam Cottage a little after four.

'I apologise for my tardiness,' he said, with a contrite expression. 'It took longer to get here than I had anticipated and I found myself stuck in Seaside Road for at least ten minutes due to a tractor performing a seemingly impossible manoeuvre in the lane.'

'That's quite all right, Mr Dale,' Mia said,' and you're not really late at all. We were told you wouldn't be arriving until around four. I hope you don't mind me asking, but is Mr Clive Dale your father?'

He looked relieved, and smiled as he visibly relaxed. 'Yes, Miss Ward. You may call me David if that makes things easier. Here are the copies you need.' He handed over a box file of papers. 'I'm more than happy to go through them with you, if you wish, and I can also run through the inventory with you. It appears to be a rather lengthy document but it really won't take more than an hour to check things off. I was the one who drew it up, so I know where everything is.'

'Thank you, David. That would be really helpful, if you're sure you don't mind. I'll make some tea and we can get started.'

'Excellent, Miss Ward. A cup of tea is just what I need.'

Was that sarcasm? One look at his face told her it wasn't and she led the way into the kitchen where Ella and Garrick were writing a shopping list.

'These are my friends, Ella and Garrick. They're staying with me for a few days to help me settle in. If it's okay with you, I'd like them to be present when we go through the papers. I didn't take it all in when your father went through them with me. I don't want to miss anything this time.'

David smiled, exchanged greetings and said he had no objection at all to Ella and Garrick's presence, but when he finally left, almost two and a half hours later, Mia got the feeling Ella and Garrick were starting to take objection to his.

'Bloody Nora. I don't think that man has an ounce of humour in his body.' Ella collapsed on a kitchen chair and slumped across the table.

Garrick slouched in a chair opposite. 'That's almost three hours of my life I'll never get back.'

'And I still think I'm none the wiser,' Mia said, grabbing three glasses from the cupboard and handing Garrick a bottle of wine to open. 'At least now we all know where everything is. And he said

I can pack up all Mattie's clothes and store them in the attic, so that's good.'

'And that Mattie didn't own a mobile phone,' Ella said. 'Which still seems weird in this day and age.'

'She was ninety-nine,' Garrick said, opening the wine and filling the glasses. 'And there's little point in having one if you live in this place.'

Ella sat upright and grabbed a glass, almost before Garrick had finished filling it. 'I need this. It's good to have the internet up and running. When I checked my emails I'd got over a hundred! Many of them were junk though, but even so. A couple of days offline and things really start to pile up.'

'Especially on the business side,' Garrick said. 'I'd got two new orders when I checked mine.'

'Does that mean you have to go back?' Mia wasn't sure if that would be a good thing, or not. It would mean he couldn't go on his date with Alexia, but Mia wouldn't really benefit from that.

'Not unless you want to get rid of me.' Garrick threw her a grin. 'As Ella always says, the good thing about having your own business is that you can work from anywhere. Depending on what you do, I suppose. I made sure I'd used up my store of wood before I moved back to London, and because Ella told me we were coming down here for a week or two, I hadn't ordered any more in. The beauty is, I can order it online and have it

163

delivered anywhere. Or see if there's a local timber merchant and go and select my own. What I'm saying is, I'd quite like to stay for a while, unless you'd rather I didn't.'

'No. I'm happy for you to stay. We'd probably better not tell the Dales though. Mr Dale senior will probably make you sign something, telling you what you can and can't do. I hadn't really realised, until Dale the younger went through it again today, quite how complicated this 'year' thing is.'

Garrick grinned. 'You're right. He would. And I suppose it all sounded complicated, but really, it's like you having a year's tenancy on a fully furnished house, all bills included. So, you're happy for me to stay on then? You can kick me out at any time. I promise I'll leave if you ask me to. And it'll only be for a month or so. Your mum will be back by then and I know Lori will be on her way here the minute the cruise ship docks in Southampton.'

Mia grinned. 'She's already told me she will. We messaged one another on Facebook. Ella's right. It is fantastic to be connected to the world wide web once more. But you don't have to leave when Mum arrives. She'd love to see you again. There're four bedrooms in this cottage, so it's not a problem. What about you, Ella? Did you mean it when you said you'd stay for longer? I'd love to have you around.'

Ella emptied her wine glass and smiled. 'I'd love to stay. Now we've got the internet again, I can work from here. I've got nothing booked in for the next two weeks anyway, and after that, I can do most of my work online. If any of them want me to go through hard copies, they can have them couriered to me. It's no big deal.'

'It's settled then.' Mia refilled their wine glasses and raised hers in the air. 'Here's to Mattie for her wonderful gift. And to us, and the coming months in Sunbeam Cottage.'

Garrick raised his glass. 'Here's to you staying the year, to us and to Mattie.'

Ella joined in. 'Here's to Mattie, to us, and to new beginnings. Cheers.'

'To new beginnings!' Mia exclaimed, smiling brightly. 'What a wonderful thought. Yep. Here's to Mattie, to us, to Sunbeam Cottage, to Little Pondale and to new beginnings.'

'New beginnings,' Garrick said. 'I like the sound of that.'

'And to all three of us possibly finding new love,' Ella added, smiling broadly. 'Or should that be 'True Love'?' She winked. 'Well, a girl can dream. And Little Pondale is bursting with opportunities on that score.'

Mia nodded, unable to stop her gaze drifting in Garrick's direction. 'Then here's to new beginnings, new love and to possibly finding 'The One'. I can't wait to see what this year has in store for all of us.'

End of Part One

The Cottage on Lily Pond Lane

Part Two:

Summer secrets

Chapter One

'How is it even possible?' Mia scrolled through the photos on her laptop, once again, one elbow balanced on the edge of the kitchen table as she slumped forward and rested her head in her hand. Not one photograph contained an image of great-aunt Matilda. Hettie Burnstall had spent the last three hours going through them all with Mia, Ella and Garrick and had confirmed that fact.

Ella's blonde curls danced around her shoulders as she shook her head. 'Mattie obviously didn't want her photo taken. Even Hettie said that every time someone pointed a camera in Mattie's direction, Mattie turned away. I'm convinced she was in hiding, no matter what you and Garrick say.'

Garrick held up a faded photograph. 'At least we know she had light-brown hair when she came to live here. Freda assured me when she took this off the wall of photos in the pub, that this is definitely a photo of the back of Mattie's head, and Hettie thought so too.' He grinned and flipped the photo over. 'Not that it's much help. But it says on the reverse, 'Christmas 1993'. Unless my maths is wrong, according to Hettie, that was the year Mattie came to live here.'

Ella took the photo and peered at it before smiling across at Mia. 'Yeah, and we now know you and Mattie had at least one thing in common. You've both got golden-brown hair.'

Garrick tutted. 'Mattie must've been seventy-four when that was taken, so her hair was obviously dyed.

Ella laughed. 'So's Mia's. Did you think Mother Nature gave her those gorgeous highlights?'

Garrick furrowed his brows as if he wasn't sure how to answer that, but Mia came to his rescue.

'Spooky that we should pick similar colours though. And similar hairstyles, if what Hettie said was true. That Mattie always had her hair cut into a shoulder-length bob.'

Ella winked at her. 'I'm not sure I'd happily tell people I've got the same haircut as my ancient, now dead, great-aunt. It doesn't exactly scream, "young, hip, independent woman," does it? I'm not saying there's anything wrong with your hairstyle. Just don't mention the resemblance to Mattie's, that's all.'

'Good point.' Mia nodded, leant back in her chair and stretched her arms in the air, tipping her head from side to side. 'I need more coffee and I'm guessing you do too. I hadn't realised how mind-numbingly boring, looking at hundreds and hundreds of other people's photos can be, nor how spending three hours with Hettie clucking and cooing over them can make me lose the will to live.'

Ella and Garrick both nodded and grinned as Mia got up to make the drinks.

'We now know what Hettie's husband, Hector looked like,' Ella said. 'I know this is mean but after spending all morning with her I'm beginning to wonder if Hector didn't throw himself into the path of that car and his death had nothing at all to do with the curse of Frog's Hollow.'

Mia gasped. 'That is mean, Ella.' She tried to stop the grin but failed. 'Possibly true though.'

'But it was kind of Hettie to look at them,' Garrick pointed out, frowning. 'As we had no idea what Mattie looked like, it would've been like searching for an *invisible* needle in a haystack without her help. And it was good of so many of the villagers to let you have access to their photos. Freda making that announcement certainly did the trick.'

'Also true.' Mia rinsed the mugs under the tap and gave them a quick once over with a tea towel. Since Freda had told everyone in The Frog and Lily on Monday night that Mia wanted to see any photos anyone had which might contain Mattie's image, several of the villagers had handed over photographs, USB sticks with photos on, and even CDs on which they'd downloaded copies. They had all been given to Freda who had passed them on to Garrick in the pub on Tuesday night. 'But I think Hettie being a nosey old biddy, had more to do with her offer than kindness. She wanted to get a peek at everyone else's photos. And I got the feeling that Justin merely wanted us to see photos of his dance slash stripper troupe. Not that I'm complaining. Seeing three half-naked men with rippling muscles covered in oil was the highlight of this morning.'

Ella giggled. 'And the DVD was the icing on the cake. But the reason I spent so long watching it over and over again was because he told us at choir practice that he was certain Mattie had attended that particular meeting of the local Women's Institute.'

Mia turned and grinned at her. 'Yeah, right. Like anyone would believe that's the reason.'

Garrick rolled his eyes. 'What amuses me is that they called that meeting, a study of the art of dance. Did you hear Hettie say that you can buy DVDs of the shows and that she has several?'

Ella shuddered dramatically before nudging his arm. 'Yep, and I never thought I'd say this, but I'm going to join the local W.I. I really like their style. Mind you, I never thought I'd join a choir, either, but last night was fun, wasn't it, Mia?'

Mia nodded, grinned and placed what was left of a packet of chocolate digestives on the table. 'Amazingly, it was. And I think I'm going to join the W.I. too. But before we do anything else, we really must make a trip to the shops. We're getting dangerously low on biscuits. This is what's left of our final packet. We've eaten the other three and this is only our fifth day here.'

'Bloody Nora.' Ella grabbed the biscuits before Garrick got a chance. 'Four each and then they're gone. Is it just me, or does it feel as if we've been here since forever?'

Garrick took his four and shoved the last four in the packet across to where Mia had been sitting. 'It definitely feels like a lot longer than five days, but that's because we've been so busy, I suppose.'

Ella bit into a biscuit and winked at her brother. 'You certainly have. Where're you taking Alexia on your date tonight?'

Mia tensed. In the excitement of getting the photos, she'd almost forgotten Garrick and Alexia were going on a date.

She'd been worried about it when he'd first mentioned it on Monday but now it was somehow worse. Not only was Alexia drop-dead gorgeous with the body of a goddess, she was also a lovely person. Mia was rather hoping the woman would turn out to be a bitch but in just the few days Mia had known her, it was obvious Alexia could be a good friend.

Last night in the pub, Alexia had persuaded Mia and Ella to join the choir. Neither Mia nor Ella could sing to save their lives but when Alexia reminded them that Tom Tyburn, the vicar, ran the choir and mentioned that Justin Lake, Rupert Day and Jet Cross were members, the choir suddenly had a definite appeal. So much so, they'd gone along. They had tried to get Garrick to join them but he said his singing voice sounded like a rhino being strangled in a mud hole and whilst Mia had no clue as to what sound that would make, it probably wasn't pleasant, so they'd left him in the pub. Mia and Ella had certainly enjoyed it. Apart from the fact that in addition to Alexia's many attributes, she also had the voice of an angel. Didn't the woman have any faults at all?

Tom had welcomed his new members with open arms – literally, and Rupert, or Bear, as Ella now called him, seemed exceedingly pleased to see them. Jet merely smiled and nodded his head at them, then hung back without a word. Once or twice during the two-hour practice, Mia had cast a surreptitious glance in his direction from her position in the front row. She'd blushed crimson each time when she'd met those incredible eyes of his looking at her, and seen the curve of a smile on his perfect mouth. The man was far too sure of himself. But he had good reason to be, with his looks and undeniable sex appeal. Even in loose-fitting jeans and a polo shirt that had seen better days, the guy was to die for. Men like Jet should be tattooed with a health warning. Or at least a heart warning.

Justin arrived during the fifteen-minute refreshment break and, after apologising to Tom and everyone for being late, spoke to Mia and Ella for the first time.

'I heard you're looking for photos of Mattie.' His smile was like an advert for teeth whitening toothpaste and he could have easily stepped from the cover of a glossy magazine. His faded but clearly expensive jeans, together with a designer T-shirt, clung to his athletic body like a second skin and his raven-coloured hair gleamed in the mellow, church lighting as he swept a lengthy lock of it from his handsome, tanned face. 'I've given Freda a couple of CDs of photos and a DVD of one of the shows we did for the W.I. because I know Mattie was in the audience. If I'd known you were coming to choir practice, I'd have given them to you here. They're copies of the originals so feel free to keep them.'

'Thanks, Justin,' Mia said, dragging her gaze from his body and once again shooting a look at Jet. She quickly averted her eyes as he raised his glass of orange juice to her and grinned. 'Um. That's very kind of you. Did you say Mattie came to see your show?'

'She came to every show we've ever done in Little Pondale. Mattie was the reason I got into dancing in the first place. She said I had a talent for it.'

That was quite a shock. 'My great-aunt suggested you become a stripper? Sorry. I didn't mean it to come out like that.'

Justin grinned. 'No problem. She didn't exactly suggest the stripping bit, although she told me after the first show that I definitely had a talent for that too. No, she saw me in a school musical when I was about nine and she said I should become a dancer. But Dad was a baker and there was no way a boy of his was going to "faff around on a stage", so I became a baker like him. When he died a few years ago, I took over the bakery, and started dancing on the side.' He winked. 'If you like what you see on the DVD, you may want to come along to one of our shows. We perform in most of the village halls within a sixty-mile radius. Our next show here is in a few weeks.'

Ella was mesmerised. 'What's the name of your dance troupe?'

'We're called The Frog Hill Hounds.'

'Oh.' Ella was clearly disappointed but she smiled. 'We'll look forward to watching the DVD.'

Justin's gaze travelled the length of her and he smiled wickedly as he turned to walk towards Jet. 'If you ask nicely, I may give you a private performance.'

Mia slapped Ella on the back as she choked on her orange juice.

'He's clearly got his eye on you,' Alexia said, smiling warmly.

Mia frowned. 'He seems nice but a bit of a Jack the Lad. Was that true about Mattie and his dad?'

Alexia nodded. 'Every word. He comes across as a player but it's all an act. He's a great guy and unlike someone else I could mention, he won't break your heart and walk away. If he's going to dump you, he'll do it nicely and he'll hang around until he's sure you're fine.'

There was a distinct edge to Alexia's voice and Mia followed the direction of her gaze. It landed on Jet who was completely oblivious and chatting avidly to Rupert as Justin joined them.

Ella must have noticed too. 'That sounds as if you've dated Justin. And not only Justin. Have you also dated Jet or Bear?'

Alexia shrugged. 'It's a small village. I've dated every single guy in my age group. Except the vicar. And my brother, Toby, of course.'

'Every guy?' Ella queried, throwing Mia a look of surprise. 'So what's wrong with the vicar?'

'Nothing. He's simply never asked me out. I considered asking him once, but Mum told me not to mess with a man of the cloth. Which is a pity, because I wouldn't mind messing with him.' She shrugged again. 'Some things just aren't meant to be though, are they?'

Perhaps Tom had felt his ears burning because he turned and smiled at the three of them before declaring that break was over and ushering everyone back into position for the second hour of practice.

Mia wanted to ask Alexia more about her ex-boyfriends – and one in particular, but as Garrick was waiting outside when practice finished, she didn't get a chance.

And now tonight, Garrick was adding to Alexia's list of men.

How – and why – had all of her other relationships ended?

Mia wasn't sure if she was more concerned about Alexia or Garrick.

Chapter Two

Much to Mia's annoyance, Garrick wouldn't discuss how his date with Alexia went. He spent the first hour of Thursday morning mowing the lawn, partly to avoid Hettie when she came to clean, no doubt, but also partly to avoid Mia and Ella's questions. The rest of the morning he simply sauntered around with a smile on his face and a far-away look in his eyes.

At least he hadn't spent the night with her. Mia had heard him come home at precisely eleven-thirty-six. Not that she had lain in bed awake, staring at the clock, waiting for him. She'd had her head buried in a book and merely happened to glance at the clock when she heard the front door close and the stairs creak. The fact that she couldn't recall one word she had read and would be hard-pressed to know what page she was on, had nothing to do with Garrick. She had other things on her mind besides him and his love life. Like making sure she added chocolate digestives to the shopping list, and other equally important stuff. Or so she tried to convince herself.

'When you eventually come down from cloud nine,' Mia snapped at Garrick during lunch which consisted of left-over pizza and the remnants of a decidedly wilted lettuce, 'do you think you could drive us to the shops?'

'Sorry. What?' Garrick clearly hadn't heard a word, and he hadn't touched his lunch.

'Will you drive us to the shops?'

He glanced from Mia to Ella and back again. 'Of course. But why d'you need me to drive you? You've got a car.'

Ella grinned. 'The breathalyser would explode if she got stopped. We stayed in last night and had the last frozen pizza, washed down with two or three bottles of wine. And get this. We played chess. Well sort of. Neither of us knows how to play it so we made it up as we went along. It's surprising how entertaining an evening can be when you don't have a TV. How much did you have to drink?'

'I didn't.' He frowned. 'You two really shouldn't drink so much. It was a beautiful evening. Why didn't you go for a walk?'

'Where to?' Mia asked. 'The pub?'

He shook his head. 'There're miles of footpaths through the countryside. There's Frog Hill. The beach. Oh sorry. Forget the beach. That wouldn't be good with your fear of water, would it? Although the tide goes out so far here that you could walk near the dunes and not even notice you're by the sea.'

'Believe me, I'd notice.' Mia studied his face over the rim of her mug of tea. 'Is that where you went? For a walk on the beach?'

Garrick smiled wistfully but didn't respond.

Ella poked him on the arm. 'Why the secrecy?'

'Let's get to the shops,' he said, still smiling as he got to his feet. 'Alexia told me about a wood merchant and I believe it's on the way. You don't mind if we stop there on the way back, do you? It won't take long to see if he's got anything of interest.' He didn't wait for an answer and was opening the front door a moment later.

Ella shook her head, slurped her tea and stood up. 'First he won't talk about his break-up with Fiona. Now he won't talk about his date last night. There's something seriously up with my brother and I haven't a clue what it is.'

Mia hadn't got a clue either and she definitely wanted to find out.

But it soon became clear Garrick had no intention of talking about his relationships.

During their shopping trip, Mia and Ella spent most of the thirty-minute journey there, asking subtle, and some not so subtle questions, all of which Garrick evaded answering. They continued their interrogation in the supermarket and were so intent on their 'mission', they forgot to browse in any of the boutiques or shoe shops in the town.

That was so unusual, Garrick made a point of mentioning it, especially as they hadn't been near a shop for almost a week.

'We'll go on a shopping spree another day,' Mia said.

'Yeah,' Ella added. 'It's not as if we need anything. We've even decided not to get a TV for a while.'

'Bloody hell,' Garrick replied, stopping in his tracks for dramatic effect. 'I never thought I'd hear my sister say those words. Or you, Mia. I think we need to find a doctor right away, or at the very least, a pharmacist. You two must be sick if you can walk past all these shops without looking in every single one. And I'll be very interested to see how long it is before you're buying a TV.'

Ignoring his facetious remark, Mia and Ella renewed their line of questioning and continued it as they drove to the wood merchant and even in the fish and chip shop where they stopped for supper, until Garrick finally snapped.

'Instead of asking me so many questions about my love life, why don't you two concentrate on your own? You can ask me until you're blue in the face but this is all you'll get. No comment. Okay? Now can we please change the subject? Finding a photograph of Mattie was a dismal failure, so what's the next step?'

Mia didn't have a clue and Ella had no suggestions. Even Garrick was at a loss. The thirty-minute journey home was a relatively quiet one. There was no point in probing Garrick further as he clearly wouldn't budge and all three of them spent the journey deep in thought.

'There's only one thing we can do,' Mia said to Ella when they returned to the cottage at eight in the evening and were unpacking the groceries. 'We need to ask Alexia.'

Ella beamed. 'That's an excellent idea. I could murder a drink. Er. What do we need to ask Alexia? About Mattie, or Garrick?'

'Both.' Mia switched on the kettle and opened a new packet of chocolate digestives. She took one out and munched on it, offering the packet to Ella, who did the same.

'Phew!' Garrick dumped three cases of wine on the worktop. 'I'll say it again. You two really shouldn't drink so much.'

'Excuse us!' Mia said. 'You drink wine too. I'm making tea. D'you want one?'

Garrick grinned. 'No thanks. I've finished unloading so I'm off to the pub.'

Mia glared at him. 'What was that about drinking too much?'

His grin broadened. 'I have no intention of drinking.' He grabbed the large bouquet of red tulips, red carnations and yellow roses he had purchased from a quaint little florist shop near the wood merchant's, and without another word, headed back towards the front door.

'So much for asking Alexia,' Ella said, grabbing another biscuit. 'She'll be busy.'

'She won't be the only one.' Mia set a determined look on her face. 'Forget the tea. We're going to the pub.'

Chapter Three

'Last night was a complete waste of time.' Mia slathered marmalade on her toast, still annoyed about her evening in the pub. Alexia had been working behind the bar so Garrick spent most of the evening chatting with her brother Toby, along with Justin, Bear and Jet. Mia took the opportunity to have a word with Alexia but Alexia had seemed a little distant. Cool even. Definitely not the friendly, chatty woman she had been before.

Ella grinned. 'Not a complete waste. I did get to spend at least half an hour talking to Justin. Am I being an idiot? I think I really like him.'

Mia shrugged. 'I don't know. Alexia said he was a nice guy and he did seem genuine last night. I got the feeling he likes you too. He spent most of the time asking things about you, not talking about himself. I'm sure that means he's interested.' She grinned. 'But I thought you liked the vicar? And before that, you liked Bear. And let's not forget you had the hots for Jet the minute you saw him.'

Ella giggled. 'Okay, I see your point. It's difficult to choose. But I think I like Justin most of all. Perhaps I should be like Alexia and go out with all of them.'

Mia frowned. 'What was up with her last night? She seemed distinctly off. I asked her how her date with Garrick went and she gave me a really odd look and said something like, 'You should know.' Then went off to serve someone else.'

'Did she? Okay, that is weird. Perhaps she thinks Garrick told us all about it and that didn't please her. How wrong can she be? So what should I do about Justin?'

'Wait and see if he asks you out. Or go to his bakery and ask to see his buns.'

Ella grinned as she bit into her toast, pulling a face as she chewed. 'We should've gone to him for our bread. After that loaf of his Hettie brought us, this supermarket stuff tastes like plastic.'

'Morning.' Garrick ambled into the kitchen, looking half asleep. 'I really hope you didn't, but did either of you say anything to Alexia? When I gave her the flowers and asked for another date, she was a bit vague.'

Ella raised her brows. 'And why should that have anything to do with us? Perhaps not every woman finds you as charming as we do.'

Mia sipped her coffee, the weight of Garrick's stare bearing down on her.

'Oh, okay. But it wasn't anything I said. All I asked was how the date went and she was already in a bit of a strop. I was just telling Ella. Alexia said something like, 'you should know,' and then walked off.'

Garrick frowned. 'That's odd. Unless she thinks I told you all about it. I'll have a word with her today.'

Ella pushed back her chair. 'I'm off to get some bread.'

'We've got bread.' Garrick pointed to the loaf on the table.

'Not that stuff,' Ella said, hurrying along the hall. 'Tasty bread.'

'What you mean is, you're going to flirt with Justin Lake.' His words fell on deaf ears as Ella shut the front door.

'She's decided she likes him the most,' Mia said, passing Garrick a mug of coffee.

'Thanks. I'm not surprised.' He looked at Mia over the rim. 'Have you decided who you like the most?'

Mia choked back her coffee.

Finally she managed, 'It doesn't really matter who I like the most, if that person doesn't feel the same about me.'

He stared at her for a moment before replying: 'No. That's true. It doesn't.'

'Who can that be?' Mia got up to answer the doorbell, thankful for the interruption.

She was so surprised to see who it was when she opened the front door, that the only thing she could think to say was, 'Bloody Nora!'

The morning sunlight made Jet's hair seem even darker. She couldn't see his eyes behind his sunglasses but the grin on his luscious-looking lips was enough to make her heart skip a beat and her legs impersonate jelly.

'No,' he said, his voice as sultry as a summer's night. 'Not Nora. Don't you remember? The name's Jet. Jet Cross.'

She half expected him to add that he had a licence to kill, but he didn't.

'Er. Hi. What do you want?'

His raised brows were evident above the rim of his glasses and Mia realised how rude that must have sounded.

'Sorry,' she said. 'Good morning. What can I do for you?'

His grin turned to a bright and sexy smile. 'Good morning, Mia. It's more a case of what I can do for you.'

The tone of his voice conjured up a number of things in Mia's mind that he could probably do for her and heat rushed to every last inch of skin on her body. She gripped the door knob a little tighter and leant against the edge of the door. All she managed to say was, 'Oh?'

'Would you like to go for a walk?' He was still smiling.

'A walk?'

'Yes. Do you have a cold? Your voice sounds a bit croaky.'

'No.' She coughed to clear her throat. 'You're asking me to go for a walk?'

'Yes.'

'Why?'

A furrow creased his brow. 'Because it's a lovely morning for a walk.'

'A walk where?'

'Along the beach,' he suggested.

Mia shook her head. 'No way!'

Jet tensed visibly but relaxed just as quickly. 'Is it me, or the beach that puts you off?'

'The beach. I'm afraid of water.'

'Really?' He seemed genuinely surprised.

Mia nodded. 'I nearly drowned when I was six. I haven't been in the sea since then. Or a swimming pool either. I can force myself to walk on a beach about twice a year, providing it's a beach I know well and that I'm with someone I feel I can trust with my life.'

'That's a shame. Especially if you're going to be living here. I wonder if there's something we can do about that.'

'About what? My fear of water? Or about me living here?' She had no idea why she had said that second part.

'Your fear. If I promise to make absolutely certain you don't drown, will you come with me?'

'It's not funny.'

'I agree. It's not. So will you come with me?'

'For a walk along the beach?'

'Yes.'

'Absolutely not.'

'Don't you trust me?'

She frowned at him. 'I don't know you. And from what I've heard, you're not a man any woman can trust.'

'Oh?' He tensed again and this time he didn't relax. 'Are you someone who takes notice of gossip, Mia? That surprises me. Mattie never did. And I knew her well.'

Mia met his eyes. 'Mattie? You knew Mattie well?' A sudden thought popped into her head but it was so unpleasant she could hardly bare to think it. Why on earth she said it, she had no idea. 'Oh my God! You didn't add my great-aunt to your list of heart-broken conquests, did you? Because that's just gross!'

The sultry tone turned to ice and the glare he gave her could have frozen her on the spot as he virtually spat out his response. 'No, Mia. I didn't. And not that it matters, but I don't have a list of conquests, or any list for that matter. I was clearly mistaken about you. I thought you were like Mattie, but you're not. Except, perhaps, in looks. I'm sorry I bothered you.'

As he turned and marched away, Mia meant to say she was sorry for offending him. Instead she said, 'You don't bother me one bit, Jet Cross. Not one little bit.' She slammed the door so hard that Garrick rushed into the hall.

'What's wrong, Mia? Who was that?'

'That was a jumped-up, arrogant pig of a man who thinks he can just click his fingers and every woman will fall at his feet. Then he breaks their hearts and moves on to the next one. Well, if he thinks he's doing that to me, he's got another think coming.'

Garrick frowned. 'Who?'

Mia gasped. 'Jet bloody Cross, of course! Who else?'

Garrick tutted. 'You shouldn't believe everything you hear. I've told you that before. What did he say to upset you?'

'He …he asked me to go for a walk! And he clearly thought I'd be so honoured I'd do exactly what he wanted.'

Garrick's frown deepened. 'A walk? I don't know why that would make you so angry. And I may not know him well but Jet Cross is the least jumped-up man I've ever met. As for being arrogant, I don't think it's arrogance at all. I think it's confidence and determination.'

'Confidence. Arrogance. Determination. Call it what you like. From the moment I saw him hold up all the traffic to manoeuvre his bloody tractor into that field, I knew he would be trouble.'

'Did you? I thought you fancied him. Ella certainly did. And the only traffic he held up, was us. I think you're wrong about him, Mia. For one thing, I bet you don't know that he and his mum were living on the breadline after his dad left with another woman when he was twelve. They were living in a cottage on Little Pond Farm and the miserable git who owned the farm back then nearly threw them out when the dad left. I don't know all the details but I was told that Mattie persuaded the farmer to let them stay and Jet worked every hour he could to build a better life for him and his mum, even though it was illegal for a kid to work more than a few hours a week. I also heard that when the farmer decided to sell up, Mattie gave Jet a loan. He was only sixteen at the time and no bank would've lent him the money. He paid her back every last penny of it until the farm was finally his outright, just one year ago. I honestly don't think the guy had time to intentionally break every woman's heart. Since the age of twelve, he's spent almost every hour working.'

To say that Garrick's words left Mia stunned, was an understatement. She would have asked him more but Hettie Burnstall arrived unexpectedly and as Hettie had brought a cake she had baked, Mia had to let her in. Garrick dashed off, saying he had to go back to the wood merchant they had visited the day before. Mia knew that wasn't true and he was simply avoiding Hettie but it gave Mia a chance to check Garrick's story about Jet.

Over tea and a slice or two of the deliciously moist, chocolate and caramel cake, Mia and Hettie chatted about Garrick and the furniture he made, until Mia plucked up the courage to ask. She tried to make her question sound casual.

'We saw Jet Cross briefly this morning and something Garrick said, made me curious.'

'Oh? What did Garrick say, deary?'

'That he'd heard that Jet's dad left, and Jet worked day and night from the age of twelve, to try to buy Little Pond Farm. Is that true, do you know?'

Hettie finished her tea and shook her head. 'Dreadful business, deary. I remember it like it was yesterday. Jethro senior ran off with a woman he met at a barn dance, leaving Sarah and young Jet with nothing but the roof over their heads. And they almost lost that, my dear. Barn dances were a regular event in those days, and Jethro always had an eye for the ladies. No one ever thought the man would abandon his wife and child, but he did, deary. He did. Jeremy Warren owned the farm back then and he was nothing but a crook and a liar. Had young Jet working all hours, and for a pittance, I don't doubt. Sarah got a job in the pub and started a little cleaning business, deary, to help pay the rent. She used to clean for Matilda, until the poor dear became too ill and that's when I took over. Cancer, my dear. Thought she'd beaten it, but it came back.'

'Cancer? Jet's mum had cancer?'

Hettie nodded. 'Terrible, it was. We all helped out with the odd gift of clothes, or bedding, or a pot of stew, a cake, or loaf of bread and such, but Sarah was a proud woman, deary, and Jet was just the same. Neither wanted charity. Whatever help they were given, they found some way to reciprocate. And somehow, deary, for all of that, Sarah and Jet managed to put some money by. When Jeremy Warren decided to sell, Jet went and got a bank loan, I believe. There was a bit of a celebration in The Frog and Lily last year when he'd finally paid it off and the farm was well and truly his, my dear. Such a shame dear Sarah didn't live to see that. Died five years ago, on Christmas Eve. But she was proud of him, and rightly so, deary. Just a shame he didn't find himself a nice young woman and settle down. That's all she ever wanted for him. But not our Jet. He was having none of that, my dear. He takes after his dad, where women are concerned. Jethro had a long line of women from what I recall. But Jet's ten times the man his father was. Very few people liked Jethro. Except the women. Everyone loves Jet.' She suddenly grinned and chuckled, tapping Mia on the hand. 'Why the sudden interest in Jet, deary? I knew it! You've fallen under his spell, haven't you? It's those eyes. I told you deary, didn't I? One look into his eyes and you'll forgive him anything.'

'No, I haven't!'

Mia jumped up a bit too quickly and Hettie nodded as if that confirmed it.

'Your secret's safe with me, deary,' she said, tapping one side of her nose with her finger. 'But listen to me. Talking ten chickens at a time again. Best get on deary, or the morning will be gone. I promised Brenda Dupont a cake today.' She picked up her bag and tapped it, putting it on the chair next to her as she got to her feet. 'That's my next stop.'

Mia had a dreadful feeling that Hettie's sudden urge to leave had more to do with her hurry to spread the news that Mia had fallen for Jet, than it did with visiting someone else, and Mia spent the next few minutes trying to convince Hettie that she had no interest in Jet Cross whatsoever.

Hettie tapped her nose again and grinned. 'Safe with me, deary. Safe with me.'

Mia was sure it was anything but. And the worst part was, it wasn't even true. Mia hadn't fallen for Jet Cross. She wasn't sure she even liked him. Although Garrick's story had made her rethink her opinion slightly and Hettie's version had reinforced that change.

'I'm back!' Ella dashed into the kitchen, a loaf of bread in one arm, a bag of iced buns in the other and a smile so wide that it must have made her cheeks hurt.

Even Hettie hesitated, clearly eager to find out why.

'Thanks, Hettie,' Mia said, forcing a smile. 'Please don't let us keep you. Thanks again for the cake. You don't mind letting yourself out, do you?'

Mia grabbed Ella by the elbow, giving her enough time to drop her goods on the table before dragging her out onto the deck and shutting the door behind them.

'What's the rush?' Ella looked startled.

Mia lowered her voice. 'I didn't want to give Hettie even more to gossip about. She thinks I'm madly in love with Jet.'

Ella frowned. 'With Jet? Are you?'

'Of course I'm not. I thought the man was an arrogant ... That doesn't matter. The thing is, Jet came here and asked me to go for a walk and I said some horrible things to him. Then Garrick told me a story about Mattie lending Jet the money to buy his farm. I asked Hettie to see if she could confirm it, and now she's going to tell the entire village I'm besotted with Jet Cross.' Mia glanced into the kitchen but Hettie appeared to have left.

'Okay.' Ella glanced over her shoulder before flopping onto a chair and tugging Mia's sleeve to make her sit. 'You lost me at Mattie lending Jet the money to buy his farm, but we'll get back to that. You said Jet asked you to go for a walk. What does that mean? Are we back in the 1930s? Was he asking you out?'

'No. I don't think so. I'm not sure. He meant an actual walk. On the beach of all places. Even when I told him I'm afraid of water.'

Ella shook her head. 'Let's not make this even more complicated. When did Jet ask you to go for this walk?'

'Today. Just before nine. He came here.'

'Jet came here? Wow. So why did you say horrible things to him?'

'Because Hettie had said he breaks women's hearts, remember? And Alexia was looking at him at choir practice when she said that stuff about Justin not being like someone else she could mention. Oh! How did you get on with Justin? Sorry. I'm so worried about this business with Jet I'd completely forgotten to ask.'

Ella pulled a serious face. 'I didn't go out to see Justin. I went out to get bread.' She grinned. 'And came back with a loaf, some iced buns, and a date for Saturday night. Well, when I say 'date', what I actually mean is tickets for Justin's next show in some village a few miles away. But we're going for a drink after and he's going to bring a friend.' Ella clapped her hands in excitement.

Mia beamed at her. 'Oh Ella! That's wonderful. Wait a minute. Why's he bringing a friend? He's not asking you to take part in some sort of threesome, is he? Because that's almost as gross as Jet having sex with Mattie.'

Ella shrieked. 'Jet and Mattie had sex! In exchange for her lending him the money to buy the farm, you mean? Bloody Nora! You've got to be joking!'

Unfortunately, Hettie reappeared and opened the back door at that precise moment. Her mouth fell open and her eyes were the size of saucers. 'I forgot my bag,' she mumbled, holding the bag in the air. Before Mia had a chance to act, Hettie had closed the door and raced along the hall to the front door, faster than Usain Bolt.

'Hettie!' Mia suddenly realised what Hettie must have heard. She got up and ran after her but when she opened the front door, Hettie was nowhere to be seen. How could the woman move so fast? Mia returned to Ella, flopped back in the chair and dropped her head into her hands. 'Bloody hell! Now she's going to tell everyone Jet and Mattie had sex. And of course, they didn't.'

'They didn't?' Ella breathed a sigh of relief. 'Thank God for that. But why did you say they did?'

'I didn't. I thought it for one millionth of a second. And I did actually say it to him. But I don't know why because I knew he wouldn't. And neither would Mattie. Oh God. This is such a mess.'

Ella sighed and shook her head. She poked Mia in the arm and giggled. 'Look on the bright side. At least now Hettie won't tell everyone you've fallen for Jet because she's got something far more interesting to tell them. Or maybe she'll tell them both things. It's just as well you've got a date on Saturday.'

Mia looked up at her. 'What? I haven't got a date. I told you. I said horrible things to him. He left and that was that.'

Ella gave a little cough. 'I'm talking about the friend Justin is bringing for you on Saturday night. Don't look at me like that. It's about time you and

I followed Garrick's lead and got back in the game.'

'Oh God, Ella. What have you done? Who's this friend he's bringing?'

Ella pulled a comically apologetic face. 'I was so excited, I completely forgot to ask. Wouldn't it be funny if it was Jet?' She giggled uncontrollably.

'No, Ella Swann. It wouldn't be in the least bit funny. We need to call Justin right now and find out who it is. In fact, you need to tell him I'm not going.'

'No can do,' Ella said, still giggling. 'No phone signal remember? And besides, I didn't take his number. And let's not forget you owe me one. I did offer to come and stay here when you got so upset about the thought of living in the countryside. And I did bring my wonderful brother along too.'

Mia sighed and cast Ella a sarcastic look.

'Yes. And look how well that's all working out.'

Chapter Four

Something had changed. And it wasn't for the better.

When Mia, Ella and Garrick had arrived in Little Pondale exactly one week earlier, they had been three single people who found a village full of seemingly friendly residents. Now Garrick was dating Alexia, although she didn't appear to be exactly thrilled about it. On Friday night in the pub, Alexia had virtually ignored him. She also behaved as if Mia had a contagious disease, clearly avoiding her at every opportunity. Even Toby, Freda and Alec weren't quite as friendly when they served them drinks. Justin wasn't in the pub, and nor was Bear. Thankfully, there was no sign of Jet either, but there was definitely an atmosphere. The locals turned and looked at Mia and her friends when they walked in but instead of friendly waves and greetings, all they offered were a few nods and more than one shake of the head. Hettie Burnstall had clearly done her worst and Mia, Ella and Garrick only stayed for one drink. When they got back to the cottage they discussed this turn of events but none of them had any idea what they could do to make things right.

Until the following morning, when Mia knew exactly what she had to do. But when she pulled back the curtains at six-thirty on Saturday morning and saw the pouring rain, her heart sank just a little.

She gritted her teeth and jumped into the shower before putting on a clean pair of jeans, a T-shirt and a cardigan. She ran downstairs and, after a quick coffee and a couple of chocolate digestives, she scribbled a note to Ella and Garrick.

Garrick's van was in the way and in the time it would take her to move that back and forth to get her car out, she could probably walk to her destination. She grabbed her raincoat and an umbrella from the hall and dashed out into the rain.

It didn't take long for her to arrive at Little Pond Farm but by the time she did, the wind had joined the rain and her umbrella had blown inside out. Her hair was hanging limp around her face and her jeans were soaking wet. The waterproof raincoat wasn't doing its job either but the walking boots she had bought were, so at least her feet were dry. Pushing open the wooden gate, she followed the mud-covered drive to the door of the Georgian farmhouse and rang the bell.

No one answered. She rang it again but still no one came.

She hadn't come this far to give up now, so she walked around the aged sandstone façade and followed a path to what appeared to be a row of large sheds. Strange sounds drifted through the early morning air, competing with the now torrential rain pummelling the ground. One was definitely machinery, another she recognised as clucking chickens and the third was mooing cows.

For a moment she stopped in her tracks. The thought of being in close contact with several farm animals was bad enough; the idea that something might be happening to them was even worse. She started to back away but the door of the barn closest to her flew open and she caught a glimpse of what was going on inside.

Mia burst out laughing in relief. She didn't know anything about farming but the octopus-like contraption attached to the underneath of the cows made it clear even to her untrained eye that the cows were being milked.

It was a moment or two before she noticed the mountain of a man standing just inside the door, staring in her direction. He wore a Macintosh like the ones she had seen in cowboy films and actual cowboy boots, covered in white elasticated booties. Beneath his mac he wore a white overall and on his head, beneath a cowboy hat, he wore what appeared to be a white plastic shower cap, although it was obviously something to do with public health and safety, Mia was sure of that.

'Howdy,' he called out. 'You gonna stand there in the rain, or you coming in the dry?'

The accent was unmistakably American but she had no idea where from. Texas maybe?

'Hello. I'm looking for Jet Cross.' Mia walked towards the barn but she didn't want to venture inside. This was as close as she wanted to get to a herd of cows, even if they were all contained in individual enclosures, which for some reason made her think back to her days at Whitley Smythe and Black and the 'pods' in which she and the rest of the admin staff all spent their working days.

'He's with the chickens,' the American said. 'Next barn along. You must be Mia.' He took off his cowboy hat and tipped it in her direction before shoving a wayward strand of blond hair back beneath the shower cap and returning his hat to his head. 'I'm Franklin Grant. Pleased to meet you ma'am.'

Ma'am? Was he for real?

'Hi. Yes, I'm Mia. Lovely to meet you too. But please don't call me ma'am.' She smiled at him and giggled. 'It makes me sound like ... well, let's just say I'd prefer to be called Mia.'

'Mia's a mighty fine name. You kinda like the rain then do you, Mia?'

Mia shook her head and wished she hadn't. A river of water poured beneath her coat and ran down her back.

'No. But I prefer it to a barn full of cows.'

He laughed heartily and it was contagious. The type of laugh that you simply have to laugh along with.

'Not an animal lover then?'

'Dogs and cats are great. Farm creatures, not so much. The barn next door, you said?'

'Right you are, Ma'am. Begging your pardon. Mia. Next barn along. I'm sure he'll be mighty pleased to see you this wet and wild morning.'

'I wouldn't bet on that. See you later, I hope.'

'You can count on it.' He tipped his hat once more, grabbed a metal urn the size of a small person, with just his fingertips, and disappeared back into the barn.

Mia trudged through increasing amounts of mud to the next barn and stood outside for a moment. Should she knock? She couldn't see a doorbell and she had no idea what the protocol was for entering a chicken barn. She erred on the side of caution and rapped her knuckles against the wood three times.

'Hello! Is anyone in there? It's Mia. Mia Ward. I'm looking for Jet Cross. Is he … oh!'

The door flew open and Jet towered before her. He didn't look as pleased to see her as Franklin thought he might. Or perhaps Franklin was being facetious. Mia hadn't expected Jet to welcome her visit but the look he was giving her made her wonder if she might be murdered and fed to the cows. Or was it pigs who ate humans?

Whatever. If looks could kill, she'd be dead on this very spot.

'What do you want?'

She smiled wanly. 'I wondered if you'd like to go for a walk.'

The tiniest of twitches tugged at his mouth.

'A walk? In the pouring rain?'

She shrugged. 'I'd like to talk and I'm already soaked to the skin. I can't possibly get any wetter.'

He raised his brows and looked her up and down before holding the door open and stepping to one side. 'I'm not. You'd better come inside.'

She shook her head. 'I'm allergic to animals.'

'That's okay. These are birds.'

He grabbed her arm and yanked her inside and she stumbled and fell against him. She quickly regained her composure and pushed away from him, brushing herself down even though she had no reason to.

'Sorry. You took me by surprise,' she said, blushing profusely.

'That makes two of us. Why are you here, Mia?'

'I owe you an apology.'

He glared at her. 'You can say that again.'

She smiled sheepishly. 'I owe you an apology.' Again, that tiny twitch caught her eye.

'Okay. Let's hear it. But just so that we're clear, are you apologising for what you said to me when I came to see you? Or are you apologising for telling everyone in the village my business? Or are you apologising for telling everyone in the village that I had sex with Mattie in exchange for a loan?'

Mia cringed. 'All three. Although technically, it wasn't me who told everyone in the village you had sex with Mattie, or about your business.'

He gave a sarcastic laugh. 'You told Hettie. That's as good as telling everyone.'

'No. I actually told Ella. Hettie simply overheard.'

He tutted and turned away. 'Oh well. That makes all the difference.' He turned back to face her. 'Do you have any idea how I felt when I heard that? Any idea how hard I've worked to get where I am? Everything I've given up to be here? No, of course you don't. And it's not just my reputation you could've so easily ruined. Has it even occurred to you what you might've done to Mattie's? Everyone loved and respected Mattie. She may not have opened up and shared the story of her life and she may have had a few odd ways, but she was highly thought of. It makes me angry to hear her name dragged through the mud.'

It hadn't occurred to Mia. 'But I didn't say that's what happened. It was all a simple misunderstanding. If everyone is so ready to believe the worst of Mattie, and of you, then they couldn't have thought much of either of you in the first place. If someone said something like that about me to Ella or Garrick they'd laugh and tell the gossiper to get a life. I don't think anyone in the village actually believed it. I'm sure they think we were the ones spreading gossip and they made it clear they weren't having any of it. I think your reputation's pretty much as it was before, and so is Mattie's. But it wasn't any of us who started the story about you being a guy who goes around breaking women's hearts. That story was out there long before we arrived. But I'm sorry if we made it worse. If I made it worse.'

He met the look in her eyes and held it with his for what seemed like an eternity but was merely a matter of seconds as water dripped from her hair and trickled down the bridge of her nose. She wiped it away with her hand.

'Okay, fine,' he said, turning away from her. 'Apology accepted. You can go now.'

Without thinking, she reached out and touched his arm. 'I'm truly sorry, Jet. I didn't mean any of this to happen. If it makes you feel any better, I think the entire village is sending me, Ella and Garrick to Coventry for this. They hardly spoke to us in the pub last night.'

He looked at her hand as if it burnt through his jacket to his skin and he waved his arm to brush her off. 'Fine. But that doesn't make me feel better. That's the last thing I'd want. Little Pondale is a friendly place. I don't want three Londoners to change that overnight.'

She persisted. 'I mean it. I'm really sorry. Tell me what I can do to make it up to you. I'll do anything you want. Anything at all.'

He raised his brows and stared at her. 'Anything? Absolutely anything?'

She narrowed her eyes and met his stare. 'Within reason. But I'm not having sex with you, if that's what you're going to suggest.'

A burst of laughter escaped him. 'It's always sex with you, isn't it? I hate to disappoint you, but that wasn't what I was going to suggest. It's far, far worse than that.'

'Worse? What could be worse?'

He laughed again. 'You do realise that you're still insulting me, don't you? I have it on pretty good authority that there are many things far worse than having sex with me.'

'I didn't mean it like that. I'm sure sex with you would be …'

'Would be …?'

'Fine,' she said, hastily clearing her throat.

'Fine? Okay. I'll take that.'

'So … what were you going to suggest I do?'

He tipped his head to one side and looked her up and down.

'Go for a walk with me.'

Mia brightened. 'Yes, I'll happily do that.'

'Along the beach?'

'Er. No. Anywhere but the beach.'

He shrugged. 'Take it or leave it. My chickens need feeding.'

'You want me to feed your chickens too?'

He grinned at her and Mia relaxed a little. 'No. Although I think you owe me that as well as a walk along the beach.'

Mia looked around at the barn filled with chickens, all clucking and scratching and leaping in the air. 'Do they bite? They look pretty wild. Do you let them out or do they live in here because that seems cruel to me?'

'You're not helping yourself, you know.' He threw her a serious look but the twitch increased in size. 'But I let them out. They're certified free range. If you look over there, you'll see the other door at the end of the barn is open.' He pointed across the barn. 'They can come and go as they please, and when the door is locked at night, they can still get out into a fox-proof area, through a chicken door. They're just sensible enough not to get themselves soaked in the rain.'

'Meaning I'm not as bright as a chicken?' She stuck her chin in the air.

'You're the one who's soaking wet.'

'Because I came here to apologise.'

'I told you. Apology accepted. I'll call for you at nine on Sunday morning. We're taking that walk along the beach, Mia, and I won't take no for an answer, but I will let you off feeding the chickens. For now. And if you give me ten minutes or so, I'll give you a lift home.'

'I can walk, thanks. And I'll do anything else apart from a walk on the beach.'

'And having sex with me,' he reminded her.

'Yes. No beach. No sex. But anything else, I'll do.'

'I'll see you at nine on Sunday. You'll need beach shoes.' He glanced at her feet and nodded. 'Those boots will do if it rains, but if it's good weather, you might want to wear flip-flops. Easier for paddling.'

'Paddling!' Mia shrieked. 'Did you say paddling? There is no way on this earth you'll get me to go paddling. I'm getting out of here before you think of something even more ridiculous.'

'See you Sunday morning,' he called after her as she shoved the barn door open and rushed headlong into the pouring rain.

Chapter Five

On her way back from Little Pond Farm Mia
nipped into Justin's bakery and casually mentioned
that Ella hadn't said who it was he was bringing
along on their date.

'That's because I didn't tell her,' Justin said.
'It's going to be a surprise.'

He had an odd grin on his tanned face which
seemed to be a darker brown today. Was that why
he wasn't at the pub last night? Was he having his
tan topped up? The grin was somewhere between
devilish and uncertain. Perhaps he hadn't said
who, because he hadn't found anyone who wanted
to be Mia's blind date. That was a depressing
thought.

It was even more depressing when she
mentioned it to Ella and Garrick over breakfast and
Garrick said that with so many single men around,
there must be one who'd want to go out with Mia.

'I'll ask at the rugby this afternoon if you
like?' Garrick offered, somewhat unhelpfully.

'Rugby? You may not have noticed but it's
bucketing down with rain out there and blowing a

gale. The fields at Little Pond Farm were like quagmires.'

Garrick shrugged. 'And your point is?'

Mia shook her head. 'My point is, rugby players are clearly insane. And obviously not as intelligent as chickens.'

'Does that mean you're not coming to watch?' Garrick asked with a grin.

'I'm staying in and reading a book.'

'And getting ready for your date tonight,' Ella reminded her.

'I'll be spending most of the day trying to think up a way to get out of it.'

But that was something she hadn't managed to do and Saturday night came far too soon for Mia. She resigned herself to the fact that she was going to have a miserable time apart from the hour or so of the evening where she and Ella would get to see three men, covered in little else but baby oil, gyrate around a stage.

Mia looked up the number for a minicab but they were rarer than the goose that laid the golden egg and she was told there was no chance in this weather. It hadn't stopped raining all day which Mia was sure was an omen. Justin couldn't take them because, as soon as he'd finished on the rugby field, he had to rehearse the show, so Mia was going to have to drive. Garrick offered but that seemed rather unfair. It was fifteen miles each way and in torrential rain. Besides, the one good thing about doing the driving was that if the evening turned out to be the disaster Mia thought it would, she could feign a headache and leave Ella to it. Justin would bring her home. The bad thing was, she couldn't have a drink. Garrick annoyed her on that score too, saying that it would be a good idea to give her liver a rest.

She was beginning to think she was so over her renewed crush on Garrick Swann. Until he said he would nip to the pub and see what was wrong with Alexia. The sudden pain in her tummy made her think perhaps she wasn't. Or perhaps the pain had something to do with the two iced buns and half a packet of chocolate digestives she had consumed that afternoon.

'Justin's meeting us in the pub next door,' Ella said, when they pulled up in the car park behind the village hall in Little Whitingdale. 'It's called The Green Man.'

'That's probably how my blind date feels. I'm feeling a little sick myself.'

'Will you stop it! We're going to have a wonderful night and your date is going to be gorgeous. I know he is.'

'That's put the kiss of death on it. Sorry. I just feel 'out of sorts' as Mum would say. Last night in the pub was a bit of a shock and all that stuff with Hettie telling everyone what we said about Jet is still upsetting me. I'm going to have a word with her about it. If she wants to continue working for me, she'll have to stop gossiping about us and repeating what she hears. How did Mattie, who clearly liked to keep things to herself, put up with Hettie for so long? I just don't get it.'

'Let's forget about all that tonight and have a good time.'

That was easy for Ella to say. She wasn't the one who had to apologise to Jet. But Ella was right. There wasn't much point in dwelling on it tonight and now Mia was determined to have a good time, no matter who her date turned out to be.

The first surprise was that the village hall was packed to the rafters with women of all ages, and not just women. There were also a handful of men. Justin had arranged for Ella and Mia to have seats at the very front, a mere few feet from the stage. They would certainly get an eyeful.

The second surprise was that Mattie had been right. Justin was an extremely talented dancer. Despite having watched the DVD, seeing Justin in the flesh was a completely different experience. Mia was expecting skimpy thongs, gyrating pelvises and thrusting hips. The show had all of those but it contained so much more. The dance routines could grace a West End stage. The timing was perfect, the men were unbelievably sexy and yet incredibly graceful too. The atmosphere in the hall was electric and yet no one stormed the stage, or tried to remove what little clothing the dancers wore. No one screamed suggestive comments or threw their knickers on the stage and when the show was finally over, everyone who wanted autographs formed an orderly queue. It was all somewhat surreal.

'Are the audiences always that well-behaved?' Mia asked Justin when he joined them in the pub.

He'd changed into jeans and a T-shirt and looked like any other average guy meeting his date for a drink, except he was deeply tanned and had a better body than your average guy.

Justin laughed. 'Not always. A couple of times over the years we've had to call the police, but most women want to have fun. One or two think we'll do more for them than dance, if you get what I mean, and you'd be surprised how angry a drunk woman can get when she's told we won't have sex with her. Men can also be the victims of sexual harassment and assault. We have to be very careful how we handle situations like that. But thankfully, it's rare. What did you think of the show?'

'I thought it was brilliant,' Ella said, a little starry-eyed.

Mia smiled and nodded. 'It was, Justin. And Mattie was right about you. You are a talented dancer. But you're also a talented baker. Your iced buns are to die for.'

'Thanks. I assume that's not a euphemism.' He grinned and winked. 'I think I ended up with the best of both worlds. Ah. At last.' He tipped his head to one side as he peered over Mia's shoulder. 'Your date has finally arrived.'

And Mia got the third surprise of the night.

Chapter Six

Mia overslept. She had tossed and turned all night and didn't drop off to sleep until after four, which meant when Garrick woke her with a mug of coffee at half past eight, she had less than half an hour to get ready for her walk with Jet. She didn't have time to talk about her date last night but Garrick seemed determined to ask questions.

'Who was he then? Ella's not in her bedroom so either she got up very early and went out, or she didn't come back last night.'

Mia took the coffee, making sure the duvet was pulled over her chest. The last thing she wanted was a repeat performance of her 'exposure' the other day.

'Thanks for this but I wish you'd called me earlier. Jet's coming here at nine. Can we chat about this later? But Ella did come home last night, so perhaps she's gone to get more fresh bread.' She grinned. 'I heard Justin say that if she popped in early this morning, he'd put a bun in the oven for her. Corny, but amusing, and the way he said it, even made me want to rush round there first thing.

I expect she set her alarm for five on the dot. Oh, my date was Bear. Bear as in the man, not as in naked.'

'Bear?' Garrick seemed almost as surprised as Mia had been. 'I didn't know he fancied you. He hasn't mentioned it and we've talked about lots of things concerning people in the village. He was the one who told me all that stuff about Jet when I was asking him about Mattie.'

'Bear told you that? That's a bit of a surprise. Either he trusted you not to share it, or he's not a man who's good at keeping private stuff, private. I must remember that, just in case. But I'm not sure he does fancy me. I think he got roped in, much like I did.'

'How did it go? Are you seeing him again?'

Mia shrugged and gulped her coffee. 'I don't know. He said he'd like to but ...'

'But what?'

'Um. Can we please talk about this later? I need to get ready.'

'It's a simple question, Mia. It won't take a minute to answer.'

Mia sighed. It was anything but simple.

'He seems to be under the mistaken impression that you've got a thing for me. He said he doesn't want to tread on anyone's toes and he doesn't want to play games either.'

'He said what?'

'I know it's crazy. I told him we're just friends and that we've known each other most of our lives but … well … apparently when you were on your date with Alexia, all you talked about was me. Well, me and your ex, Fiona. And that was a real surprise because whenever Ella and I ask you about that, you tell us to mind our own business.'

Garrick dropped onto the edge of the bed and shook his head. 'I … I don't remember doing that. Alexia asked about my previous relationships and I told her I'd moved back down south after living with someone for several years, but I'm sure I didn't say much more than that. As for talking about you.' He looked Mia in the eye and frowned. 'Perhaps I did, a bit. But only to explain why I was here and what good friends we are.'

Mia sighed again as Garrick looked away, shook his head and studied his hands instead.

Since Bear had told her that last night, she had been hoping it was true. Wondering if, deep down, Garrick could possibly feel the same about her as she did about him. Picturing them going on a date. Imagining that starry far-away look in his eyes could be for her and not Alexia.

'At least we now know what Alexia meant when she said, "You should know," to me on Thursday night. And why she's being cool towards us both. I think you have some explaining to do. Perhaps you should tell her I'm going to be dating Bear. That might set her mind at ease.'

He jerked his head around to look at her and the crease between his brows was deep.

'Are you?' He stared into her eyes. 'Going to be dating Bear, I mean?'

Mia nodded. 'If he asks me. Yes. He's good-looking. He's fun. He's a vet.'

'What's that got to do with it?'

Mia shrugged and sighed once more. Until the ringing of the bell made her jump and spill her coffee all over the duvet.

'That's Jet!' she shrieked, as Garrick leapt off the bed. 'He's early. Oh God, Garrick. Will you go and talk to him and tell him I'll be fifteen minutes at the most. What's the weather like?'

'The weather?'

She grabbed her dressing gown and dashed across the room. 'Yes. Is it raining or sunny?'

'Why don't you open the curtains and look out the window?' Garrick swept the duvet off the bed and walked towards the bedroom door with the duvet tucked under his arm.

'I haven't got time. Just tell me for heaven's sake.' She hovered just inside the doorway of the en-suite.

'Sunny. In fact, it's a beautiful day. At least it was.'

She did a double-take at that. There was something in his tone that made her wonder what he meant. But she didn't have time to ask. Jet was waiting and she had less than fifteen minutes to make herself look beautiful. Well, perhaps not beautiful but at least half-human.

She did it in fourteen, although her hair was wringing wet and swept up into a pony tail and the dress she'd struggled into was a bit too tight and revealing for a Sunday morning stroll along the beach. It was more appropriate for a night of dancing and romance beneath the stars. But she didn't have time to change. She rushed downstairs, through the kitchen and out onto the deck where Jet and Garrick were sitting drinking coffee. When she saw the look on Jet's and Garrick's faces as they turned towards her, she was rather pleased she hadn't changed.

'Wow!' Garrick said, turning a deeper crimson than Mia's dress.

Jet merely looked her up and down but in such a way that left her in little doubt that he liked what he saw. The twitch she'd come to expect from him turned into the broadest, sexiest grin she'd ever seen. If she hadn't been able to hold on to the backdoor frame, she might very easily have fallen into his arms right then and there.

Jet got to his feet, thanked Garrick for the coffee and looked Mia in the eye. 'Ready?'

She nodded and Garrick said he'd see them later, stood up and went inside, briefly touching Mia's arm as he passed her in the doorway.

She smiled up at Jet. 'Sorry if I kept you waiting. I overslept. I was out on a blind date last night, which turned out to be with Bear, and I didn't get much sleep.' Her statement didn't seem to bother him one bit.

'No rain today.' He grinned again, glancing at her sandaled feet. 'You know what that means.'

She shook her head. 'No way, Jet. I thought I made it clear, I'm afraid of water.'

'You did. Let's go.'

He took her hand in his and she glanced down at their clasped hands. It was as if she'd slid hers into a perfectly fitting glove. But it was more than that. It made her feel safe, somehow. It made her feel she could face anything. Even, eventually, a walk along the beach with him. Until, instead of walking back inside, he led her down the wooden steps and onto the garden path which in turn led to the sand dunes. And the beach. This was a bit too soon. She tried to pull back but his grip was firm and he strode ahead. Unless she wanted to be dragged, she had no choice but to fight him, or go with him. To her surprise, she chose the latter.

'Are you seeing him again?'

'What? Who? Garrick?' Jet's question was so sudden and coming on top of the very real fear bubbling up inside her, she had forgotten she'd tried to tease him with news of her date.

'Bear.' He glanced down at her and when she met his eyes, she saw genuine concern. He stopped and turned to face her, still clutching her hand in his. 'You really are afraid, aren't you?'

'Of dating?'

Jet grinned. 'Of water. Why would you be afraid of dating? There's nothing to it. Boy likes girl. Girl likes boy. There's nothing frightening about that.'

'That's easy for you to say. My love life up till now has been a complete horror story.'

He laughed and his grip on her hand tightened a fraction as they walked on. Or perhaps she imagined it.

'I suppose, if I'm honest, mine hasn't exactly been a bed of roses. Despite what you may have heard. Bear's a great guy though. Nothing frightening about him. Unless you're facing him on the rugby field. That's a different matter entirely.'

'I'll bear that in mind. No pun intended.'

'The answer's yes then?'

'Um. Are we still talking about dating? Or have we gone back to my genuine and all-consuming terror when it comes to water?'

'You're seeing Bear again?'

She nodded. 'If he asks.'

'You mean he hasn't?'

She shook her head. 'There ... um ... seems to have been a bit of a misunderstanding.'

'About you and Garrick, you mean?'

'Yes. How did you know that?'

He met her eyes again but this time he didn't stop.

'I've seen the way you look at him. And the way he looks at you.'

'The way he looks at me?'

'You're not trying to deny the way you look at him then?'

'Um. Yes. I mean. No. We're friends. Good friends.'

'But you'd like him to be more than a friend, wouldn't you, Mia?'

This time she stopped. Her mouth fell open and she stared at him, wide-eyed. How on earth did he know that? He grinned at her and coaxed her to continue walking by a gentle pull on her hand.

'Yes,' she admitted, bowing her head so he wouldn't see her eyes. She was equally surprised and relieved that she'd finally told someone else how she felt, but astonished that the person was Jet. 'But he's not interested in me in that way.'

'Isn't he? Have you asked him?'

'No! I haven't asked him.'

'Why not? Women are supposed to be equal to men. Isn't it time they did the asking? All you have to say is, 'Would you go out on a date with me?' What's the worst that could happen?'

'He could say no and our friendship would be ruined.'

'Why would it? You're not going to stalk him, are you? All you say is that if he doesn't have feelings for you as anything other than a friend, you don't want the friendship to change.'

'Sounds simple but I don't think it's quite that easy in reality.'

'It's only difficult if you make it so. Ask the question, Mia. You might be surprised by the answer.'

She suddenly burst out laughing. 'This is so surreal. Garrick is dating Alexia. I've just been on a date with Bear. You're giving me advice on how to get Garrick to go out with me and yet you're the one walking hand in hand with me. Neither Garrick nor Bear have done that.'

Jet smiled down at her. 'Not just walking hand in hand, Mia. Walking hand in hand at the water's edge.'

Mia's head turned from side to side like someone possessed by a demon. She had been so preoccupied by the conversation that she hadn't even noticed that they'd left the garden, walked over the sand dunes and were now within spitting distance of the sea. She froze on the spot, her free hand shooting to his arm which she clung to as if her life depended on it. She swallowed, blinked and tried to stop her heart from exploding from her chest. She gulped in rapid breaths of salty, sea air as the gently lapping waves pounded in her ears. It was a miracle she didn't faint.

'You're perfectly safe, Mia.'

Jet's voice was soft and soothing but she could hardly hear it above the roaring of the sea and the screeching of the gulls circling overhead, even though she knew neither one was making the dreadful noises she could hear. It was just her fear kicking in and exaggerating every sound, every movement, every horror. She let out a scream, screwed her eyes tightly shut and buried her head against his chest, throwing her arms about his waist and holding on for dear life.

He wrapped his arms around her and held her tight. 'I'm so sorry, Mia. I truly am. I hadn't realised you would be this terrified. I wouldn't have brought you so close if I'd known. Both Garrick and Ella said you can walk along the shore if you feel safe. And you are safe, Mia. I promise you. Nothing bad's going to happen, Mia. You're safe and sound. Trust me. I'll take care of you. Now we can walk away, or you can take a few deep breaths and open your eyes and look at me.'

She shook her head maniacally.

'Okay. Just take your time. I'm here. The water isn't going to touch you. I won't let it. I'll succeed where King Canute failed. I'll hold back the tide from you.'

He joked but Mia didn't find it funny.

'It may mean I'll have to sweep you up in my arms but you don't mind that, do you? How much do you weigh? Not much from the look and feel of you.'

He gently poked her with one finger whilst keeping his arms tight around her.

'If you were one of my chickens, I'd have to fatten you up. Nothing worse than a scrawny bird. Not that I'm saying you're scrawny, or a bird, because you're not. In fact, I think you're pretty near perfect.'

225

She gave a little gasp at that.

'You know what people are going to say if anyone sees us standing here like this, don't you? Still, I guess it's as good a way as any to see how Garrick really feels. And Bear for that matter. Jealousy can do incredible things to spur a man on, you know. Feel free to jump into this conversation at any time, Mia. Any time at all. But there's no need to rush. It's Sunday and I've got all morning free. The tide won't turn for a while. I checked the tide tables. And it takes several hours to come in. It's still going out for the next fifteen minutes and it's at least ten feet further away than it was last time you looked.'

'No, it isn't,' she mumbled into his chest, breathing in his musky aftershave.

'Sorry. I didn't catch that. Look at me, Mia. Please look at me.'

Slowly, very, very slowly she raised her head to look up at him.

'There,' he said, his voice husky and a look of tenderness in his eyes. 'That's not so bad, is it?'

She gingerly shook her head.

'What about if you turn around and look at the sea now. Don't panic. I'll keep my arms around you.' He began to twist her gently around until her back was against him and his arms were around her front. 'Lean against me and put your hands in mine. You're perfectly safe. Now breathe slowly in and out. Deep breaths in and deep breaths out.'

Mia did as she was told and slipped her hands in his, resting her arms on his forearms and making him hug her close as she filled her nostrils with sea air and let her chest rise and fall rhythmically. Something inside made her want to do this.

'Okay?' He put his head against hers and whispered in her ear. 'I'll never let anything happen to you, Mia. You have my word on that.'

For the first time in more years than she could remember she was standing on the sand, within inches of the sea. And as amazing as it seemed, she felt safe and unafraid.

Chapter Seven

'I can't believe you did it,' Garrick said when she returned to the cottage.

'I wouldn't have been able to if Jet hadn't distracted me with, let's say, an interesting conversation. I was so engrossed I didn't realise how close we were to the water until he pointed it out.'

'That must've been some conversation,' Ella said, having got back from Justin's at the same time as Mia returned from her walk. 'Are you sure it was the conversation and not Jet's dreamy eyes?'

Mia grinned. 'His looks may have had something to do with it.'

'So Bear's now history?' Garrick didn't sound pleased.

'No. If Bear asks me out, I'll go. Unless someone else I like asks me first.'

Garrick frowned. 'Jet didn't ask you out?'

Mia sighed. 'I wasn't talking about Jet, but no, he didn't. Garrick? Will you go with me to the beach tomorrow? I want to go each day until I'm brave enough to go alone. And I want to check the tides to make sure it's going out, like it was today. That'll make me feel safer, somehow. Will you show me how to do that? I can Google it, I suppose.'

'Of course I will. If I'd known you were eager to fight your fear I'd have taken you myself long ago, but you always screamed blue murder when anyone suggested it. What made you do this now?'

Mia laughed at that. 'Jet made me. Seriously, I had no intention of facing my fear. I'm a wimp. I'll admit it.'

Every day for the next week, Mia went to the beach, even if it rained, which it did on two of the days. She still couldn't go alone and she didn't get as close to the sea as Jet had taken her, but each day she got a little closer and each day was a triumph to her.

On Tuesday, it was Bear who took her, having asked her in the pub on Monday night if he could see her again. Mia was so pleased that all the villagers seemed to have forgiven her, Ella and Garrick and had welcomed them back into the fold, that she didn't dare say no in case she upset them all again by refusing him. It was ridiculous, but Mia hadn't been thinking clearly for a few days now. Not since Jet had come to the cottage on the Friday morning and Hettie Burnstall had spread her gossip. Mia had meant to have a word with Hettie on Monday morning about that, but her hour had clashed with Mia's beach walk and Mia had left it to Ella to pay Hettie. She planned to speak to her on Thursday, but by then, things had settled down so well and Hettie seemed more subdued than she had been. Once again, Mia put it off.

A walk on the beach during lunchtime with a semi-terrified woman probably wasn't the date Bear had in mind, but the hour they spent together on Tuesday made Mia see him as a possible boyfriend. When he asked her on a date for Saturday night, she happily said yes.

Garrick took her again on Wednesday and she almost plucked up the courage to ask him if he felt more for her than friendship, but he spent most of the time talking about how things had improved with Alexia since he'd told her Mia was dating Bear, so Mia pushed the question to the back of her mind.

On Thursday, Justin and Ella went with her. Justin held hands with both of them and Ella told him that was the only chance he would get to have a threesome, so he'd better make the most of it. The poor guy looked terrified until he realised she was joking.

'Bloody Nora,' he said, mimicking Ella. 'You nearly gave me a heart attack. I thought you meant it.' He was surprisingly strait-laced for a man who spent most Saturday nights covered in baby oil, gyrating on a stage.

Garrick accompanied her on Friday. Once again, he spent the entire time saying how wonderful Alexia was and how he was sure they'd soon be having sex. Mia was surprised they hadn't already. He seemed to spend every evening in the pub and Alexia made it pretty obvious she was willing. Perhaps Garrick was back to his former self and his spontaneity was over.

On Saturday, Bear took her to the beach as part of their date. The times of the tides were gradually changing and low tide had been at three, so when they arrived just after eight it was high tide and the sea was choppy. Mia wasn't yet brave enough to venture too close, and for some reason Bear didn't inspire the same confidence in her as Jet had done. They walked across the dunes and Mia kept one eye focused on the sea, just in case. Afterwards, they went to The Frog and Lily for a drink and something to eat. Jet, who Mia hadn't seen since Sunday was there and as soon as she saw him she raced to the bar to tell him where she'd been.

'I've walked on the beach every day since Sunday,' she said, beaming at him.

He glanced over her head towards Bear and nodded to his friend. 'That's great, Mia. Mattie would be proud of you.'

She rather hoped he would be proud of her, but he didn't seem that interested.

'I hoped to see you at choir practice on Tuesday but you didn't come.'

He shook his head and studied his pint of beer intently. 'Busy week. Lots to do on the farm.'

'Maybe I can help.' He shot her a doubtful look and she hurried on: 'I'd like to do something to thank you. If it hadn't been for you I wouldn't have felt the sand between my toes this week, or smelt the salt air up close, or felt the sea spray on my cheeks, or watched the gulls soar over the waves and dogs chase sticks into the water.' She saw the twitch of his lips but it vanished before it had a chance to take hold.

'That's nice. I'm pleased for you. But you'd have done it eventually, with or without me.'

'I wouldn't!' She lowered her voice from the shriek. 'Is something wrong? Have I done something else to annoy you?'

'No. I'm tired that's all. It's felt like a very long week. So you're dating Bear. How's that working out for you? I assume you didn't ask Garrick.'

'Shush.' She glanced around and waved at Bear who was chatting to Toby at the other end of the bar. Garrick and Ella stood beside him, as Alexia leant provocatively on the bar, her ample bosoms a fraction of an inch from Garrick's hand. Not that Garrick seemed to notice. 'I'd like to keep that just between you and me. As you can see, everything's rosy with Garrick and Alexia.'

'Is it? If my girlfriend wore a T-shirt that low cut and stuck her breasts that close to me, I wouldn't be chatting to her brother, I can assure you.'

Mia gasped as Jet drank his beer. 'She's working. He can hardly have rampant sex with her on the bar, can he?'

Jet sniggered. 'Rampant sex? Okay. I'll go with that. I'm not suggesting they have *rampant sex.*'

'Don't make fun of me,' she snapped. 'What's wrong with rampant sex?'

'Nothing whatsoever. I wouldn't mind a bit of rampant sex myself.'

The twitch was back and this time it spread across his mouth until it reached his eyes, which seemed to dance as he looked at her. Or perhaps that was wishful thinking.

'Then why did you laugh like that when I said it?'

'It's always about sex with you, isn't it? As I was saying before you snapped at me, I'm not suggesting they have sex, rampant or otherwise, but he could at least show some interest.'

'It's not always about sex with me. I can't even remember the last time I had sex. Oh yes, I can. That's why I got fired. Not that we did have sex. My boss just thought we had when he found us sprawled across his desk.' She saw the look of curious amusement on Jet's face. Why on earth had she said that? 'It was an office party and he was my boyfriend.' She cleared her throat. 'But this isn't about me. Are you suggesting Garrick stands there with his eyes as good as clued to Alexia's boobs? How romantic.'

'No. Tell me more about the desk.'

'No. What should he be doing then? In your opinion.'

Jet put his pint glass on the bar and moved closer to her, sliding an arm slowly around her waist and leaning forward to whisper in her ear. 'He could do this, for starters.' He drew away from her so suddenly that she nearly lost her footing. 'Sorry. I forgot you're here with my mate.' He grabbed his glass and knocked back his beer in a matter of seconds. 'Come on.' He took her hand in his and for one brief moment she thought he was going to take her out of the pub. Instead, he took her back to Bear.

'Hi mate.' Bear slapped Jet on the arm. 'What were you doing over there?'

'Apart from trying to seduce your new girlfriend, you mean? I was discussing something with Alec, until Mia came over to tell me that she's as good as beaten her phobia.'

Bear smiled. Either he hadn't heard the seduction part or it didn't bother him. 'She still has a long way to go, but she's making steps in the right direction. And I hear she has you to thank for it.'

Jet shook his head. 'Nope. She has herself to thank for it. She overcame her fear herself. I just stood behind her and admired the view.'

'You did a lot more than that,' Mia protested.

'Right place, right time. That's all. Got to go. See you at training tomorrow?' Jet directed the question to Bear.

'Yeah. See you tomorrow, mate.' He nodded, smiled, turned his attention to Toby and ordered some drinks.

'You're leaving?' Mia hoped that didn't sound as desperate as it felt inside.

'Chickens to put to bed.'

'Let me help. I can help. You made me feel safe near the water. I'm sure you'll make me feel safe in a barn filled with chickens.' Damn. She hadn't meant to sound so keen. And she'd forgotten she was on a date.

Jet raised his brows and smiled, shaking his head. He leant forward and lowered his voice. 'Now that's romantic, Mia.' But before she got a chance to reply, he turned and walked out of the pub.

Chapter Eight

Other than a short walk along the beach on Sunday morning, Mia spent most of the day scrolling through the photos on her laptop yet again. She still couldn't believe that Mattie could have lived in such a tiny place as Little Pondale for twenty-five years and that the only confirmed photo of her was the back of her head at a Christmas party in The Frog and Lily, the year she arrived.

What was also odd was that everyone Mia had spoken to said how much they liked and respected Mattie, how wonderfully friendly and caring she was, and yet not one of them – not one – could tell Mia anything about Mattie's life before she arrived in the village. It seemed Mattie knew everything about everyone, but no one knew anything about Mattie. She had a knack for getting people to open up and bare their souls, it seemed, whilst keeping the door to her own, very firmly closed.

Mia was at a loss to know what to do next to try to discover anything about Mattie and expected the week to be much the same as the week before. She would continue to ask questions in the hope that someone would finally shed even a small patch of light on Mattie's history. She would strengthen her determination to beat her fear of water. And she would revel in the peace and tranquillity of country life, something to which she was slowly growing accustomed.

But early on Monday morning the peace was shattered by what sounded like a woman's scream. Leaping out of bed, Mia rushed into the hall, bumping into Garrick.

'That wasn't a fox,' she said, having become acquainted with the vixen's nightly call. 'That was human.'

Garrick nodded and raced downstairs with Mia at his heels. Ella stood, shaking in the doorway.

'Ella!' Mia shrieked. 'What is it? Are you okay?'

Ella shook her head and pointed a quivering finger at the doorstep.

Garrick ran to her and pulled her back into the hall before a burst of laughter escaped him. 'Bloody hell, Ella. It's only a frog. And it isn't even real.' He bent down and picked it up, holding it in the air. He squeezed it between his fingers and it sounded like a mouse. Ella screamed and hid behind Mia.

'You know she doesn't like frogs,' Mia said, giving Garrick a reproachful look.

'It's a dog's toy,' he said, squeezing it again so that it emitted a second squeak.

'It's a bloody frog!' Ella yelled. 'I don't care if it's not real. Keep it away from me. I can't stand the things, you know that. And it's all your fault. If you and Barry Hopkirk hadn't put one in my bed when I was a kid, I wouldn't be the wreck I am now whenever I see one close up.'

'Sorry, sis. I'll take it to the pub with me later. For now I'll chuck it in my van.'

'You're going to take a toy frog to the pub?' Mia queried, fighting back a grin. 'Are you sure you want to do that?'

'Someone may be missing it. As I said, it's a dog's toy. Someone's dog must have dropped it.'

Ella glared at him. 'On our doorstep? Don't be ridiculous. Bloody Nora! This is that curse of Frog's Hollow thing Hettie told us about!' She shot a worried look at Mia. 'But none of us have been to the place, have we?'

'I haven't,' Mia said, more concerned now that she had been reminded of the curse.

Garrick shook his head. 'It's nothing to do with a curse. If it wasn't left by someone's dog, one of the foxes could've taken it from someone's garden, thinking it was edible and dropped it here when it realised it wasn't. There are any number of reasons why it might be here, but not one of them is because of a curse, Ella, so forget that right now, or Mia will start panicking about it.'

'Yeah,' Ella said, taking a deep breath. 'You're probably right. There's nothing to worry about, Mia. But please put it in your van right now,

Garrick. Just looking at it is making me feel queasy.'

Garrick smiled reassuringly, grabbed his keys and with nothing on his feet, he tip-toed down the drive towards his van and tossed the frog inside.

'Where were you going at this time in the morning?' Mia glanced at her watch. 'Or need I ask?'

Ella forced a smile. 'I was going to get some bread, but I'm not sure I'm up to it right now. I think I need to sit down. Bloody frogs. I can't stand the things.'

'It doesn't stop you going to the pub,' Mia pointed out.

Ella gave her a shove. 'Not even a frog could do that. Actually, it could, but a picture of one doesn't bother me, it's only when I see them in the flesh, or something that looks real that I break out in a cold sweat.'

'I'll make coffee,' Mia said, taking Ella by the arm and leading her into the kitchen. 'I love these light mornings, don't you? And just think, in a little over a week, it'll officially be summer. Bear told me that around here, summer starts on the first of June, so we're already two weeks in. Farming communities often go by the meteorological calendar, apparently. Or was it the lunar calendar? Or the Julian calendar?' She shrugged. 'I can't remember. He was telling me about Midsummer Night and that's how we got on to the subject. It's actually on Midsummer's Eve that they all go naked bathing in the pond, so he said. That's the 23rd of June. It's all a bit confusing because summer for us starts on the 21st of June and that's the longest day, but Midsummer's Day was set way back when and it's always on the 24th. I think that's what he said.'

'What in God's name are you babbling about?' Ella asked, flopping down onto a kitchen chair. 'If that's your way of getting me to forget the frog, telling me about naked bathing in a pond that's the source of this whole business really isn't helping.'

'I thought knowing that summer is sort of here, at least in Little Pondale, might cheer you up. Added to the fact that you'll soon get to see all the guys in the village, naked. Although I expect you've already seen Justin starkers. Come to think of it, I've as good as seen that.'

'I haven't.' Ella opened the packet of chocolate digestives Mia handed her. 'We've fooled around but we haven't stripped off and leapt into bed yet. He wants to take things slowly.'

Mia shook her head as she filled the kettle. 'That man continues to amaze me.'

'Which man?' Garrick joined them and sat across the table from his sister.

'Justin,' Ella said. 'We're talking about the Midsummer thing. It's on the 23rd apparently.'

'I know. It's already in my diary.'

'You keep a diary?' Mia was surprised.

'A work diary so that I can schedule orders, but I put personal things in it too. Did you know as far as most of the village is concerned, it's already summer and–'

'Yes, we know,' Mia and Ella said simultaneously.

'But did you know there's a Village Fête, a Kite Festival, the Frog Hill Run as well as the naked bathing?'

'My cup runneth over,' Ella replied sarcastically. 'These country folk certainly know how to have a good time, don't they? Although, those things do all sound as if they might be fun. Apart from the running bit. When are they?'

'End of June, early July, I think. The Village Fête's in August. Alexia told me about them last night.'

'That means Mum will be here for them. Her ship docks on the 21st. She messaged late last night to remind me and to say she'd like to come straight here. I told her that would be great. It's okay with you two, isn't it?'

'Of course,' Garrick said. 'Besides, it's your cottage. Well it will be, in a little over eleven months.'

Ella nodded. 'Absolutely. Ooh! She'll be here in time for the naked bathing. Now that will be fun.'

Mia put three mugs of coffee on the table and flopped onto a chair. 'Dear God. That's all I need. My sixty-year-old mum running around naked with people half her age, especially as she's got a better body than I have. Not that I'll be there. For once in my life, I'm rather glad I'm afraid of water.'

'There's nothing wrong with your body,' Garrick said, his face flushing. 'Will Lori really want to do that?' He laughed. 'Why am I asking? Of course she will.'

The frog was completely forgotten and none of them thought any more about it.

Until the following day, when Hettie popped round unexpectedly.

'I hear there was a frog on your doorstep yesterday,' she said excitedly the second Mia opened the front door. 'You didn't mention it when I came to clean.'

Mia sighed and tried to block the doorway with her body, but Ella called out from the kitchen that the coffee would get cold, which Hettie took to be an invite, even though Hettie didn't drink coffee and Ella had intended the comment as an excuse for Mia to get rid of her.

'I'd rather have tea, deary,' Hettie called out, smiling at Mia as she stepped forward and Mia had no option but to let the woman in.

'We've got a rather busy morning,' Mia said, following Hettie along the hall.

'Don't mind me, deary. I'm just popping in to see how you all are. What an awful thing to happen. Which one of you was it meant for?'

'Was what meant for?' Garrick asked, joining them in the kitchen from the garden where he'd been trimming the hedges.

'The frog, deary. Oh my. You look as if you've just stepped out of one of those calendars filled with half-naked men.'

Hettie's gaze swept over him and Mia was convinced Hettie licked her lips. But she couldn't really blame her. Garrick did look the part with his jeans hanging loose about his waist, his bare, lightly tanned torso damp with sweat and his mop of sandy-brown hair sprinkled with bits of leaves.

Mia cleared her throat and dragged her gaze to her mug of coffee which she gulped as if she hadn't had a drink for days.

'It's hot out there this morning,' Garrick said, a touch defensively, his handsome face reddening beneath Hettie's scrutiny.

He turned away and grabbed his shirt from the back of a chair where he'd left it, sliding it across his broad shoulders and loosely buttoning it to halfway. The white cotton clung to his frame and had the effect of making him even more appealing, rather than less.

'If you weren't my brother,' Ella said, grinning at him over the rim of her mug, 'I'd quite fancy you myself.'

That made him blush all the more and the strange and awkward silence was only broken a second or two later when the kettle rather noisily clicked itself off.

Ella made tea for Hettie and poured Garrick a coffee. 'You've heard about the frog then?'

'Oh yes, deary. Yesterday evening in the pub. I popped round right away but you were all out. You were with that sexy young Justin, of course, deary.' Hettie nodded at Ella as she handed Hettie the cup of tea. She smiled at Mia and sat down. 'You were with gorgeous Rupert, dear. And you, you handsome devil ...' She reached out and poked Garrick on the hip. '... Well, all I can say is if only I were a few years younger, Alexia Bywater would have serious competition, deary. I was a pretty young thing you know and my body was curvier than hers. Flexible too. I could wrap my legs around my neck, you know, dear. Probably still could if it weren't for a touch of arthritis.'

A rather unpleasant vision of Hettie with her legs wrapped around Garrick's neck popped into Mia's head as Garrick choked on his coffee and Ella made a curious sound, almost like a clucking chicken.

'But listen to me, talking ten chickens at a time. It's wonderful to see you all settling in to village life so quickly, dears. I hope this frog and the curse won't put you off. Which one of you was it who went to Frog's Hollow, did you say?'

'We didn't,' Garrick half-snapped at her before shaking his head. 'Sorry. But the frog yesterday had nothing to do with any curse, Hettie and even if it did, we haven't been to the place, not on a Monday or any other day, so why would the curse come to us?'

'It's a puzzlement, deary, I'll admit. Some might say that it's a sign you're not meant to stay here. Not me, of course. I want you all to stay. I would've put a pound on it, myself, but I'm not one for gambling. But others think you'll leave. That means you won't inherit though doesn't it deary, so I suppose you feel you've got to stay. I've no idea why Matilda did that. But then she did have some rather peculiar ways, deary.'

'What did you say?' Garrick stared at her in disbelief.

Hettie looked flustered and fiddled with the handle of her cup. 'It's all a bit of fun, deary. Nothing to get upset about. Village life can get a little dull sometimes and little things like this help liven it up. No harm was meant, deary.'

'What?' Mia wasn't sure why Garrick looked so cross.

He sucked in a breath and let it out. 'I thought you weren't going to tell anyone about the conditions of your inheritance. About the fact that you'll only inherit if you stay here for one year.'

'I wasn't.' Mia looked from him to Ella to Hettie. 'I haven't. But now everyone will know.' She glared at him.

'Everyone already knows, Mia.' His voice was strained and it was clear he was trying not to let anger get the better of him. 'Didn't you hear what Hettie said? She clearly said that people think

245

you'll leave which means you won't get your inheritance. If Hettie knows, so does everyone else. And it's pretty obvious they do, because unless I'm mistaken, they've all been making bets on it. Whether you'll stay or go. I'm right aren't I, Hettie?'

Hettie's bottom lip quivered and she blinked several times, her fingers shaking as she put down her cup and nodded. 'I'm so sorry, deary. I didn't mean to let that slip. It's this business with the frog. It's got me all a-jitter. And I can't keep a secret to save my life. Never could. No matter how hard I try. It's a weakness, deary.'

'What?' Mia stared at Hettie before turning to Garrick then Ella. 'I don't understand. How could Hettie know?'

'Don't look at me,' Ella said, holding up one hand. 'I haven't said a word about the will or the terms of your inheritance. Not even to Justin.'

'Neither have I,' Garrick said. 'How do you know about it, Hettie?'

She shook her head. 'Please don't be mad with me, deary. I can't think straight when people are cross with me. I heard it somewhere but I can't think where. In the pub I expect. That's where I hear most things. That's where I heard about the frog yesterday.'

'It wasn't because you searched through Mattie's things and found something then? Or because you eavesdropped on a conversation?' Garrick was almost hostile.

'No! Eavesdrop? Me? I wouldn't do such a thing. It's almost dishonest. If I hear a conversation as I'm standing at a door or as I'm passing by, that's a different thing entirely but to actually suggest I'd stand and listen at keyholes and such, never. Never in all my days. And to suggest I'd search through dear Matilda's personal papers and belongings? Well, I've never been so insulted in my life.'

She got to her feet, swayed slightly and gripped the back of the chair with one hand while clamping the other to her chest. Her rosy cheeks drained of colour and her eyes filled with tears.

'Bloody Nora!' Ella shrieked, leaping to her aid. 'She's having a heart attack. Call an ambulance, Garrick!'

'No, no deary,' Hettie croaked softly. 'It's not a heart attack. I've had one, so I know. Just a palpitation. I'll be fine once I'm home.'

She made a move as if to leave but Mia grabbed her arm.

'You're not going anywhere until we're sure you're okay, Hettie. And we're certainly not letting you go home where you'll be alone. Sit down and take deep breaths.'

'Don't you trouble yourself over a silly old fool like me, deary. And I won't be alone. Prince Gustav will be with me. And my darling Hector, of course.'

'A rat and a ghost,' Garrick said, his mobile pressed against his ear. 'Sorry Hettie, but Mia's right. You're staying here and we're calling a doctor at the very least. I'd never forgive myself if something happened to you. I'm sorry if I caused this. I apologise for the things I said. Jesus! Why can't ... Bugger! I forgot there's no bloody phone signal here.'

He dashed towards the living room to use the landline but Hettie grabbed his hand.

'Call Rupert if you insist on phoning someone,' she said.

'He's a vet, Hettie! I'm calling 999.' Garrick looked at her as if he thought she'd also lost her mind, and eased her fingers from him.

Hettie tutted. 'I'm not senile, deary. He's also one of those community first responder people. Trust me. He's the man to call in an emergency. Not that this is an emergency, deary. I'm much better now. I'm sure I'll be as right as ninepence if I might have another cup of tea.'

'Of course,' Ella said. 'I'll make a fresh one right away.'

'I'll run across the lane and get Rupert,' Garrick said. 'It'll probably be quicker than finding his number.' He raced to the front door.

Mia took one of Hettie's hands in hers and smiled reassuringly. 'We'll take care of you, Hettie. There's nothing to worry about, I'm sure.'

Hettie smiled back. 'Bless you, deary. Bless you all. But the only thing that worries me, is how that frog got on your doorstep.'

Chapter Nine

Bear confirmed that Hettie had not had a heart attack on this occasion but that she did have one in the past.

'It was a few years ago now,' he said, as he sat at the kitchen table with Mia, enjoying a cup of coffee and a chocolate digestive.

Hettie was resting on the living room sofa, propped up with cushions at her back, a blanket over her legs and Ella plying her with cups of tea, while Garrick hovered in the background, clearly blaming himself for Hettie's current state.

'So you're the man to call in an emergency?' Mia smiled at Bear, who seemed more appealing now that he was not only a vet but also a quasi-doctor.

'Not just in an emergency, I hope,' he said, leaning closer to her. 'Are you doing anything tonight? Do you fancy playing a bit of doctors and nurses in my cottage?'

The suggestion took her by surprise and for a moment she didn't respond until she remembered it was Tuesday, and shook her head.

'Choir practice, remember?'

'How could I forget? I meant after choir practice. I'd like to do a little practising of my own. You're looking very sexy in that summer dress.' His gaze swept over her. 'But not quite as sexy as when I first arrived. From what I saw of the nightdress you were wearing beneath your dressing gown, it left little to my imagination. And now I've made you blush, you're looking even sexier. I haven't got any appointments booked in for the next hour. I know we've only been on two dates but we could make this the third. How do you fancy coming back with me now and I'll give you a thorough examination?'

Mia's mug nearly slipped from her fingers and it took a second or two to compose herself. Was he actually suggesting they go back to his place and have sex while Hettie lay virtually prostrate on the sofa? So far, they'd only shared one brief kiss on Saturday night after their date and while it was nice, it hadn't blown her mind. He was handsome, yes. He was fit, in every sense of the word and he was sexy. But did she want to sleep with him? She hadn't thought that far ahead. Clearly he had. And right at this moment, he reminded her of an excited puppy, eager to play with his new toy.

She shook her head and smiled apologetically. 'As tempting as that offer is, Bear, I think I must decline. I can't leave Ella and Garrick with Hettie the way she is. It wouldn't be fair. Besides, what if something happened? I'd be mortified if the village found out you and I were having sex while Hettie gasped her last breath.'

His face fell and he scowled. 'That woman will outlive the lot of us, believe me. And no one would find out. I'm not the sort of guy who blabs about his sex life to all and sundry.'

'I wasn't suggesting you were, but things seem to have a way of getting out in this village. For example, what have you heard about me and this cottage?'

He frowned. 'I don't get what you mean.'

'I mean. What have you heard about my inheritance?'

'Oh that.' He fell back against the chair and shrugged. 'Only what everyone else has.'

Mia leant forward. 'And what has everyone heard?'

He tipped his head to one side as if he still didn't follow her line of questioning. He gave a nonchalant shrug. 'That Mattie made it a condition of her will that you have to live here for one year before you can inherit her estate.'

Mia gasped. 'And who told you that?'

Again the shrug. 'I can't recall. I think I heard it in the pub.'

'And that was it? Someone in the pub just came right out with that?'

'What is this? Twenty questions? I honestly don't remember. Why? Isn't it true?'

'Yes it's true. But it wasn't supposed to be common knowledge.'

He shrugged again but this time he grinned. 'No point in trying to keep something like that secret around here. Oh, I also heard that if you don't stay the year, you only get a small sum of cash. The rest of Mattie's estate goes to the next in line.'

'What? You even know that! Do you also know who the 'next in line' as you call them, is?'

He seemed confused but then a wicked grin spread across his lips and he suddenly leant forward, almost knocking heads with her. 'Come and have sex with me and I'll tell you everything I know.'

She leant back as far away as she could get. 'Tell me everything you know or you won't stand a chance in hell of so much as kissing me again, let alone having sex with me.'

'That's cruel.' The grin grew wider. 'But I like a feisty woman. God, you're hot, Mia! Do you have any idea how turned on I am right now? Please come and have sex with me! I'm begging you.'

She looked away and only then did she spot Garrick hovering in the doorway. His face was flushed and from the expression he wore he could happily have killed someone.

'I think Hettie's feeling a lot better.' His voice was cool and controlled, which was completely at odds with his face. 'Please don't let us keep you,

Rupert. I'm sure you've got people and their pets waiting to see you.'

Bear seemed oblivious to Garrick's demeanour but he frowned when Garrick came to join them.

'As it happens, I haven't. I was just telling Mia that I've got an hour or so to kill. I've invited her to come and take a look around my surgery. You don't mind if we leave you and Ella to it, do you mate?' He got to his feet and smiled. 'There's nothing wrong with Hettie that a bit of attention won't cure.'

'Actually, I do. Sorry. But we were in the middle of something when Hettie had her episode. We really need to get on with that. I'm sure you understand. There's plenty of time for Mia to go and see your surgery, if she really wants to.'

Bear glanced at Mia and she quickly took her cue.

'Yes. Sorry, Bear. Perhaps another time. Although I'd appreciate an answer to my question before you leave. Do you know the name of the person 'next in line'?'

'What?' Now Bear looked cross. 'No. No one does. There's a bet about that …' He stopped suddenly and coughed. 'Right. I'll leave you to it.'

'Oh no you won't!' Garrick stood in his path and although Bear was broader by a couple of inches and taller by the same amount, Garrick appeared more threatening at that moment. 'Not until you explain that bit. Did you say there's a bet

253

about who'll inherit if Mia doesn't stay? Or that there's a bet as to whether she'll stay or go? Because Hettie alluded to something similar and we'd rather like to know what's going on.'

Bear glanced from Mia to Garrick and then to Ella as she joined them.

'What's going on? What have I missed?'

Garrick didn't take his gaze from Bear. 'Rupert was just going to tell us about a bet the village seems to have regarding Mia. We're waiting, Rupert.'

'Mate ...' Bear gave an ingratiating smile. '... There's no need to get a strop on. It's just a bit of fun. When we heard Mia was coming from London and the condition in the will, we simply all wondered how long she would stay. You know what it's like on a Friday night in the pub. Banter flies back and forth. Someone, and I can't remember who so don't even bother to ask, said they would bet a fiver she wouldn't last a week.'

Mia gasped and he grinned at her.

'Nothing personal, Mia. We hadn't met you then. Anyway, someone else said they'd take that bet and make it one month. It all kicked off from there until someone suggested we do it properly and run a pool. The bets run from a week – which has obviously been and gone – all the way up to you seeing it through and staying the year. Then one started on who inherits if you leave, but that one's not as popular.'

Mia shook her head in disbelief. 'And I thought this was a friendly village.'

'It is a friendly village,' Bear protested. 'It's just a bit of fun, Mia.'

'Really?' Ella said. 'Is that why someone left a frog on Mia's doorstep yesterday morning? As a bit of fun? Or was it a feeble attempt to try and scare her away?'

'Frog? What frog?' Bear appeared genuinely surprised. 'That toy frog Garrick brought into the pub, you mean? How could that scare anyone?'

'It bloody well scared me!' Ella shrieked. 'I can't stand the things.'

'I'm sorry. I had no idea. But it wasn't me and I don't think anyone in the village would do something to purposefully scare you, or Mia, or anyone. Honestly. The bets are just a bit of harmless fun.'

'Until someone gets hurt,' Garrick said.

Mia shoved back her chair and looked Bear in the eye. 'Well, Rupert, you can tell everyone in the village that unless they put money on me staying here for the year, they can kiss their bet goodbye because I'm staying. And there's not a thing that you or anyone else can do to make me leave. I actually thought I might even make it my permanent home, but now I'm not so sure. I don't think I've ever been so disappointed in so many people, in my entire life. And you can tell them all that in the pub too.' She turned towards the back door.

'Mia. Please. Don't be like that.' Bear sounded contrite as he reached out and touched her arm, but she shook him off.

'And you can take your *surgery* and shove it up your arse, Rupert bloody Day!'

She shoved the back door open and stormed into the garden, tears of anger and frustration pricking at her eyes.

But as she picked up her pace and ran towards the dunes, a question popped into her head.

Had Jet Cross placed a bet, and if so, how long had he given her to stay?

And more importantly, who had he named as the 'next in line', because for some bizarre reason, she was beginning to think the person named in the sealed codicil, could very well be him.

Chapter Ten

Mia got within twenty feet of the sea before she realised where she was, and when she stopped, her heart thumped in her chest and her breath came in gasps. It was partly due to the fact that she was so unfit, but it was also obvious she wasn't over her phobia yet.

Garrick was calling her name and he quickly closed the distance between them, pulling her into his arms and holding her so close she could hear the drum of his heart as the warmth of his body melded with hers.

'For a minute there I was terrified you were going to run right into the sea. It may be summer but that's water's still freezing. I would've killed you if I'd had to come in and drag you out.'

His voice was tender with an equal measure of concern and reassuring humour.

Mia giggled into his chest. 'There's not much chance of me ever running into the sea. My fear will always kick-in. But if I had, you could've simply left me.' She looked up at him, safe in his embrace.

'No, I couldn't, Mia.' He smiled and gently brushed a wayward lock of hair from her face. 'In fact, I'm beginning to wonder if I'll ever be able to do that.'

'What?' She didn't dare to hope. 'Let me drown?' She grinned at him as they stared into each other's eyes.

'I think you know what I mean.'

She slowly shook her head, her gaze still locked with his. 'Do I, Garrick?'

'Don't you? I think it's pretty obvious, even though I've done everything I could to try to deny it. I'm terrified I'll lose your friendship.'

'You'll never lose my friendship, Garrick. I'll always be your friend, no matter what.'

'But I want to be more than friends, Mia.' He let out a heavy sigh. 'There, I've said it. I know you probably don't feel the same and I know you're about to inherit a fortune. I probably couldn't have picked a worse time but when I came in and saw Bear leering all over you, that was the final straw. I couldn't take it anymore.'

'But you're dating Alexia. You're besotted with her.'

He shook his head. 'I'm not besotted. She's gorgeous, yes, and I thought … Well, if I'm going to be completely honest, I was still in love with Fiona when I came here. I had hardly seen you over the last few years, but the minute I saw you again, I felt something. I thought it was just a rebound thing, you know? Then I saw Alexia and

258

she reminded me so much of Fiona and, I'm ashamed to say this, but I thought I could have a fling with her and that would get Fiona out of my system, once and for all. But Fiona's been replaced by you. No. That didn't come out right. I don't mean replaced. I mean. God, I don't know what I mean. I wish I'd never opened my big mouth but it feels as if I've been keeping this secret for too long. The more I tried to fall in love with Alexia, the more I wanted you.' He let her go and ran a hand through his hair. 'I'm sorry, Mia. You probably think I'm a complete jerk.'

'No I don't, Garrick. But you are still dating Alexia, aren't you?'

He shook his head again and kicked the sand with his shoe. 'I won't be after I tell her it's over.'

'You're going to do that?'

'Yes.'

'Why?'

'Because I can't pretend any longer.'

'But I thought you couldn't wait to have sex with her and … and you took her all those flowers.'

'I was overcompensating. I was trying to make myself believe I felt something for her but I didn't. I don't. And when it came to sex.' He laughed mockingly. 'I can't believe I'm saying this, but I couldn't bring myself to go through with it. And I don't mean I couldn't do it physically. I'm saying I simply didn't want to. I'm not one of those guys who can have meaningless sex just for the fun of it. I wish I were, but I'm not.'

'I'm very glad you're not. But Alexia's gorgeous and has the body of a goddess. I'd do anything to have a body like hers.'

'Would you? That's odd. I'd rather have you in my arms any day.'

'You would? You mean it? You prefer me to Alexia?'

He nodded. 'No competition as far as I'm concerned. And it's not just about your body. I like so much more about you.'

'What exactly are you saying? That you like me? That you fancy me? That you … that you don't want to have sex with Alexia but you wouldn't mind having sex with me? Is that what you're saying?'

He laughed and nodded. 'Yes to all of that. Only I was hoping I could find a more romantic way to say it. I think I've rather cocked it up though, haven't I?'

Mia slipped her arms back around his waist and leant into him, looking up into his eyes and seeing surprise mingled with hope. 'Nope. But I do have one question.'

He wrapped his arms around her again and pulled her close. 'Just one?'

Mia nodded. 'Garrick Swann? Will you please go out on a date with me?'

He laughed. 'Bloody Nora, Mia! Absolutely.'

'Oh. But you've got to finish with Alexia first. And I know I don't have to say this to a lovely man like you, but do it gently, won't you?'

He beamed at her, grabbed her hand and they hurried back towards the cottage.

'I'm going to tell Alexia right now, and then Mia Ward, you and I are going on a date. And before you ask, it's not going to be to The Frog and Lily.'

Chapter Eleven

Mia could understand the way the villagers had reacted when they thought she and her friends were spreading gossip concerning Jet and Mattie, but now that she knew they were making bets regarding her inheritance, since before she arrived in Little Pondale, she didn't feel quite as amicable towards them. There was also the added problem of her short-lived relationship with Bear. Despite the fact they had only shared one kiss, it might be awkward for both of them now that she and Garrick were an item. And Alexia had not been exactly thrilled by Garrick's news.

'You may want to consider avoiding her for a couple of days,' Garrick suggested to Mia and Ella later that afternoon. 'And perhaps you should consider giving choir practice a miss. I tried to break it off as pleasantly as I could but it seems Alexia has an issue with what she sees as rejection.'

'What did you say to her?' Ella asked, having been over the moon to hear that Mia and her brother were going on a date. 'It's about time,' had been her reaction when they had told her.

'I said that I thought she was beautiful and fun to be with. That any man would be lucky to have her by his side. But that I had rushed into asking her out when my heart still yearned for my ex-girlfriend and that since then, I had come to realise that I might have feelings for someone else. I added that it would be great if we could still be friends and that I hoped I hadn't caused her any distress as that was the last thing I had intended. I didn't get a chance to say more. She went ballistic. Called me every name under the sun and threw a pint of beer at me. Along with the glass.'

'Bloody Nora,' Ella said. 'Well, at least we know she isn't perfect. The woman has a temper.'

Mia frowned. 'She must've cared for you far more than any of us thought if that was her reaction.'

'I think I could've worded it better,' Garrick said, taking Mia's hand in his. 'I'm clearly not good when it comes to breaking up with people. Or with trying to ask people out.' He grinned. 'But we'd only had a couple of dates and we hadn't had sex. I thought she'd call me a jerk or something more colourful perhaps and then laugh about it.'

Ella punched him on the arm. 'If you even think about breaking up with Mia, you'll have me to answer to. And I won't just throw a glass of beer at you. I'll throw the entire barrel. Not that you will consider breaking up with Mia, will you?'

'That's unfair,' Mia said, laughing. 'We haven't been on a date yet. We've been friends for years and we like one another a lot. I was so jealous of Alexia, but for all of that, there are no guarantees when it comes to love. Things may not work out between us no matter how much both of us want them to. I hope, if it does ever come to either one of us wanting to break up, we'll still be friends, regardless. And I promise I won't throw anything at you if you dump me. But I think your break-up speech could do with a bit of work.'

'It was crap, wasn't it? But hopefully, that's the last time I'll need a break-up speech. And I promise, if this doesn't work out between us and you ever want to finish with me, I'll take it like a man and only sob in a corner once you've left me.'

'Oh God,' Ella said. 'I'd better go and tell Justin what's happened. I think it's better if he hears the news from me. And if you two can take your eyes off one another for five minutes, could one of you go and check on Hettie? She was fast asleep when I left her twenty minutes ago. She's absolutely fine now I'm sure, but what are we going to do about her? Are we going to send her home alone or should we ask someone to stay with her?'

'I still feel responsible,' Garrick said. 'And I don't think she should be alone tonight, do you?'

Mia sighed and shook her head. 'No. I think you're right. I think she needs to stay with us. And that means we'll have to postpone our date.'

'Bloody Nora.' Ella got to her feet. 'This relationship has ended before it's even started! I can look after Hettie. You go on your date.'

Mia frowned and so did Garrick. 'It wouldn't feel right,' they said in unison, and smiled.

'We've got all the time in the world,' Mia added.

'Absolutely. We can go on a date when Hettie's back to her old self. Let's stay in tonight and I'll cook something nice for supper. Why don't you ask Justin if he wants to join us, Ella?'

'I'll ask,' she said, dashing towards the door, 'But it's Tuesday and it's choir practice so he'll probably go there. I'll tell him to tell the vicar we won't be going and – Jesus!'

Mia jumped to her feet a nanosecond after Garrick and they raced to Ella's side. On the doorstep lay a bunch of dead flowers.

'Do you get the impression someone is sending us a message?' Ella said. 'First the frog, now this.'

'It's me they're meant for,' Mia said, as Garrick clasped her hand in his.

'Not necessarily.' Garrick bent and picked them up. 'I gave Alexia flowers, remember? This may be her way of telling me what she thinks.'

'Yeah,' Ella said, sarcastically. 'Because throwing a pint glass at your head may not have got the message across, you mean? And dead flowers say so much more.'

'Coo-ey,' Hettie called out from the living room. 'Is everything all right?'

'I'll go,' Mia said. 'I don't want to sound like a drama queen but I think it may be a good idea if you go with Ella, Garrick. Just in case.'

'Safety in numbers?' he smiled, reassuringly. 'This is just a childish prank. I'm sure no one in the village is planning to harm us.'

'Perhaps not. But I'd feel more at ease if you went. I'll be fine with Hettie.'

He kissed her on her forehead and followed his sister out, tossing the flowers in the rubbish bin on the way. When they had crossed the lane and were walking beside the pond, Mia closed the front door. And then went back and locked it, shaking her head at her need to do so, and forcing a grin, but not in an entirely confident way.

'What's happened, deary?' Hettie asked.

Mia explained the events since Hettie's episode, as briefly as she could.

'Good heavens, deary. So Garrick has finished with Alexia and you have finished with Rupert and now Garrick and you are going out. And someone has left a bunch of dead flowers at your door. And you're upset with the entire population of Little Pondale because of two silly bets. Have I got that right, deary?'

'Yes. Except they're not silly bets. They're serious because there's a great deal of money involved in Mattie's estate and it seems someone doesn't want me to inherit. The whole thing was supposed to be confidential so how did anyone find out about it in the first place? And why now? Why didn't this start when I arrived? I'm pretty certain Mattie wouldn't have mentioned the terms of her will to anyone. Her new solicitor who took over from his dad, definitely wouldn't have told anyone either and he doesn't even know who the 'next in line' is, so how can anyone else?'

'I see, deary. Well, when you put it like that, I understand why you're upset. But if the frog and flowers are meant to make you leave, dear, perhaps they only started now because it began to look as if you're here to stay. When you arrived, most of us thought you'd soon be bored living here – yes, even me, deary. But then it looked as if all three of you had found love with local people. Garrick and Alexia, Ella and Justin, and you and Rupert. You all appeared to be settling in, deary. But I don't think anyone does know who the 'next in line' is. Everyone was simply guessing. It really was just a bit of fun, deary. But yes. I know. We shouldn't be having fun about such a serious matter. I may be an old fool but I do understand that. Now that you've explained how upset you are, that is, my dear.'

Mia nodded. 'I see your point. So you think that now I'm dating Garrick, perhaps it'll stop with the frog and the flowers, because we don't have any ties to here. But there's still Ella and Justin.'

'Yes, deary. I couldn't say if it'll stop or not, but I do know none of us in Little Pondale would wish you any harm. I think young Garrick's right. It's just a childish prank. Isn't that what he said? Perhaps I might offer a piece of advice. Why don't you have a quiet word with Freda and tell her how you feel, dear? I'm sure once she knows you're upset, she'll cancel the bets and give everyone back their stakes and that'll be the end of it.'

'Will it? I'm now dating the man who has just dumped the daughter she idolises. Plus, whoever left the frog and flowers may not have placed a bet. That person or persons may know something we don't. It's a toy frog and dead flowers so far, and I'm glad you think no one would wish us any harm, but what might they do next, I wonder?'

Hettie reached out and squeezed Mia's hand. 'Now, now deary. I think you've been reading too many of those thrillers. This is Little Pondale, my dear. Nothing sinister happens in Little Pondale. Except for the curse, and as you haven't been to Frog's Hollow on a Monday, or any day, I'm sure the curse won't harm you.'

'You said earlier that it might. That perhaps we we're meant to be here.'

'Nonsense. That was me just being a silly old woman who likes a bit of attention, deary.' She let out a long, raspy sigh and shook her head. 'The truth is, I'm lonely, dear. Prince Gustav doesn't talk much and Hector's always busy these days. He's preparing for his next life, you know. I'm sorry if I've said or done anything since you've been here to make you feel unwelcome. And I'm sorry I repeated what I heard the other day. I want you to stay, deary. Matilda would definitely want you to stay. Don't let these silly things upset you, my dear.'

Mia smiled at her, and after a moment or two she asked: 'Why do you always call my great-aunt Matilda and not Mattie?'

Hettie shrugged. 'I suppose it's my way of showing her respect. And of keeping a little bit of her special to just me. I know that's silly deary, but she meant the world to me. I expect I probably got on her nerves, but she was kind and caring, and always willing to listen. She was the one who gave me Prince Gustav, deary. She knew I liked rats. She said it would be good for me to have another living creature in my home. I'm allergic to cats, and dogs are too much trouble to look after. She was right, bless her. Matilda was always right. I thought of her as one of my very best friends.'

'Really? Um. When we first arrived, I got the impression that you thought she wasn't very friendly. I can't recall your exact words but it was about becoming friends immediately then you changed it to friendly neighbours and said something about everyone being friends in Little Pondale, unless some people choose to keep themselves to themselves and have little secrets, or some such thing.'

Hettie raised her brows. 'Did I?' She rubbed her chin with her finger and thumb and thought for a moment. 'Oh yes, deary! I remember. It was when I said how much you resembled dear Matilda, and that I'd seen a photo of her as a girl. Oh deary me. That's because I talk ten chickens at a time, my dear. What I meant was that we didn't become friends immediately, we became friendly neighbours immediately. But after a while, we did become friends. Good friends, I think. Although I'm sure I thought more of dear Matilda than she did of me. But that's just fine, deary. No, no. The person I meant when I said about keeping themselves to themselves and having little secrets, wasn't Matilda.'

'Oh? Who was it then?'

Hettie looked around as if she thought someone might be listening before leaning closer to Mia. 'It was Grace, my dear. Grace Tyburn. The vicar's grandma.' She leant back against the cushions. 'Matilda didn't keep herself to herself. She joined in with everything in the village, and neither did she have little secrets, deary.' Hettie chuckled. 'Matilda's entire life was a secret. But we all loved her anyway.'

'Grace Tyburn?' Mia shook her head. 'I haven't met her yet. She's been unwell since we've been here. But wait! The photograph! You just said you saw a photo of Mattie as a girl.'

Hettie nodded. 'I did, deary.'

'Then where is it? There aren't any photos in this cottage and none of the photos we've seen were of Mattie as a girl. Do you know what happened to it?'

Hettie shook her head. 'No, deary. I don't. You're right though. I wonder where it's gone. There definitely was a photo. I believe it fell out of a book Matilda was holding, but it was a long time ago and I may be wrong about that, my dear. I bent down, picked it up and took a quick glance before I told Matilda she'd dropped it. I recall she had her back to me at the time, deary, and when I said how pretty she was as a girl, she turned around, looked somewhat surprised and then looked very sad. She gave me a weak little smile and took the photo back, saying something about it being another lifetime. And we never spoke of it again. And now, my dear, I'm feeling as fit as a flea, so I'd better get home and feed Prince Gustav.' She folded back the blanket but Mia laid a hand on her arm.

'You're not going anywhere, Hettie Burnstall. You're staying in the spare room tonight and until we're sure you're fine. Either we can go and feed Prince Gustav, or if he's in a cage or something that we can bring here, that's what we'll do.'

'Yes, he's in a cage. But you'd bring him here to me? You'd do that? You'd have a rat in your home?'

'He wouldn't be the first rat I've let into my home, Hettie. Although that one had two legs, not four. But, yes of course we'd do that. When Ella and Garrick get back from Justin's we'll get Prince Gustav for you.'

'You're just like dear Matilda. She would've done the same. Not everyone would you know, deary. Not everyone is as kind as they like to pretend they are.'

'I think that's Garrick now,' Mia said, hearing Garrick's laugh. She went to the front door and let him in. 'I locked it. Oh, hello Justin. It's lovely to see you.'

'I hear there's been some excitement,' he said, grinning at her as he walked into the hall. 'In case you're curious, I didn't bet on whether you'd stay or go and I didn't guess who gets the lot if you leave. And no, I don't know who spread that news. Ella's already grilled me. I can understand why you're upset, but they didn't mean any harm. We're a friendly, close-knit community and we try to welcome strangers but it takes a while to get to know someone. We may do things you wouldn't and vice versa. Is it really worth falling out over?'

'What about the frog and the flowers?'

He shrugged, saw Hettie on the living room sofa and waved at her. 'It's all happening here, isn't it? I don't know what the frog and flowers mean and I accept that's a bit creepy. I don't know who would do a thing like that in Little Pondale. But I'll keep my eyes open and my ear to the ground and if I discover anything, I'll let you know. In the meantime, try to forget about it. Garrick will take care of you, I don't have any doubt about that. As long as Alexia doesn't kill him, that is. That woman's got a bit of a temper. And I'm speaking from experience. But it'll blow over soon enough. She'll be all hell fire and fury for a day or so and then she'll be as sweet as pie again. Take my word for that.'

Chapter Twelve

Hettie and Prince Gustav stayed at Sunbeam Cottage until Saturday and there were no further 'incidents' during that time. They only left then because Hettie insisted she didn't want to overstay her welcome.

'I'm as right as ninepence, deary and it's time I went home. I haven't seen or heard from Hector since I've been here and I miss him, deary. I know I'll have to get used to that once he starts his new life, but until then, I want to make the most of our little chats. You understand, deary, don't you?'

Mia didn't. Talking to the dead wasn't something she believed in, but it was obvious that Hettie did, so Mia went along with it for her sake.

'Of course. But we'll pop in to check on you and you can call us on the landline at any time, night or day if you feel even a tiny bit unwell.'

Mia and Garrick still hadn't been on a date but they had shared a few lovely kisses, each one more passionate than the last, and now that Hettie was going home, and Ella was going to Justin's Saturday night show in a village thirty miles away,

274

Mia was hoping she and Garrick would share more than just kisses on Saturday night.

None of them had been to the pub, or so much as seen any of the locals other than Justin – which was odd bearing in mind the size of Little Pondale, but apart from Mia's daily walks along the beach with Garrick, none of them had been out much. Mia had spent a lot of the time looking through Mattie's attic room and safe for the missing photo, as well as clues to Mattie's life, but found neither. She also spent a considerable number of hours, sitting in the sunshine in the garden with Hettie and Prince Gustav. To her surprise, she was growing rather fond of both of them and Hettie shared more snippets of her conversations with Mattie, but nothing threw any light on the ongoing mystery. In the evenings, all of them sat on the decking, drinking wine. Ella had been working, having been sent a children's book to edit, which meant she was in her element. Children's books were her favourites and Garrick said that was because Ella was just a big kid herself, which Ella didn't deny. Garrick had been working too. He had an order for a baby's cot which he was crafting out of oak, with intricate designs at its head and foot.

After Mia and Garrick had accompanied Hettie and Prince Gustav home and made sure the two of them were settled in, Garrick had gone to the shed to continue with the cot and Mia had taken him coffee just before noon. She marvelled as she watched him work.

'I love what you can do with your hands,' she said.

He stopped and pulled her into his arms. 'I hope you'll be saying that tonight.'

He kissed her deeply and let his hands give her a taste of what she could expect.

'Bloody Nora,' she said, breathlessly grinning up at him, her heart pounding in her chest when he eased himself away. 'If that was anything to go by, I won't be saying much at all, except, perhaps, don't stop.' She gave him a questioning look. 'Why did you?'

'Stop?' he queried, with a devilish grin. 'Because I don't want a garden shed to be the first place we make love and if I'd carried on, I think we both know that's what would've happened.'

Mia ran a finger down the front of his T-shirt. 'Ella's busy working on the book and Hettie's gone. We could go upstairs right now. I think I'm pretty good with my hands too.'

His grin broadened. 'I don't doubt that for a second and believe me, I'd like nothing better, but I need to get this finished and once you and I get into bed, I don't think either of us will be getting out for a couple of days at least. I'll have this done by this evening and then I can give you my undivided attention. Is that okay with you?'

She let out a long, dramatic sigh. 'I suppose it'll have to be. But you'd better make the wait worthwhile, Garrick Swann, I'm telling you that right now.'

He pulled her back into his arms and smiled down at her. 'I promise you, Mia Ward, it'll be worthwhile. It'll be like all your birthdays and mine have come at once.' He kissed her again and if that kiss was anything to go by, he was probably right.

She eased herself away. 'I'd better go then. The sooner you finish that baby's cot, the sooner you can jump into mine.' She turned to leave but he grabbed her fingers in his.

'Mia?' He looked serious all of a sudden.

'Yes?'

'Do you want kids?'

She sniggered. 'Right now?'

He shook his head and looked her directly in the eye, all hint of amusement gone, and a furrow of concern creased his brow.

'I'm serious. You do want kids, don't you? You want a family?'

She moved closer to him and placed her hands flat against his chest. He slid his arms around her as if he were frightened she might break.

'Yes. Of course I do. But why the sudden question? Why the concern?'

He shook his head again and took a deep breath and when Mia looked into his eyes, there was a definite hint of sadness about them.

'Because I want kids more than anything in the world. Having a family is incredibly important to me. The most important thing, in fact.'

'O-kay,' she said tentatively. This was a worrying turn of events and definitely not something she'd seen coming. 'Um. That's fine. That's great, even. But why are you asking me this now?'

He sighed deeply. 'Because that's the reason Fiona and I broke up. She didn't want kids. She wanted her career. She just forgot to mention it until the day that I proposed.'

Mia's hands dropped to her sides and her legs momentarily buckled beneath her. Had a truck just hit her in the chest? That's what it felt like. Garrick had proposed to Fiona? That was news. And not the most pleasant news either.

'Wow! I wasn't expecting that.' She stepped away from him and studied the wood shavings on the floor. Was a piece of her heart amongst them?

'I'm so sorry, Mia. I hadn't meant to blurt it out like that. Please don't back away from me. It's over. Fiona is history. You and I have a future together. I'm sure of it.'

'Because I want kids? What would've happened if I'd said no? Would you have dumped me too?'

He ran a hand through his hair and shook his head. 'It sounds awful when you say it like that, but if I'm honest then the answer has to be yes. This is so important to me, Mia.'

'Obviously. So even though you loved Fiona enough to want to marry her and, I assume, spend the rest of your life with her, because she didn't want kids, you suddenly fell out of love. Is that what you're telling me?'

'No! I still love her. Loved her. I still loved her when I came here. I told you that. That's why I acted like a jerk with Alexia. Jesus! I'm screwing this up, aren't I?'

'Frankly, Garrick. Yes you are.'

He reached out and pulled her to him and although she wanted to push him away, she didn't. Because she also wanted to hold him and feel his arms around her. She wanted things to go back to where they had been before he'd asked that bloody question.

'That's why I had to ask you now, Mia. Before we took things further. I … I'm falling in love with you. Have fallen in love with you, I think. It would break my heart if this ended here and now. But if you'd said you didn't want kids, then it would be better to end it now than later, when it would hurt us both even more.'

'Then why didn't you ask me about kids, before you asked me out?'

Again he shook his head. 'I don't know. I wasn't thinking about kids when I rushed after you that day. All I was thinking about was how jealous I'd felt when Bear was suggesting you go back and have sex with him. And when I held you in my arms, I had to tell you how I felt. But it was you who asked me out, remember?'

'How could I forget? So in that moment, and each day since then, until right now, you had …

forgotten how important kids are to you? You'd forgotten the need to ask me if I wanted them? Is there anything else you've forgotten to ask me? Do you have a checklist or something?'

'Mia! That's not fair. I'm sorry. I didn't mean this to happen. I didn't mean for us to happen. I'm so confused. But I don't have a list. I promise you.' His arms tightened about her. 'I swear to you. That's the only thing.'

'Kids? But what if there's a problem? I mean, what if one of us can't? Medically, I mean. Or should that be physically? Anyway, what I mean is, what if it's not possible for us to have kids naturally? Would you want to do all that IVF stuff? And what if that didn't work? Would you dump me after that?'

'No! Of course not!'

'Really? So even though kids mean the world to you, if it turned out we couldn't have them, you'd be okay with that? You'd still love me?'

'Yes, of course I would. And besides, we could adopt.'

'Adopt? So, it's not a matter of you needing to have your own kids? You'd be happy with any kids, just as long as there were kids?'

He nodded and smiled, as if that made things better. 'Yes, of course.'

'What if I didn't want to adopt?'

'Why wouldn't you? You said you want kids.'

'I do. I'm just asking hypothetically.'

He shifted his feet and frowned. 'Then I think we need to establish that now. I want kids, Mia. I want a family. If that's not what you want, then, as much as I care for you ... as much as I think I love you, maybe we shouldn't take it further. But please, please, say you do. I want you, Mia. I want you in my life. If you want a family too, then why is this such a stumbling block?'

She looked into his eyes and melted. What was she doing? She did want kids. Maybe not as desperately as he clearly did but she wanted them. She wanted a family. She wanted kids and grandchildren and great-grandchildren. She wanted all of that. But most of all, she wanted true love. She wanted 'The One'. And right here, right now, she was pretty sure that Garrick was 'The One'.

'I do want kids, Garrick. I do. And, yes, I'd be happy to adopt. I want a family too. The only difference is, I don't think I could give up someone I loved if they didn't feel the same. It's early days between us and I can't believe we're having this conversation now, but if we do have a future together I'd need to know that you feel the same way about me. That I was really 'The One' for you, no matter what.'

'Of course,' he said, as he leant in to kiss her.

And when he did, he made her feel that perhaps she was worrying for nothing.

Perhaps, she was 'The One' for Garrick Swann.

Chapter Thirteen

Once it creeps in, doubt has a way of taking hold. And Mia was having doubts. Well just one doubt – but it was a big one.

Surely when you found 'The One', you would love them so much you would give up anything for them. Even kids. All that would matter to you would be that you were with 'The One'. Or perhaps that's what fairy tales were for. Perhaps in real life people didn't do that. But she would. She was sure of that. Yet Garrick clearly wouldn't.

All of Saturday afternoon it had niggled away at her. During the fabulous dinner Garrick cooked for them, it had munched on her brain, and later, after several passionate kisses when Garrick had carried her upstairs in a dramatically romantic gesture, it had been there between them, plucking at her heart.

Sex with Garrick was everything she knew it would be; his hands had lived up to their promise and even gone beyond and he did things to her she'd only dreamt of. His stamina would have made an Olympian proud and his attentiveness could not be faulted. She had moaned his name so many times and still he'd given more. He was the perfect lover. Caring, kind, considerate and gentle, yet demanding, possessive and passionate at the same time. His kisses made her want to weep with joy, his caresses, scream with ecstasy and when, moments before they finally fell into an exhausted sleep, he said, 'I love you, Mia.' She should have felt as if she held the universe in her arms.

But she didn't.

When twilight crept between the curtains and the first bird chirped in the tree closest to her bedroom window, she turned to look at Garrick. He was sound asleep, a contented smile lingering on his lips. She turned away, slid out of bed, threw on her dress that Garrick had tossed on the floor last night in his hurry to touch her bare flesh, and silently made her way downstairs. A stream of warm air wafted in with the promise of a hot day when she opened the back door. She grabbed a bottle of water from the fridge and walked into the garden.

Birds twittered in the trees while a gentle breeze teased the leaves and flicked at the tufts of grass scattered here and there as she made her way across the soft golden sands of the dunes, grains seeping between her bare toes. Gulls swooped in the distance over the sea and when she reached the flat carpet of darker sand, it was cool beneath her feet. She walked towards the shore where tiny bubbles of white tickled the sand, and somewhere, not too far away, a dog barked, but she concentrated on the water's edge. Could she inch a little closer? She closed her eyes and breathed in the salty air, plucking up her courage as her name drifted softly towards her on the summer breeze.

'Mia.'

'Jet?' Her eyes shot open. She wasn't imagining it. Jet was really here.

Excitement bubbled up inside her as she turned and watched him walk towards her. His long legs quickly covering the expanse of sand between them, his white cotton shirt billowing softly in the breeze and his dark hair dancing around his face. His jeans were wet up to his knees and he was carrying a pair of walking boots in one hand as a bundle of wet fur, flapping ears and lolling tongue ran along beside him.

He beamed at her. 'It's good to see you. And that you've overcome your fear.'

She returned his smile in kind. 'It's good to see you too. And I haven't completely overcome it, but I'm getting there. I still haven't put my feet in yet. Is that your dog?'

'No, she's my new girlfriend.' He laughed and the mellifluous sound reminded her how much she'd missed hearing it. 'And she's a great improvement on the last. She's loyal, loving, and she doesn't worry about what she eats. Although I'm not sure if that's a plus or negative. Her name's Mattie. You're not allergic to dogs, if I remember rightly. Just basic farm animals.'

'And chickens. Mattie? You've named her after my great-aunt? What made you decide to get a dog?'

'The bastard who dumped her in the middle of a field, tied to a post,' he growled.

'Someone dumped her? And you've adopted her?' She bent down and tickled one very wet ear and Mattie turned in circles trying to lick Mia's hand.

He nodded and his smile returned. 'People are always telling me it's time I let a female move in with me. I hear you got your man.'

'What? Oh, Garrick you mean?'

He cocked one brow. 'Is there someone else?'

'No. Of course there isn't.'

'Alexia took it well, no doubt.'

'Absolutely. She gave him a free pint.'

He grinned. 'So I heard. I also heard you've been looking after Hettie. That was very kind of you.'

'Kindness didn't come into it. She drives me nuts, but I think I'm beginning to like her. I wasn't sure about her at first, and I hated that she helped to spread those things about you. But that was really my fault. She's very lonely, you know.'

'I know. And that's not all I heard.' He looked her in the eye, suddenly serious. 'I heard that someone's been leaving you unwanted gifts. Is that true?'

She nodded. 'Yes. A frog on Monday. Dead flowers on Tuesday. But nothing since. I think someone was hoping it might scare me away.'

'A toy frog and some dead flowers? It'll take more than that to scare you away, if you're anything like Mattie. And I mean your great-aunt. Not my dog. Although you do have similar hair to my dog, especially tied back in that ponytail.'

'Thanks. How kind. You're always so charming. But you said the other day that I was nothing like my great-aunt.'

'That was because I was cross with you. I have a feeling you're very like her. She wouldn't let anyone scare her off. And I don't think you will either, will you Mia?'

'Not a toy and some flowers, no. But if I feared for my safety, or my friends' safety, I might.'

'Are you scared?' He sounded worried.

'No. Not yet. But I have the strangest feeling this isn't over. Don't ask me why, it's just there.' She looked him directly in the eye. 'How long did you bet I would stay? And who did you name as the 'next in line'?'

He frowned. 'Now who's being charming? You're always so ready to think the worst of me, aren't you? I didn't bet. I don't believe in gambling in any shape or form. My dad used to bet on the horses. I saw what it can do to a man. It nearly ruined us. And that was before he ran off with another woman.' He gave a bitter laugh,

286

shook his head and grinned. 'Sorry. I didn't mean to bore you with my family history. Although I expect you've heard it all anyway.'

'You didn't bore me. I'd like to know more about you. You and your family, I mean. I'd like to know more about everyone in the village, not just you. I don't have a particular interest in you.' She was digging herself into a hole.

'I know you don't,' he said, glancing out to sea.

Mia petted Mattie again to fill the awkward silence.

'If I were a betting man,' Jet said, looking at her once more. 'I would've bet you'll stay. And I really hope you do. Mattie wanted you to.'

'That sounds definitive. As if you actually know that's what she wanted as opposed to merely assuming it.'

'I do know that's what she wanted. She told me so herself.'

'She did what?' Mia stood upright and glared at him. 'When? Why haven't you told me this before?'

'I was going to. I intended to tell you everything I knew about her. That's why I came to the cottage and asked you to go for that walk that day. The day you told me to bugger off, only not in those exact words. Then afterwards, well, I just thought I'd let things take their natural course.'

'So when did she tell you? And what exactly did she say? Did she tell you how she knew about me? And why you? Or did she tell other people too? Did she tell you about her will? Did she mention who is next in line?'

'So many questions.' He let out a sigh. 'Okay. She told me the day I ...' He hesitated. 'Well, you already know that Mattie lent me money, because you accused me of having sex with her in exchange, so there's no point in trying to keep it a secret. But it was, until you and Hettie made it public knowledge. Until then, everyone believed I'd borrowed the money from the bank. Anyway, she told me the day I repaid the final instalment of the loan she gave me. That was a year before she died.'

'I really am so sorry for that, as I've told you. But why did it have to be a secret anyway? It was a straightforward loan, wasn't it? So there was no reason to hide it.'

'Except that privacy was extremely important to Mattie. She didn't want people to know her business – or mine.'

'Then why did she come to live in a village like this? Finding out each other's business seems to go with the territory.'

'Really? What have you found out about Mattie so far then?'

'That she ...' Mia sighed. 'That she liked to keep secrets. Okay. I get your point. No one knew anything about her, it seems. And yet she seemed to know a lot about them. Everyone I've asked said that she had a way of getting into their soul. Only they didn't use those words. That she could extract every tiny detail of their lives. And yet at her wake, everyone realised just how little they knew about her. The only thing they did know was that she had a great-niece named Mia. Me. And that she had a nephew she loved dearly but who had died young. My dad. Except it also seems that they did know the details of her will and someone may know who inherits if I leave. So that's one secret she didn't manage to keep. Oh, and Garrick told me about the loan, so that wasn't a secret either. And it was Bear who told him, so you obviously must've told Bear.'

He frowned. 'Bear told Garrick?'

'Yes.'

'When?'

'I don't know. But Garrick told me the day you came to the cottage and I told you to …' She grinned, '… bugger off. He said that I was wrong about you and what Bear had told him. Why? Are you saying you didn't tell Bear?'

'I don't recall doing so. But perhaps I did. There have been a couple of occasions where alcohol may have loosened my tongue, as they say.'

Mia frowned. Jet must've told Bear, otherwise, how would he have known? Jet took a small rubber ball from inside one of his boots and threw it in the sea for Mattie to chase, staring after her as she bounced over the tiny waves rippling the shore.

'So anyway,' Mia prompted. 'You paid Mattie back and she told you that she'd left me the cottage? That's a bit weird.'

He took a second or two to respond and he smiled fondly as if he were reliving the conversation.

'She told me that there was no need for me to make the final payment, but I insisted. That's when she said that she only had one person to leave her money to and a few thousand pounds here or there wouldn't make much difference. She said she'd put a condition in her will because she wanted you to come and live here, not just sell up without spending any time in Little Pondale. I don't know if she told anyone else, but she told me she hadn't and that she'd appreciate me keeping it to myself. Which I have.'

'Unless you also blurted that out when you got drunk and told Bear about the loan. Don't look at me like that. You said it yourself. You can't recall telling him and yet he knows, so perhaps you told him everything. Maybe you should ask him.'

'I intend to.'

'Did she say anything else? The 'next in line' bit, for example?'

'She didn't mention a 'next in line'. She said she was certain you'd stay so the condition wouldn't be an issue.'

'So why put it there in the first place?'

'I just told you why. Because she wanted you to live in Little Pondale.'

'But why? That's what I don't get.'

He shrugged. 'Don't ask me. She didn't say and I didn't question her decision. It was her money, after all. And her will. The only other thing she did say was that she wanted me to keep an eye on you. And I have. Since the day you arrived. Until I realised that Garrick could take better care of you than I ever could because he's living in the cottage. And that you'd prefer that anyway. But I'm still keeping an eye on you, Mia. For Mattie's sake.'

She would have asked him to elaborate but Garrick called her name and marched towards them, wrapping his arm around Mia the second she was within his reach.

'Hello Jet.' Garrick's greeting didn't sound that friendly.

'Hi.' Neither did Jet's response. 'It was great to see you again, Mia. But I'd better get Mattie home and dry her off. I'll see you both soon, I hope.' Without another word, Jet walked off in the opposite direction, with Mattie leaping and bounding at his heels.

'You were a bit off with Jet,' Mia said, looking up at Garrick.

'Was I? I woke up and found you gone and I spotted the two of you from the window. I saw you deep in conversation and perhaps I was a little jealous.' He spun her round to face him and pulled her into his arms. 'Last night was incredible, Mia. I was hoping for a repeat performance. Let's go

291

back to bed. It can't be more than six a.m. And it's Sunday. I can't think of a better way to spend a Sunday, can you?'

He kissed her, gently at first, before deepening the kiss until she couldn't think of anything better than spending the day in bed in Garrick's arms.

They ran back to the cottage, laughing and excited, hand in hand, but as they burst into the kitchen, they came face to face with Freda, Alexia, Toby and Alec and everyone fell silent as if someone had just died.

'Bloody Nora!' Mia said. Then realised she'd said that out loud.

Ella, who was making coffee, yawned and turned to Mia giving her an apologetic smile.

'Look who the early bird brought in.'

'We're sorry to call so early,' Freda said, sitting upright like some matriarch while her family sat around her. 'But we feel we need to clear the air and we're all early risers so what better time than now?'

Mia could think of several much better times but that, she thankfully managed to keep to herself. Garrick wrapped his arm protectively around Mia's waist and Mia saw the hostile glare Alexia gave her, though it was soon replaced by a simpering smile.

'Clear the air about what, exactly?' Garrick asked, his voice cool but polite.

'Alexia's behaviour, for one,' Freda said. 'I don't suppose you expect her to apologise but that was no way for a daughter of mine to behave, so she will.'

'I'm sorry, Garrick,' Alexia said, her smile little more than a twisted line on her lips.

'There's no need,' Garrick said. 'I'm sure I deserved it.'

'That's as may be,' said Alec, glaring at him. 'But at least you were honest and hadn't taken advantage, so we'll leave it be and say no more about it. You're welcome back to our pub at any time.'

'Which brings us on to the bit we really came here about,' Toby said. His smile was friendly and looked genuine. 'The bets. We didn't mean any harm by them and they were made before we met you. We were aware that Mattie thought the world of you but all we really knew was that you lived in London, worked at a big accountancy firm and that your dad was dead. We also knew you never came to visit Mattie so we thought that made you an unpleasant sort of person. No wait.' He held his hand up as Mia tried to interrupt him. 'Please let me get this out, Mia. Then you can have your say.'

Mia nodded. 'Okay.'

'Thanks. We believed Mattie visited you all the time instead. We didn't know you'd never met her, until you came here and told us. We thought you were possibly one of those yuppy types from London who would swan about in high heels and designer clothes, crying if you so much as chipped a false nail and who wouldn't be seen dead in the country unless it was to stay at a stately home and go shooting pheasants or something. If we'd known you were an ordinary, lovely, friendly girl, just like one of us, we wouldn't have done it. We're cancelling the bets today and repaying everyone their money. You're welcome to come and see it for yourselves and we're inviting you to lunch, on us. We want you to feel welcome in Little Pondale, Mia. We all want you to stay. Okay. Now you can have your say.'

'Thanks, Toby. I appreciate that more than you can imagine. And I can understand why you felt the way you did. I do feel welcome here. We all do. Or did. But someone doesn't want us to stay, do they? The frog and flowers didn't get there by themselves.'

The Bywater family looked at one another, shaking their heads and shrugging.

'We don't know who would do something like that,' Freda said. 'But we'll keep our eyes open and if we ever find out, believe me, that person will wish they had never set foot in this village.'

Ella passed around mugs of coffee and tea and handed mugs to Mia and Garrick.

'We're all okay then, are we?' Ella said. 'Because I have to say that not feeling welcome in the only pub in the village has been a bit of a pain in the bum.'

'We're all okay, if Mia says we are,' Freda said, raising her mug as if making a toast.

'Aye,' Alec nodded. 'I'll go along with that.'

Alexia sighed before smiling wryly. 'I can forgive and forget. It was obvious Garrick wanted to be with you all along. I'm sorry about the bets thing, Mia, and I'm sorry I threw a glass of beer at you, Garrick.'

'Mia?' Toby queried. 'Garrick?'

'We're all okay,' Mia said, smiling.

Garrick nodded. 'Whatever Mia says is fine with me. We're all okay. And I'm sorry too, Alexia. I'm sure there's a man out there just waiting to meet you. You're gorgeous and–'

'G-ar-rick,' Ella's voice held a note of warning. 'Shut up and drink your coffee or I'll throw something at your head.'

Everyone burst out laughing, including Alexia.

Chapter Fourteen

Mia was relieved that things had settled down and that they could return to The Frog and Lily and feel welcome once again.

Garrick said he was pleased too, but he just wished they had waited until Monday to come round, because they had scuppered his plans to spend the day in bed with Mia. When she suggested a very early night instead, his good mood was restored.

Mia was glad that she and Ella could go to choir practice on Tuesday but was disappointed that Jet wasn't there. Bear still seemed a little cool towards her and when she walked over to him to ask if Jet had had a word with him, he was almost defensive.

He glared at her. 'About what?'

'About whether … never mind. It's not my place to bring it up. I'm sure he'll talk to you himself.' She turned away to return to Ella and Justin but he reached out and touched her arm.

'Are you going to the top of Frog Hill to watch the sunrise on Thursday?' His tone had become warm and friendly, the way it used to be when they first met.

'Why Thursday?'

'It's the Summer Solstice. And the official start of summer. Most people go to the top of Frog Hill because you get a great view as the sun rises over the sea, don't you, Tom?'

The vicar was handing out orange juice and stopped and smiled. 'Don't I what? I missed the first bit. Lovely to see you again Mia by the way. We missed you both last week.' He nodded towards Ella who was standing arm in arm with Justin a few feet away.

'Get a great view of the sunrise from the top of Frog Hill? I was telling Mia about the Summer Solstice.'

'Ah yes. You get a superb view from there. I often go to watch an early sunrise, but never on a Solstice.' He grinned. 'I can't be seen to be supporting a pagan ceremony, after all. Some of the locals here would stone me. If you're interested, Mia, people congregate at twilight, so it means being up and out around three-thirty. It's quite a climb because you can only drive about halfway but most people walk. The sunrise is around a quarter to five so that'll give you time to get there and settled.'

'A lot of us go,' Bear said. 'Apart from Jet.'

'Jet isn't interested in watching a sunrise?' Mia queried.

'Oh, he's interested but he likes to do his own thing, doesn't he, Tom?'

Tom nodded. 'Yes. I believe he likes to watch it at ground level. He goes to Rainbow's End, or he has done every year as far as I'm aware. If you're not keen on the hike up the hill, you could always go there and watch it. I'm sure Jet wouldn't mind you sharing the experience with him. Excuse me, you two. I can see Alexia wants a refill.' He jiggled the jug of orange juice in his hand and hurried towards Alexia.

'What's Rainbow's End?' Mia asked Bear.

'It's a rocky outcrop, I suppose you'd call it. From your cottage, you simply walk along the sand and around the other side of where Frog Hill meets the beach. Just a bit further on is Rainbow's End. It's called that because the rocks are all different colours and tones, from pale yellow to a dark, almost black. It's the sediments and minerals in the rock or something. Geology was never my strong subject. It's worth a look just to see the colours change when the sun hits it. That's why Jet always goes there. He's very in tune with the earth. I suppose that's why he's a farmer. Oh. I think we're about to start the second half. Might see you at the Solstice, then?'

'Yes. Maybe.'

But Mia had no intention of climbing Frog Hill to watch the Summer Solstice, or at least the sunrise part of it. If she was going anywhere, it would be to Rainbow's End, and she spent the whole of Wednesday trying on dresses to find one she wanted to wear. It was just as well that Ella and Garrick had gone to London for the day. Their Uncle Bert was having an operation and although it was nothing serious and certainly not life-threatening, the family were all gathering to visit him.

'Why don't you come with us?' Garrick asked in bed that morning.

He had as good as moved in to Mia's room since Saturday night. Not that she was complaining. Each night she spent with him was better than the last and she'd had more sex over the last few days than she'd had in her entire previous relationship with 'the rat'.

'No,' she said. 'Mum will be arriving on Thursday evening. She's driving from Southampton and I want to make sure everything's ready for her. You don't mind if I move your things from the other back bedroom to the spare room at the front, do you? I'd like Mum to see the gorgeous view each day, and you're spending every night in my room anyway.'

'Of course I don't mind. I'll move my stuff before we leave today. Are you sure you won't come with us?'

Mia nodded. 'If I spend today in London, I'll be racing around all day on Thursday and I don't want that. Besides, a day apart will do us good. We'll be even more excited to see one another when you get back.

'I don't think it's possible for me to get more excited than I am right now,' he'd replied, that devilish grin spreading across his mouth as his hands slid over her naked hips and he pulled her close.

'I see what you mean,' she said, giving him her sexiest smile. 'I'm feeling pretty excited myself.'

That meant Garrick left two hours later than he'd planned but the delay was not entirely down to his and Mia's sex-drive. Ella had spent Tuesday night at Justin's and it seemed the two of them had been similarly excited on Wednesday morning. Or possibly more so, because when Ella finally returned to Sunbeam Cottage she told Mia that Tuesday night had been the first time she and Justin had made love, and that it had been the best night of her entire life. All she told Garrick as they said goodbye to Mia and headed out the door, was that she'd need to sleep all the way to London and probably all the way back. Mia understood exactly how she felt, so in between trying on dresses, she'd taken an afternoon nap.

It was the landline phone that woke her up and when she looked at the bedside clock before answering it, she was horrified to see that it was eight-thirty in the evening.

'Hello, Mia?' It was Garrick's voice. But why was he calling on the landline and why did he sound so anxious?

'Garrick? Is everything okay?'

'No. Mum's had an accident. It's not serious so don't panic but we're stuck in A&E and have been for a couple of hours. I don't know what time we'll get back tonight but it's going to be way past midnight by the looks of things. We need to get Mum seen and then depending on what they say, either settled here in hospital or settled back at home.'

'Oh my God, Garrick! Don't even think about coming back tonight. I don't want you racing around these country lanes in the dark, especially as there's no need. You and Ella stay at your parents' house. I'll be fine. Call me as soon as you have any news about your mum. What happened?'

'She tripped and fell. We think she's broken her ankle but she says the whole of her left leg hurts so it may be her leg that's broken. I suggested Ella stay and I come back but then we realised that if Mum needs to be carried and lifted, Ella can't do it and Dad's back's playing up again, so neither can he. I'm worried about you though. I said you should've come with us.'

'And spent the evening in A&E? No thanks. I'll be fine. Give Ella and your mum and dad my love. I'll see you tomorrow. Now try to stop worrying. I'm sure your mum'll be fine. And I'll be fine. I may even go and spend the night at Hettie's. I'm sure she won't mind.'

'That's a brilliant idea. Do that. That'll stop me worrying.'

'Okay. I will. Bye, Garrick.'

'I love you, Mia,' he said.

'I love you too,' she replied, before hanging up.

Then she cursed herself under her breath.

She did love him. That was true.

So why had she spent the day trying on dresses?

And why had she just lied to him?

There was no way she was going to spend the night at Hettie's.

And why was she counting the hours until sunrise?

Because it sure as hell had nothing to do with the Summer bloody Solstice.

Chapter Fifteen

Mia's head shot from the pillow and she sat bolt upright when her alarm went off at three a.m. Her eyes were burning, her throat was sore and her body must have been used by rugby-playing ghosts all night because it ached and creaked as she clambered out of bed.

She padded to the shower then dried her hair as best she could. She dabbed her mascara brush over her lashes but couldn't really focus so gave it up as a bad job and swiped her lipstick across her mouth, climbed into the dress she had chosen, slipped a cardigan over her shoulders and slid her feet into her sandals. She clumped downstairs, still half-asleep and, after two mugs of coffee and a few digestive biscuits, headed out into the garden, illuminating the path with the torch on her mobile until she made it to the open sands of the beach.

The stillness was amazing as was the near-silence that surrounded her. All she could hear was the gentle lapping of the waves somewhere in the distance. She hadn't checked the tides, but the sea looked a long way off and she was sure it wouldn't be a problem. Besides, Jet would be there if she succumbed to her fear, and there was no good reason why she should.

She breathed in the salty air and watched as the sky grew lighter by the minute. Twilight would give way to the sunrise before too long; she just hoped she wasn't too late to see it hit the rocks of Rainbow's End. She increased her pace to make sure she didn't but when she turned the corner of the bottom of Frog Hill where the hill met the beach and saw the long strip of rocky land that was obviously Rainbow's End, there was no sign of Jet.

She hurried onwards and clambered up onto the rocks at the base of Rainbow's End, then walked along the crest of the rocky outcrop. It protruded quite a way from the bottom of Frog Hill and she could see that to get the best view of the soon-to-be sunrise, she needed to move further along. She hadn't gone very far when she spotted what looked like a chair, carved out of the rocks. It was misshapen and obviously made by the elements rather than man but when she sat on it, it felt like a throne of sorts and she smiled, remembering Jet's remark about King Canute and holding back the tide.

She wasn't sure how long she sat there but the sun was rising. She could see it peeking slowly over the horizon and she kept looking back towards Frog Hill but there was still no sign of Jet. The sun crept higher and all colours of the rainbow danced around her legs as the rays hit the rocks of

Rainbow's End. It was beautiful beyond description and she had never seen anything like it. No wonder Jet loved it here. Except he wasn't here. Where was he? She yawned and stretched and watched the sun. She glanced towards the top of Frog Hill and thought she could make out some people but from this distance she couldn't tell who they were.

She yawned again and as the rays of the sun reached out to her and warmed her skin she could tell it was going to be a sweltering day. Her lids were heavy and so was her body. She closed her eyes for a second, basking in the warmth, and the waves in the distance were like one of those CDs people buy to soothe themselves to sleep or into meditation. She leant further back against the rock and revelled in the peace and tranquillity. Jet might not have turned up which was very disappointing, but this was bliss. Just the warm summer breeze, the rays of the sun bathing her skin, the sound of the waves.

The warmth, the sun, the waves.

The warmth, the sun, the waves.

The warmth …

She jolted awake and opened her eyes, and was overcome with terror.

The sun was full in the sky, the breeze had dropped away and the tide had come in.

There was water in front of her.

Water to her right.

Water to her left.

Water lapping at the rocky outcrop and one little wave licked her toe.

She pulled her feet back and tried to force herself to stand as another wave greedily leapt up and licked her foot.

The tide was coming in fast.

Very fast.

She had to move.

She frantically looked about her and her heart skipped a beat.

The sea wasn't just on three sides, it was all around her.

The rocky outcrop of Rainbow's End had become an island, separated from the bottom of Frog Hill by the sea.

She pulled her mobile from her bag only to realise she couldn't get a signal.

She was alone. She couldn't phone for help and as she stared wildly around her, there wasn't another person in sight. They were probably all still in bed, or at the top of Frog Hill, safely away from the encroaching sea.

A wave sucked at her foot and she screamed and ran, slipping and sliding on the uneven rocks as she made her unsteady way towards the shore. To her terrified eyes, it wasn't getting any closer.

'Help me!' she screamed at the top of her lungs. 'Please! Please! Someone help me!'

'Mia!' The sound of her name was a beacon of hope.

'Jet!' She screamed.

But it wasn't Jet who waded through the knee-deep water towards her, a look of reassurance on his handsome face. It was Tom Tyburn, without his vicar's garb, and wearing nothing but a pair of swim shorts. If she hadn't been so terrified she would have been even more astonished than she was, because it struck her even then that he was tanned. His agile body was perfect in every way and when he reached out for her and lifted her into his arms, he held her safe and secure above the hungry waves.

'I've got you, Mia. You're safe. There's nothing to fear now. I'm here. I won't let the water touch you. Close your eyes and rest your head against me.'

Her heart pounded in her chest but she did as she was told and didn't open her eyes again until he finally deposited her gently on the ground several feet away from the shore on the rocks at the foot of Frog Hill.

'What happened?' he asked. 'Why were you on Rainbow's End on your own?'

'I … I wanted to see the sunrise,' she eventually managed, shivering and shaking as if her body was having its own seismic event.

'But why did you come here alone when you're still so terrified of water?'

'I … I didn't know the tide came in so far. I must've nodded off and didn't see it. I thought Jet would be here.'

'You thought Jet would be here?' he repeated as if he didn't understand.

She managed to meet his eyes, and nodded.

He shook his head and sighed.

'I saw Jet this morning. He was going up Frog Hill. He told me he fancied a change this year.'

Mia almost burst into tears but she bit her lip and forced herself to fight it. She stared at Rainbow's End and remembered that the water had only come up to Tom's knees.

'How far does the tide come in?' she asked.

'Not that much further than it is now. The highest it would get is probably up to your waist and that would be on a very high tide, which today isn't.'

So there was no likelihood of any real harm coming to her. Other than that created by her own fear. And yet she couldn't shake the feeling that she had somehow been manipulated into coming here.

But the only people who had mentioned Rainbow's End to her were the man who had just saved her, and Bear. And she was only here because she wanted to see Jet. Had Jet heard she had been discussing this place with Tom and Bear? Had he known that she would come here to see him? Had he changed the habit of a lifetime and gone to the top of Frog Hill precisely so that she would be alone on Rainbow's End during an incoming tide?

Or was she being completely ridiculous because she was so tired and afraid? Jet hadn't asked her to come here. No one had. She was here because she wanted to be. That was no one's fault but her own.

'You must think I'm really stupid to be so afraid of water just a few inches deep. But I can't help it. And I'm finally trying hard to overcome my fear.'

Tom shook his head. 'I think no such thing. I know you nearly drowned when you were very young. That must have been terrifying. Some fears, however irrational they may seem to others, are very real indeed. I turn to jelly and break out in a cold sweat at the mere sight of a spider.'

Mia looked at him and smiled. 'No you don't. You're just saying that to make me feel better, aren't you?'

He shrugged his shoulders. 'You'll have to wait until we see a spider. I think you're very brave to try to overcome your fear. I hope today hasn't set you back. Let's just sit here and admire the view until you've regained your equilibrium.'

Mia's gaze wandered over Tom's agile body. It was easy to admire, although that wasn't the view he meant and she grinned as she dragged her eyes from his firm thighs, towards the horizon. Looking at the sea once more sent a shiver down her spine but after taking several more deep breaths, all she felt, was tired.

'Thank you for saving me, Tom.'

'Anytime. I'm just glad I decided to go for an early morning swim today. It was only because I couldn't sleep last night. Otherwise I'd still be in my bed, for at least another hour.'

'Which is exactly where I'm going to be,' she said. 'If you'll help me to my feet. I'm still a little shaky. Oh God! I didn't mean I'd be in your bed, Tom! I meant I'll be in mine. I'm so sorry.'

He laughed. 'I thought my luck had changed. Don't worry, Mia. I knew exactly what you meant. But … if you ever do decide you'd like to be, I'd welcome you with open arms. Now let me take you home. To yours of course. Sadly, not to mine.'

Chapter Sixteen

Mia did not tell Garrick or Ella about what happened at the beach when they arrived back at the cottage late that afternoon. Their mum had suffered a broken ankle and a nasty bruise on her leg but other than that she was fine, and had insisted they could leave her in their father's loving care but it was obvious Garrick was worried and Mia didn't want to add to that.

'I can't believe how much I missed you,' Garrick said, sweeping her into his arms and kissing her, the moment he arrived. 'Did anything exciting happen while I was away?'

'I've been busy preparing for Mum's arrival,' Mia lied, avoiding his intense gaze. With her mum arriving any minute, she didn't have time to explain and she had no desire to relive the whole experience. Besides, she didn't want to worry him. She was also still trying to get her head around that odd remark Tom had made, about her being welcome in his bed. That had been a total surprise, but he was probably only joking.

'I'll cook something for supper,' Garrick said, after kissing her again. 'I expect Lori will be tired and she'll want an early night. I wouldn't mind one of those myself.' He winked. 'Is it still okay for me to sleep with you while your mum's here?'

Mia laughed at that. 'First, there is no way Mum will want an early night, and second, yes of course it is, but maybe not tonight. I think she'll want to spend most of the night catching up and I know I'd like to spend some time alone with her. You don't mind, do you?'

'No,' he said, but his expression said otherwise.

Mia was right. When Lori arrived at Sunbeam Cottage, a little after seven, she was full of life.

'It's so wonderful to see you, darling.' Lori hugged Mia so tightly, Mia could hardly breathe, as Garrick brought Lori's bags inside. 'I've missed you more than ever this time. But isn't this place divine? It's like something from the pages of one of those posh, country magazines. I can't wait to have a nose around. And Ella, sweetheart. How are you? You're all looking so well. It must be the country air. Especially you, Garrick. But I haven't seen you for such a long time. When my darling daughter told me you two were an item, I couldn't believe it. I'm so happy I could cry. But listen to me prattling on. I'm just so excited to be here. And with my daughter so happy.' She squeezed Mia again and planted several kisses all over Mia's face.

Mia laughed and returned her mum's kisses. 'Oh, Mum. You have no idea how pleased I am to have you here.'

'Would you like to have a shower or a nap before supper?' Garrick asked. 'I'll take your bags upstairs.'

'Nap? Good heavens, no. And I had a shower on the ship before we disembarked. I can't wait to go to The Frog and Lily. I've heard so much about it and I'm dying to meet all the different people Mia's told me about. Besides, I could murder a G&T.'

Ella laughed. 'The life and soul of the party, as usual, Lori.'

'Just a little slower these days,' Lori said, linking arms with Mia. 'But first, I need a quick tour of the cottage.'

Mia proudly showed her mum around and Lori ooh-ed and ahh-ed in every room. Apart from the dining room.

'Did Matilda use a rowing machine? And in the dining room, of all places.'

Mia laughed. 'No, Mum. That's mine. We weren't sure where to put it and we never eat in here. We use the table in the kitchen. The bedrooms, as you'll see, are rather special and now with all of us here, we don't have a room we can use for junk. We thought of putting it in the attic but that room's special too.'

'Do you use it? The rowing machine, I mean?'

Ella laughed at that. 'She treats it like a work of art. A sculpture or something.'

'Then it can go in the room I'm having,' Lori said. 'I could do with losing a few pounds.'

Mia tutted. 'That's right, Mum. Make me feel guilty.' She laughed.

After Lori had seen all the rooms, including the attic, she declared: 'Your great-aunt Matilda may have been trouble as far as her family were concerned, but from where I'm standing, the woman is nothing short of an angel. To leave you all this.' She shook her head and smiled, brushing away a tear of obvious happiness. 'Well. What can I say? Have you discovered anything about her yet?'

'Sadly, no we haven't.' Mia shook her head, as they headed back downstairs. 'And the weird thing is, there are no photos of her and no one knows anything very much about her. She's a total enigma, Mum. But I'm not giving up. I'm determined to find out who she was. And where she got her money from. Because it obviously wasn't her family.'

'I think it's so exciting,' Lori said. 'And the locals have made you all so welcome. I can't wait to meet them all. Shall we go?'

'What about supper?' Garrick looked disappointed and possibly a little surprised.

'Will it keep?' Lori asked, to which Garrick nodded. 'Then we'll have it when we come home. That's the one thing I did notice on my way here.

A definite shortage of curry houses, and I do like a good curry after a few drinks in the pub.'

'Which is why Garrick has cooked a curry,' Mia said, smiling tenderly at Garrick.

'Have you really, Garrick?' Lori beamed at him and then at Mia. 'He's a keeper, darling.'

'I know he is,' Mia replied, and they headed out to The Frog and Lily.

'All these cottages are so quaint,' Lori said, walking arm in arm with Mia. 'Do you know all your neighbours?'

'Most of them. There're a couple I still don't think we've met and one or two we've only seen to nod to.'

'Is that the vicar?' Lori pointed at Tom who was strolling down the lane towards them.

'Yes it is,' Mia said, before calling out as loud as she could, 'Hello, Tom. It's lovely to see you. I haven't seen you since choir practice.' She pulled a face and prayed that he would understand. 'This is my mum, Lori. She's come to stay for a while.'

'Hello, Mia and hello, Lori. I'm very pleased to meet you. You have a wonderful daughter. Hi Ella. Hi Garrick.'

'I know,' Lori said. 'And I've heard nothing but good things about you. I'd love to join your choir practice if I may?'

'Of course. The more the merrier.'

Mia breathed a sigh of relief. Tom obviously understood. 'We're going to the pub. Why don't you join us?'

'Thanks for the offer, but I'm going to see my gran. She's still a bit under the weather and I promised I'd read to her. Perhaps I'll see you there tomorrow night.'

'I'll be in there every night,' Lori replied, laughing. 'Oh good heavens. That made me sound like some sort of lush. I'm not, Reverend, believe me.'

'I do,' he smiled. 'Please call me Tom. We're all friends in Little Pondale. Enjoy your night.'

'He seems lovely,' Lori said. 'And very handsome in his way. And who's this gorgeous hunk? Two fabulous men walking down one little lane. I think I'm going to like Little Pondale.'

'That's Justin.' Ella ran to him and he swept her up in his arms as if he hadn't seen her for a year instead of only one night. Then he kissed her so passionately it made the blood rush to Mia's own cheeks.

'Wowee!' Lori gave a long, low whistle. 'I'm definitely going to like this village.'

'If you like that,' Garrick said, 'you'll love Saturday night. Not only is Justin and his dance troupe performing in the church hall, but it's Midsummer's Eve and all the locals go skinny dipping in the pond at Frog's Hollow.'

Mia cringed. 'I wasn't going to tell Mum about that until after it had taken place.'

'Why ever not, darling?' Lori asked, a crooked smile on her lips and a glint in her eye. 'I like the sound of both of those, especially the skinny dipping,'

'That's why I wasn't going to tell you. There's no way I want my mum parading around naked in front of half the village!'

'Why not?'

'Because I won't be going and I don't want the likes of Jet Cross, Rupert Day, Toby Bywater and all the rest of them, thinking that it's because my mum's got a better body than me.'

'No one would think that, darling. Is it that, or are you embarrassed at the thought of me parading around with people half my age? I hope it's not that, because I'm not embarrassed or ashamed of my body and neither should you be.' Lori gave Mia a quelling look and her tone became serious. 'It's my body and there's not another like it. Just as there isn't another like yours.'

'Luckily for everyone else.'

'I'm serious. Your dad and I didn't bring you up to feel inferior to anyone. You're special, darling. We all are. We're all one-offs. Be proud, be loud, be awesome, and never be embarrassed or ashamed, as we say in my book club. It doesn't matter if a person is slim, or not so slim, tall, or not so tall, has webbed feet or six fingers on each hand, we're all unique and we should wear our uniqueness with pride. I'm up for this. And you, Ella? If that gorgeous young man of yours will ever put you down.'

'We're going,' Ella grinned. 'Oh, and Justin, say hello to Lori.'

'Hi, Lori,' Justin grinned, before kissing Ella again as he carried her up the lane, with her legs wrapped around him.

Dear God. This was all Mia needed. To have her sixty-year-old mum running around naked with the younger half of the residents of Little Pondale.

Chapter Seventeen

It was Midsummer's Eve and Lori was still determined to join in with the naked bathing in the pond at Frog's Hollow, especially since she had met the rest of the young men in the village, in the pub on Thursday night. To Mia's discomfort, Lori seemed particularly eager to see what Jet would look like in the buff, and Lori had spent most of that night in Mia's room discussing it. Was it any wonder that when Mia did eventually fall asleep, with her mum curled up beside her, she dreamt of Jet, in all his naked glory. Not that she knew what he would look like naked, but she had a pretty good imagination.

They had been given all the details of the event in the pub on Thursday night and that had given Mia a tiny beacon of hope. Traditionally, the women were allowed to go in first, which meant that the water would hide everything. Then they were joined by the men. No one was allowed to touch but they were allowed to look. But when Mia, Ella and Lori went to Frog's Hollow to do a little recognisance on Friday afternoon, Mia's beacon was snuffed out. In spite of its name, Frog's Hollow was a place of beauty and the water in the pond was clear and crisp and clean. It was fresh water from a natural spring that had been widened many centuries before, not the dug-out muddy pond she and Ella had imagined.

'That won't hide a thing,' Ella said, grinning.

'No it won't.' Lori rubbed her manicured hands together and smiled eagerly.

'Kill me now,' Mia said. 'I'm so glad I won't have to do this.'

Why on earth Ella and Lori and even Garrick wanted to was a mystery to Mia and during the interval in Justin's show on Saturday, Mia grew increasingly concerned. Especially since she had realised that it wasn't merely the villagers her mum would get to see starkers that night, but also Garrick Swann. The thought of her boyfriend being naked in front of her mum, was more than a little disturbing.

'Do you really want to do this tonight?' she asked Ella and her mum.

'After watching these three young men,' Lori said, 'I'm keener than ever.'

'Me too,' Ella added. 'Justin's bringing along the other two in the troupe.'

'The more the merrier,' Lori trilled. 'Will Tom, the vicar be there?'

'It's a pagan thing,' Ella said. 'Or a witchcraft thing, or something along those lines. So I doubt it. It's definitely not a Christian thing. And the vicar running around in the buff probably wouldn't go down too well with some of the old fogies in the village.'

Lori grinned and licked her lips. 'That's a pity. I'd like to see what he keeps hidden under that cassock.'

'You and me both,' Ella said. 'I've seen him in a suit, and he looked pretty decent in that. But I've never seen him in casual clothes.'

Mia still hadn't told them that she had seen him in only swim shorts. Or about what happened on the beach.

'I need some air,' she said. 'I'm getting a bit of a headache.'

'Don't you dare run off,' Ella said. 'You might not be taking part in the bathing but you're coming with us, aren't you?

'God no! And I don't think it would be right if I did. I'd be the only one with clothes on.'

'You could take them off. Just not go in the water.'

'Yeah right! And be even more on display than the rest of you. No thank you very much.'

When she pushed open the door of the church hall and stepped outside, she was very tempted to run, especially when she heard a dog bark and saw Mattie rush towards her.

'Hello Mia,' Jet's voice wasn't quite as friendly as the last time. 'I was hoping I'd bump into you.'

'Hello, Jet. I was hoping I had become invisible.'

He frowned. 'Is that another of your ways of telling me to bugger off?'

'What? No. I was being facetious. Ella and Mum are intent on going to this Midsummer's Eve thing tonight and I really, really, really, don't want my mum to go.'

He relaxed. 'Why not?'

'Because she's my mum. And she's sixty. And she'll be surrounded by people half her age. But that's why she wants to go.'

He grinned at her. 'Ah yes. I noticed on Thursday night in the pub that Lori had a very keen interest in Pagan festivities.'

'A keen interest in seeing lots of naked young men. She's particularly keen on seeing you.'

Oh my God! Why had she said that?

He raised his brows. 'Is she? I can't think why. I'm sure she'll be disappointed.'

'You're going then?'

'I go every year.'

'Why? I really don't see the point. No pun intended.'

He sniggered. 'The water's very cold.'

Mia frowned at him. 'You think this whole thing is just a riot, don't you? I'll say one thing for you. You've definitely got a sense of humour. However weird it may be.'

'Thanks. I'll take that as a compliment. The first you've ever paid me.' He grinned. 'I think it's a bit of harmless fun that's been going on round here for centuries. No one is forced to participate. No one breaks the rules. No one comes to any harm. It's no different than going to a nudist beach.'

'I wouldn't want to go to one of those either.'

'You won't be taking part, obviously. Is that just because you're afraid of water? Or is it also because you're afraid of being naked? Are you a bit of a prude, Mia? They say the ones who talk about sex all the time are the ones who never do it.'

'What? I'm not a prude! It's the water. Being naked is fine. I'm happy being naked. I do it all the time. I dance naked. I sleep naked. I would swim naked if I weren't afraid of water. But I don't like the thought of being naked in front of so many people, I'll admit. That doesn't make me a prude. And as for sex. You're the one who talks about it all the time, not me. I'm having plenty of sex, for your information. Every chance I get, in fact.'

'That's painted a very detailed image for me. Thanks for that. If you beat your fear of water, you can always participate next year. I'd quite like to see that. Why didn't you go to watch the sunrise on Thursday?' His face became serious as he changed the subject.

'I did.'

He frowned. 'I didn't see you. And I looked for you, believe me.'

'That's because you went to Frog Hill whereas I went to Rainbow's End.'

'Rainbow's End? You went to Rainbow's End. Alone?'

She'd done it again. She'd said something in front of him that she had not meant to.

'Yes.'

'Why?' A deep line furrowed his brow. 'Why would you go to Rainbow's End?'

'I told you. To see the sunrise.'

'It's better from the top of Frog Hill, so everyone says.'

'Apart from you. You think it's …'

And again! What was wrong with her?

'I think it's better from Rainbow's End, is that what you were about to say? So you went there because you thought that's where I would be? Or you went there to see if I was right?'

'To see if you were right. Not to see you. Why would I want to see you?'

'I don't know, Mia. Why would you? Perhaps to ask me more questions? Or perhaps there's another reason.'

Of course there isn't. I've got a boyfriend and we're in love.'

'So I've heard. What time were you there?'

'Why?'

'Because when the tide comes in, Rainbow's End is surrounded by water. Not deep water, but water all around. And the tide would've been coming in before sunrise.'

Mia coughed and stepped from one foot to the other. 'I didn't notice. I didn't stay long.'

'You're lying to me.'

'How can you …? No, I'm not!'

'Yes you are. What happened, Mia? Did you get caught by the tide? Are you okay?'

'Of course I'm okay. I'm standing here, aren't I?'

'Looking like you're having palpitations.' He reached out and took her fingers in his. 'Tell me what happened.'

'Nothing happened.'

'Please don't lie to me, Mia.'

'Okay! I was tired and I nodded off and the tide came in and I panicked. But luckily for me, Tom came along and he rushed out and saved me and took me to the shore. Happy now?'

He stiffened and clenched his jaw. 'No, Mia. I'm not. I'm happy you're safe. But I'm not happy you put yourself in that situation. Promise me you'll never do anything like that again. Not without me there. Not without someone there.'

'You said yourself the water isn't deep. I was panicking, that's all.'

'And it's the panic that could've caused you harm. Please, Mia. Promise me.'

'Okay, okay. I promise. But you've got to promise not to tell Mum. Or Ella. Or Garrick.'

He looked perplexed. 'Why not?'

'Because I don't want them to worry. You almost went ballistic when I told you, so imagine how people who love me would feel.'

'I know how they would feel. I won't say a word. I promise. But if you and Garrick are so in love, I think he'd want to know. Keeping secrets like that is not a good thing to do when you're in a relationship.'

'Really? How would you know? From what I've heard you've never stayed with a woman long enough to have a real relationship.' She gasped. 'Sorry! I don't know why I said that.'

'Don't you?' He held her gaze for a second before he turned away. 'I'd better get Mattie home. I've got a date with a pond.'

'I'm sorry, Jet,' Mia said, hoping he would stay.

'So am I, Mia,' he replied, but he carried on walking and if anything, he increased his pace.

Chapter Eighteen

Mia went to bed long before her mum and Garrick came home, but she heard them giggling and chatting as they stumbled up the stairs. As soon as Garrick got into bed, he reached for Mia and tried to kiss her but for some reason she pretended to be asleep. She got up before him in the morning. She wasn't quite sure why, but the whole thing felt weird. Probably because she hadn't been a part of it.

'You've got to come next year,' Ella said when she came back from Justin's later that morning. 'It was really fun. No one leered at anyone or anything, but we did all take a sneaky peek. And Bloody Nora! I've revised my opinion of one or two of the men in the village.' She laughed.

'Was Jet there?' Mia had not meant to ask and he had told her himself he was going. But even so, she had to check.

'Oh, he was there all right. And let me tell you, Mia. That man can stand out in a crowd. And

I met Franklin Grant for the first time. He says he's met you.'

Mia rubbed her forehead and nodded. 'I met him at Little Pond Farm.'

'Lori was pretty taken with him. And I think it was reciprocated.'

'What? He's about our age!'

'He's thirty-eight. But he likes mature women.'

Mia sighed. 'I know Mum wants to have a good time, and I know she's never really got over Dad's death, but I'm beginning to worry about her.'

'Why? I think she's got the right attitude. She believes in living life to the full. It wouldn't do us any harm to follow in her footsteps.'

'Perhaps you're right. I just don't want her to do anything she may regret.'

'Why not? You and I do it all the time. It's part of living life. One thing you can be sure of with Lori, is that she can take care of herself. Is she up yet?'

'No. She likes a lie-in on a Sunday. And after last night, I doubt we'll see her much before noon. Garrick's not up yet either.'

Ella grabbed a chocolate digestive from an open packet. 'What did he say about last night?'

'Nothing yet. I was asleep by the time he got home and he was asleep when I got up. Why?'

Ella shrugged. 'No reason.'

'Was Alexia there?'

Ella nodded. 'But nothing happened with them, so don't start thinking it did. I just wondered if he said anything about Jet.'

'Why would he say anything about Jet?'

'Because there was a definite atmosphere between Jet and Bear and Garrick. I don't know why or what it was about, but there was something. Even Justin noticed it. He said that Jet had been acting weird lately and he thinks it may have something to do with you. He also said that Bear told him it may be connected to your inheritance.'

'My inheritance? I'm not sure I'd listen to what Bear has to say because he seems to be saying a lot recently. It was Bear who told me …' She let her voice trail off. She'd almost said that it was Bear who told her that Jet would be at Rainbow's End the other day and that she was starting to wonder if he'd done that on purpose. 'I mean it was Bear who blabbed about Jet's loan from Mattie. I think he's a bit of a gossip.'

Ella shrugged. 'I'm keeping out of it. But I wondered if Garrick had mentioned it, that's all. It's the Kite Festival next Saturday. They were all talking about it last night. I think we need to get some kites and learn how to fly them so we can take part. We've got six days including today. That should be enough. It can't be hard to fly a kite, can it?'

It was very hard to fly a kite as Mia, Ella and Lori soon discovered. Garrick said there was no way he was getting involved so they left him alone each day while they went out to hone their dubious skills, but he joined them at the top of Frog Hill on the day of the Festival Competition.

The day was perfect for flying kites. The sky, a cloudless, baby blue was a pristine backdrop for the colourful kites and the lengths of trailing ribbons. The wind was warm as it travelled across the English Channel all the way from the Mediterranean and wavered somewhere between a force 3 and 4. Many of the villagers took part and half the battle was to ensure your kite didn't crash into someone else's. Several people seemed to be targeting one another's and screams of delight filled the air as the kites ducked and dived above the crowd.

'There's definitely a knack to this,' Ella shouted. 'And we haven't got it.'

'But at least it's fun,' Mia yelled, avoiding a near-crash and laughing hysterically as she managed to outmanoeuvre her opponent.

Lori pointed out, 'It's all good exercise and will be doing wonders for our bingo wings.'

'I don't have bingo wings,' Ella protested loudly.

'Give it time and you will,' shrieked Lori, laughing. 'Unless you use Mia's rowing machine.'

By the time the competition ended, the three of them could hardly speak but Lori won third prize, although none of them were sure how.

'It's because I winked at the judges,' she confided as she showed off her prize. Which was a much better kite than the one she had. 'I'm going to keep this up. I really enjoyed myself.'

'So did I,' Mia said, searching the crowd for one face in particular but looking away the moment she spotted him. Why did she need to know Jet was there? It was getting a bit annoying. It was as if he had some invisible hold on her and she couldn't break free. But she laughed when she saw Mattie chasing back and forth after various kites and leaping in the air in a bid to catch them despite each one being far out of reach of her furry paws.

The Festival lasted for the entire day and it wasn't all about kites. There were stalls selling cakes and sweets, and others selling refreshments. Some sold sunglasses and sun hats and others sold handmade goods such as cotton cushion covers, and crocheted shawls. There were games and races for children and the llamas Mia had seen on the very first day she arrived, were paraded back and forth for everyone to stroke and ooh and ahh at. Mia kept her distance.

'Allergic to llamas?' Jet appeared from nowhere and stood beside her.

'They come under the same category as farm animals as far as I'm concerned.' She tried to sound cool but her heart appeared to be soaring like her kite had been, twenty minutes earlier.

'I'm sure they'll be delighted to hear that. Well done on the kite flying. Is that a skill you acquired in London? Or something you've picked up recently?'

'Very recently. We only started last Sunday.'

'Then I'm doubly impressed.'

'That's made my day, as I'm sure you can imagine. Did you enjoy Midsummer's Eve?'

'Very much so, thanks. Did you?'

Mia glared at him. 'I went to bed early.'

'That sounds like fun. Naked?'

'What?' She intensified the glare.

'Just curious. You said you sleep naked, remember?'

She tried to appear nonchalant though she felt anything but. 'Yes. Naked apart from my perfume.'

'I like your perfume. I could breathe it in all day.' He moved a little closer.

Goose bumps ran up and down her spine. 'I'm so glad. I'll buy you some for Christmas. It'll make a change from smelling cow manure.'

'I hope you're not implying that I smell like cow manure.' He looked hurt.

'No! You always smell divine. I mean, fine.'

'That's good to know. Where's the love of your life?'

'Who?'

'Garrick. The man you're so in love with.'

'I know who I'm in love with.'

'Do you, Mia?'

She tutted. 'Yes. Of course, I do. He's getting some drinks, I think. I simply didn't hear what you said.'

'Have you told him about Rainbow's End?'

She glared at him some more. 'No. And you promised you wouldn't.'

'I did promise. And I won't say a word. I'm just surprised you haven't.'

'There's no need. It's over and done with.'

'Is it? I haven't seen you on the beach since then.'

'I'ye been busy learning to fly a kite.'

'You haven't been back since it happened, have you?'

'How do you know that?' Did the man have super-human powers?

'Because I know you better than you think. Don't let it set you back, Mia. You know what they say. If you fall off a horse you get straight back on.'

'Which is why I don't ride horses. I'll go back to the beach when I'm ready.'

'I hope so, Mia. It's important.'

He turned away and Mattie followed at his heels as usual.

Mia had a sudden and rather ridiculous urge to do the same, but Garrick returned, bearing drinks and she turned to him instead.

Chapter Nineteen

Lori was settling in. She had met Hettie and to Mia's surprise they had hit it off immediately. It was only after listening to one of their conversations that she realised her mum and Hettie talked alike. Not in the words they used or the tone in which they said them, but in their pattern of speech. They had a knack of stringing a number of sentences together, each one often about a completely different matter and hardly stopping for breath. Garrick had said something about it the evening Lori arrived.

'For a moment there I thought it was Hettie talking and not your mum,' he had said.

When Lori discovered Hettie enjoyed reading similar books to her, and mentioned her own book club, Hettie was all for starting a book club in Little Pondale.

'We could meet at one another's cottages once every fortnight, deary. How long does it take most people to read a book because I can read a book a day, unless it's one of those days where my dear Hector wants to chat, or dear Prince Gustav requires more attention than usual. Men are like that, aren't they deary? One day they're off doing their own thing and the next they're all like lost little boys and can't do a thing unless you do it with them. Don't you find that, deary? But listen to me talking ten chickens at a time. Mia dear, your lovely mum and I are going to start a book club. I'm sure you and Ella will want to join dear, especially as Ella edits books and everything.'

'That's wonderful, Hettie,' Mia had said. 'But are you sure that's a good idea, Mum?'

'I think it's a fabulous idea. We could even ask the men to join. I've always been one for equality. Men like reading romance and women enjoy a good murder. We could vary the selections. But would getting hold of books be a problem in the village? There's no public library for miles. Such a dreadful thing they're closing so many libraries these days. When I was a girl I lived in the library. In fact, that's where I met my dear, departed husband, Ernest. You're so lucky that Hector still comes to chat with you, Hettie. Ernest came to me for the first year or so. At least I like to think he did. Mainly in my dreams but every morning when I awoke, I half expected to find him there in bed beside me, our conversations had seemed so real. So let's get the book club started next week, shall we? I'm in training for the Frog Hill Run. I'll have to walk most of the way but it sounds like a fun morning and following behind a group of very fit men in shorts has an appeal all of its own. Don't you find that, Hettie?'

Mia had left them to it, but she later discovered that Lori was not the only one signed up to do the Frog Hill Run. Somehow her own name and Ella's too had been added to the list of participants. When she saw Jet's name on the list, she began her training right away, but as the mornings grew hotter with each passing day, so her wish that she could venture into the sea to cool off, increased. With Garrick by her side, she resumed her daily walks along the beach, although the walks had turned into a run, and she still hadn't told him why she had stopped for that week after the Summer Solstice. Fortunately, Tom still had not said a word about it. He didn't even mention it to her.

The friendship between Lori and Franklin Grant also grew warmer with each passing day, and Mia continued to be undecided as to whether that was good or bad.

'What's Franklin Grant like?' Mia asked Jet one morning when she spotted him walking Mattie along the beach. It was an exceedingly hot morning in the middle of July and the first time she had ventured to the beach alone since that fateful day in June. He was wearing khaki shorts and his tanned torso was bare as he paddled in the sea with Mattie by his side. At first she had been tempted to run the other way when she realised it was him. They hadn't seen much of each other since that day at the kite festival and she was still uneasy about the way she felt that day. But the opportunity to get to talk to him alone, outweighed any doubts she had and she slowed her pace to a walk and stopped several feet away from the edge of the water.

'What?' he said, putting one hand to his ear. 'I can't hear you. You'll have to come closer.'

'Don't be ridiculous. You can hear me. And there's no way I'm getting nearer to that sea. What's he like?'

The twitch tugged at the corners of his mouth and burst into a smile. 'It's good to see you on the beach again. If you stand there long enough, the sea will come to you. The tide is on the turn.'

'What?' Mia stepped back until she saw the look on Jet's face which for some reason made her step forward again. 'You once said you'd hold the tide away from me. Can I count on you to still do that?'

'You can count on me for anything, Mia. Anything at all.' He stared at her for a second or two then shook his head. 'Franklin Grant. Hmm. You've met him. Several times by now I should imagine. Haven't you formed your own opinion?'

'Yes. But you know him better and you've known him for much longer. I'd like your opinion.'

'Why?'

'Because he seems to be interested in my mum.'

'Lori's a very interesting woman. Who can blame him?'

'What's that supposed to mean?'

He walked towards her but Mattie looked from him to the sea and decided to stay where she was.

'It means exactly what I said. You mum's an interesting woman. She's also a very attractive woman. I can't blame him for liking her.'

'She's also several years older than he is.'

'So?'

'So.' She frowned at him. 'How would you feel if your mum started having an affair with a much younger man?'

'Absolutely astonished. She's been dead for five years.'

His remark took her so much by surprise that she couldn't think of anything to say other than, she was sorry, and she shouldn't have mentioned his mum. Especially as Hettie had told her how Sarah Cross had died, although she didn't mention that bit to Jet.

He shrugged. 'Why not? I think about her often. She's dead but she's not forgotten. And I'll tell you something for free. I'd give anything for her to be alive and having fun with any man, even if he was half her age. Life is short, Mia. We shouldn't spend it doing what other people think we should. We should do what is right for ourselves. Providing it's legal and it doesn't cause harm to others. Unless you fancy Franklin yourself, and that's the problem here, I'd say let her get on with it and have some fun.'

'I don't fancy Franklin! I'm in love with Garrick!'

'Ah yes. I keep forgetting. How is Garrick? We haven't seen him at rugby training for some time.'

'Garrick is fine. He's better than fine, he's fabulous. I didn't think you trained over the summer.'

'Fabulous? High praise indeed. We train throughout the year. But during the summer, a lot of our training is done in the pub.' He grinned. 'Seriously. Why haven't we seen much of Garrick? Nothing I've said or done, I hope.'

'He's been very busy. He's getting lots of orders and his business is thriving.'

'And he's spending all his free time with you? I can't blame him for that. I'd do the same if I had the chance.'

'You'd do what? I really can't figure you out, Jet Cross. One minute you behave as if you're some sort of guardian angel hovering in the background watching over me because Mattie asked you to, the next, you behave as if you hardly know I exist.'

'Oh, I'm aware you exist, Mia, believe me. But I've never said I was a guardian angel. Mattie asked me to keep an eye on you and I have. Although I haven't done a very good job because if I had, you wouldn't have been at Rainbow's End that day. But there's nothing I can do to change that now. It's nice to know you think of me as some sort of guardian angel though. Not so long ago you probably would've called me a peeping Tom. Or a devil.'

'Yuk! I can't imagine you staring into people's windows so I would never have called you a peeping Tom. A devil?' She shrugged. 'Possibly. But I think it's nice that you're keeping an eye on me. Not because I like you looking at me. I mean, looking out for me. But because it's good to know you're doing what Mattie asked you to. That shows you're a decent man.'

He pulled a face. 'Decent? Hmm. I'd rather have fabulous. But we can work on that. I always like to have something to aspire to.'

She tutted. 'The day I refer to you as fabulous will be the day hell freezes over.'

He grinned. 'Global warming's real you know. That may be sooner than you think.'

'I wouldn't bet on it.'

'I told you, Mia. I'm not a betting man.'

Their gaze locked and Mia couldn't drag her eyes from him. His grin broadened and he moved slowly towards her. She wanted to back away but her feet wouldn't move. To her amazement he took her hand in his and that feeling she had experienced that very first time, swept over her again. As if her hand had slipped into a perfectly fitting glove.

'Would you like to paddle?' He said, his voice little more than a whisper.

The spell was immediately broken.

'No way!' She backed away. 'I'm not ready for that.'

He squeezed her hand but then abruptly released it. 'I'll be here for you when you are ready, Mia. Remember that.'

She wasn't sure it was just paddling he was talking about.

He turned away. 'Mattie and I had better get home. The farm won't run itself. Oh. But don't worry about Franklin. He's a really great guy. I'd even go as far as to call him fabulous.' He grinned before becoming serious again. 'The only problem is, he's returning to the States at the end of August. But I'm pretty certain he'll have already told Lori that.'

Chapter Twenty

The morning of the Frog Hill Run was sweltering. Forecasters predicted it would be the hottest day so far this summer and that temperatures would reach thirty degrees centigrade at least. Not the ideal weather to be running up a hill. Not the ideal weather to be doing anything other than sipping a cold drink beneath the shade of a parasol, or swimming in the azure sea. And Mia wished more than anything that she could do both. Sipping the drink was easy. Swimming, not so much. She still hadn't managed to paddle her toes in the sea. At least not willingly. What happened at Rainbow's End still gave her palpitations.

But she was determined that, before this summer was over, she would put at least one foot in the cool, refreshing waters of the English Channel. The only fly in that particular ointment was that every time she imagined herself doing that, it was Jet who stood beside her and held her hand reassuringly in his, not Garrick, the man she loved.

She didn't understand how she could be so in love with one man and yet feel so close to another. Especially as, during the two months and a bit, she had been in Little Pondale, she hadn't got to know much more about Jet Cross than she knew the day she arrived. That he was confident, gorgeous, sexy to the core, had a reputation for breaking women's hearts, and for some reason, a man she was drawn to, despite not wanting to be. The only things she did know about him, were from his past. Even that, she'd heard from other people. Jet rarely seemed to talk about himself. At least, not to her.

'We're ready for this,' Ella said, as she, Mia and Lori stood in line at the foot of Frog Hill.

'Speak for yourself,' Mia said. 'I'd rather be back in bed.'

'So would I,' added Lori. 'And not alone.' She winked at Franklin who stood beside her.

He momentarily took Lori's hand and Mia let out an involuntary gasp. She quickly looked away. Jet was right. She would rather her mum be out and having fun and if that meant being with Franklin Grant, then it was her mum's choice and Mia would have to learn to live with it.

Garrick was at the finish line, waiting to cheer them on and it was Jet who came and stood behind her at the start line.

'Am I in the way? Do you want to get in front of me?' Mia asked him as he seemed to be edging ever closer to her body. His warm breath brushed her neck and sent tingles down her spine.

'No thanks. I'm enjoying the view. Besides I'll be in front of you soon enough.' He grinned.

'Oh yeah. I wouldn't be so sure about that. Eat my dust, sucker.'

He burst out laughing. 'In your dreams.'

'Would you like to put your money where your mouth is? I've got five pounds in my T-shirt pocket that says I'll beat you.' She turned to him and stuck her chin in the air.

His gaze drifted down to the little pocket over her left breast and he grinned.

'Forgetting for one moment that it's a bit weird to have five pounds in your pocket when all you're doing is running up a hill and back down again and there's nothing you can buy either going up or coming down. I've told you before, I'm not a betting man. Although I'd very much like to put my mouth where your money is.'

Mia gasped. Had he just said what she thought he had? She was so astonished at his comment that she missed the starter's gun and Jet shot past her, grinning at her over his shoulder. Had he done that on purpose?

It took her some time to catch him up and even then, it was obvious that he slowed his pace so she could do so.

'Is it too late to change my mind and take that bet?' He grinned as Ella, Lori and Justin all ran past. 'But if you win, I owe you a fiver. If I win, well, like I said, I'd like to put my mouth where your money is. Is that a deal?'

344

'No! And you're not a betting man.' She tried to outrun him.

He easily caught her up and he ran along beside her regardless of whether she picked up speed or slowed her pace. He wasn't even the slightest bit out of breath as they neared the top of the hill and just before the finish line of the first part of the race, he grinned at her and winked. 'Some things are too good a bet for any man to resist. Even a die-hard like me.'

He ran past her and reached the finish line as Garrick stepped out of the crowd and caught Mia in his arms.

'Now we get to start again and run back down,' Ella said, puffing and panting beside her in Justin's arms.

Like Jet, Justin was breathing naturally as if he'd just taken a five-minute walk, not run up a hill with a ten-degree incline in some parts of it. So was Franklin who was holding Lori's hand and smiling at her as she took several gulps of water. Lori didn't seem as exhausted as Mia which was both a relief and an irritation. Mia definitely needed to increase her fitness levels.

There was now no sign of Jet. He seemed to have disappeared into the crowd, but Mia spotted Mattie jumping up and down as someone Mia didn't recognise held her lead so Jet couldn't have gone far. A few minutes later he reappeared and took the lead from the man, smiling and thanking him as if he were a friend. Which of course, he probably was. Mia didn't know who Jet was friends with other than those in the village whom she'd met. He probably had friends all over the place. And possibly girlfriends too.

Did he have a girlfriend? The thought hadn't occurred to her before but now that it had, she had to know. She hadn't seen him with anyone but he was gorgeous, single and a red-blooded male. The probability was high. She would ask him the moment she got a chance. Not that it mattered, of course. She simply wanted to know.

They formed the line for the start of the run back down and this time, Jet stood nowhere near her. Typical of the man. When she didn't want him there he always popped up but when she wanted to ask him something, he was nowhere near her. And this time he didn't wait. He shot down the hill like a bullet from a gun and was long gone by the time Mia touched the finish line, puffing and panting as much as she had after the run up. She most certainly needed to work on her fitness.

But why Jet had disappeared was a mystery. Everyone else was going to the pub or mingling around the stalls that seemed to pop up at each of the events in Little Pondale.

It was only much later that Mia found out where Jet had gone and why, and it was Hettie who came to Sunbeam Cottage to tell her.

'It's Grace, deary,' Hettie said, looking flustered. 'Grace Tyburn, the vicar's grandma. She passed away during the Frog Hill Run. The vicar's beside himself, my dear. I was never very close to Grace and I may not entirely like the vicar but one thing I'll say about them was that they were devoted to one another. I was walking back from watching the run and I saw him running down the lane with Rupert. The next thing I see, deary, is Rupert dashing up the lane and racing back down again with Jet. I went to see if I could be of any help, because I knew at once that it must have something to do with Grace, but she had gone, my dear. I came away because there was nothing I could do. Rupert's notified the necessary people and Jet stayed to provide comfort for the vicar, dear.'

That surprised Mia more than anything. That Bear – and Tom – looked to Jet for support at such a time. But then again, didn't she feel safe and somehow comforted whenever Jet was around? Well, maybe not always comforted. Sometimes she felt downright annoyed. And sometimes she felt something else entirely. But that was a topic she had no intention of dwelling on right now. Or anytime in the future come to that.

'Is Tom okay?'

Hettie shook her head. 'Not from what I saw. But I'm sure he will be. Jet may be a heartbreaker but he's also the man you need at times like this, my dear. He sat by his dear mother's bedside for hours at a time and she told me herself what a great comfort he was. And I know Matilda thought a lot of Jet. She was often at the farm, or he came here. You wouldn't think they had a lot in common would you, deary? But they clearly did. I'm not sure what Tom Tyburn will do without his grandma. As I said, they were devoted to one another, deary. Absolutely devoted.'

That was the first time Mia thought she'd heard Hettie say Tom's name, other than when Hettie had first told her about all the single men in the village on the day Mia had arrived. It was also the first time Hettie had mentioned that Jet had been a frequent visitor to Sunbeam Cottage and Mia wasn't sure how she felt about that. But of course, he would have visited. Mattie had given him a loan and he had paid it back. That was probably why he came. And they were obviously friendly. She already knew that.

So why did she suddenly feel uneasy?

Chapter Twenty-One

Sweltering summer days surrendered to sultry summer nights as the days seemed to fly on wings and life in Little Pondale resumed a steady pace.

Tom's grandmother, Grace was buried two weeks after the Frog Hill Run and choir practice was resumed shortly after. His grandmother's death had hit Tom hard and Mia hadn't realised quite how devoted he had been to her, despite what Hettie had said. He walked around the village as if in a trance and struggled with his church duties. Everyone helped as best they could and offered comfort as often as needed.

One particularly hot morning, Mia got up very early, just as twilight broke and long before the sun had shown its face. She left Garrick asleep in bed and walked barefoot to the beach. The gentlest breeze tugged at her dress and her hair fell loosely over her shoulders. It would be the perfect morning for a swim – if only she could ever brave it.

A figure suddenly appeared from beneath the glass-like water and she realised it was Tom. He spotted her on the shore and waved and she waited for him to join her on the sand.

'How are you, Tom?' she asked, smiling affectionately.

'Good days and bad. It'll take time to adjust, I know. Everyone has been so kind. It's humbling to know so many people are there for me, especially as the role is usually reversed. I should be comforting them, not the other way around.'

'We all need comfort sometimes, Tom. If there's ever anything I can do, I sincerely hope you'll tell me. And I still owe you for not telling anyone about my near-death experience. Oh God! I'm sorry. That was tactless. So was blaspheming, I suppose. I'm not very good at this as you can tell.' She tried to make a joke of it for want of knowing what else to do.

'Don't worry,' he smiled wanly. 'There's never a right or wrong thing to say at times like these. Just knowing people care is the important thing. And knowing you care means a lot to me, Mia. I don't think you realise how much.' He stepped towards her and took her hand in his. 'Life is short, Mia. My grandmother was a grand old age but she let a lot of life pass her by. My grandfather died when I was young and many years later, Gran had a chance of having love in her life again. But she worried about what people might think and she let it slip out of her hands. She should've spoken out. She should've taken a chance. But instead she lived the rest of her days wondering what might have been and cursing herself for not grasping life by the coat tails.'

'I'm sorry to hear that, Tom. That's such a shame. My mum may have an opportunity at finding love again and I nearly tried to stop her. But someone pointed out to me that I should let her live her life. It's important to take our chances when we can. Even if it risks our hearts being bruised and our pride being trampled underfoot for a time.'

'That's precisely how I feel,' he said, staring deeply into her eyes. 'Mia?'

'Yes, Tom?'

A deep furrow formed between his brows and he licked his lips in a nervous fashion. He shook his head, took a deep breath and the words tumbled out of him so fast that Misa wasn't sure she heard correctly.

'I know you probably don't feel anything for me but I love you, Mia. I really, truly love you.' He pulled her into his arms.

She was so astonished that before she had a chance to stop him, he'd kissed her on the lips.

He let her go just as quickly and the expression on his face was a mixture of jubilation and mortification.

'I am so, so sorry, Mia! I have no idea what came over me. Please, please forgive me.'

He almost looked ready to burst into tears. The poor man was in serious distress.

She forced a comforting smile. 'Don't worry about it, Tom. There's no harm done. You're going through a terrible time. You're not yourself, I know that. Please, let's simply forget it happened. I won't mention it if you don't. It'll be another little secret between us. Just like the secret of Rainbow's End. Okay?'

He let out a long, sad sigh. 'Just like Rainbow's End.' He smiled sheepishly. 'Thank you so much, Mia. And thank you for being so … so understanding. I suppose I'd better go and put some clothes on.' He pointed to his swim shorts and smiled again. 'This means the world to me, Mia. Thank you. I won't forget today.'

He wouldn't be the only one.

Mia wouldn't forget being kissed by a vicar, in a hurry. Especially as it was actually a pleasant experience. Or it would have been if she hadn't had a boyfriend.

Chapter Twenty-Two

Mia didn't tell anyone about the kiss she and Tom had shared and the next time she saw him, after an initial moment of awkwardness, everything had been as it was before, except that he was still obviously grieving over his grandmother, Grace.

The days grew hotter and the nights more sultry and passion seemed to fill the air. Everyone was falling in love, or appeared to be. Everyone except Tom, although if what he had said that day on the beach was true, he was in love. It was simply unrequited. Ella and Justin spent nearly all their free time together now. Garrick seemed to be even more attentive and more passionate with each passing day. Lori and Franklin had now officially become an item, even though she said she was fully aware he would be returning to the States before too long.

Even Hettie had found a 'new friend'. He had heard of the book club, thanks to an on- line group Lori had set up and he travelled from a nearby village to come to the fortnightly meetings. After only two, it was clear, according to Lori, that it was more than reading books that interested him, but everyone was still surprised when Hettie turned up at The Frog and Lily with Fred one evening and told them, with a girlish giggle, that she and Fred were on a date.

Bear was now dating a friend of Alexia's, from the town, fifteen miles away, but Mia hadn't met her yet and Alexia was dating one of the members of Justin's dance troupe while Toby was dating the same man's sister. It all sounded very friendly, but that didn't stop Ella from questioning why Alexia and Toby had suddenly fallen for people they'd known for years. Until Mia pointed out that she had known Garrick for years and they had only recently fallen in love. She didn't add that she'd had a crush on Garrick on and off for most of her life.

There was one other person who now had a girlfriend, so Garrick told Mia early one morning. It was on the day of the Little Pondale Summer Fête.

'I didn't know Jet Cross had a girlfriend, did you?' Garrick asked, putting a shopping tote bag on the kitchen table.

Mia dropped the vase she was washing but thankfully it landed back in the bowl of water with a splash as she spun around to face him. 'A girlfriend? No. I didn't know. Did he tell you that?'

Garrick shook his head. 'No. But I saw them together this morning.'

'What makes you think it was his girlfriend? Did he say it was?' She gripped the edge of the sink with one hand and turned back to stare into the soapy water.

'No. It was when I was on my way back from Little Pond Farm. I went to get eggs, milk and cheese and Franklin served me. When I came back down the drive, I heard a woman laughing and looked back towards the house. Jet was leaving the house with a buxom blonde on his arm.'

'A buxom blonde?' Mia cleared her throat. 'Well that doesn't necessarily mean she's his girlfriend, does it?'

'I suppose not. But from where I was standing, she was certainly behaving like a girlfriend. As I said, she had her arm through his and they were laughing and looking at one another as if they were the best of friends.'

'Perhaps they are. Friends, I mean.'

'I've never seen the woman before. And they looked very friendly. She was even adjusting his shirt collar as they walked towards a gleaming red sportscar. It was early, don't forget. It's only eight, now. She had obviously either spent the night, or she's a very early visitor.'

'Perhaps, like you, she was there to buy provisions.'

Garrick laughed. 'She wasn't dressed like a woman shopping for food. She was dressed like a woman on a date. Perhaps he'll bring her to the

Summer Fête. Then you'll see her for yourself and you can decide if she's his girlfriend or not.'

'Why should I care if she's his girlfriend? It's none of my concern. He's single. He can have a girlfriend if he wants.'

'Okay. There's no need to bite my head off.'

'Sorry. I'm just feeling tired this morning. It's going to be another scorching day by the feel of it. I'd rather spend the day standing under the shower than go to this Summer Fête.'

Garrick came and slid his arms around her waist. 'The shower sounds pretty good to me.' He kissed her neck but she moved her head away.

'Is something wrong, Mia?' He turned her around to face him. 'You seemed fine when I went out. Now, less than twenty minutes later, you're suddenly feeling tired. This doesn't have anything to do with the fact that Jet may have a girlfriend, does it?'

'No! No, of course it doesn't. I told you. I don't care if he has a girlfriend or not. I'm just surprised no one's mentioned it, that's all. And yes, I'm suddenly feeling tired.' She wrapped her arms around him and held him tight.

'We could always go back to bed for an hour or so,' he said, easing her away and kissing her softly on the lips.

'Yes,' she said. 'Let's do that. I can't think of anything I'd rather do right now than go to bed with the man I love.' And she stood on her tiptoes and kissed him.

She had to do something to get Jet Cross and a buxom blonde out of her head.

Chapter Twenty-Three

'So this is the Annual Summer Fête,' Mia said, as she walked hand in hand with Garrick amongst the stalls and tents surrounding the village pond.

Garrick smiled lovingly down at her. 'That's what it said on the flyer.'

Mia was hoping to see Justin and Ella. She had missed Ella this morning because she and Garrick had gone back to bed and by the time they got up again, Ella had left the cottage. If Jet had a girlfriend, surely Justin would know? And if he knew, he'd tell Ella. Why hadn't Ella mentioned it? Failing that, Lori was meeting Franklin here. Franklin would definitely know. He was staying at Little Pond Farm. He would know who came and went.

Everyone in the village was at the Summer Fête, and that meant Jet would be here somewhere. Jet and possibly his new girlfriend. Mia wasn't sure whether she wanted to see them or not. She'd rather know first from Justin or Franklin. Then at least she could prepare herself.

Prepare herself for what? She was in love with Garrick. She was Garrick's girlfriend. Why was she getting so distressed at the thought of seeing Jet with a woman? It didn't make any sense.

And then she saw him. And he smiled.

And suddenly it did.

It made complete sense.

Yes, she was in love with Garrick.

But she was also, clearly, more than a little in love with Jet.

'Hello, Mia. Hi Garrick,' he said, smiling as he looked Mia in the eye.

He was alone. And Mia breathed a sigh of relief.

Until a beautiful, buxom blonde around Mia's age rushed up and grabbed his hand.

'Jet!' she shrieked. 'There's a fortune-teller. Let's go and get our fortunes told.'

He smiled tenderly and Mia was sure a bone in her ribcage must have broken because something had just pierced her heart.

'It's not really my scene, but fine, if that's what you want, let's do it.'

Was Jet always so easily persuaded? Or was it just this woman's ample charms?

'Oh, sorry,' he said, grinning at Mia as if he knew what she was feeling. 'This is Tiffany. Tiff. This is Mia and her boyfriend, Garrick. Oh, and here comes Mia's mum, Lori and Mia's best friend, Ella. Franklin and Justin, you already know.'

Mia turned to see Lori and Franklin and Ella and Justin just feet away, walking towards them, smiling.

'Hi everyone,' Tiffany said. 'Jet and I were about to go and have our fortunes told. Why don't we all go? Won't that be fun?'

Mia couldn't think of anything worse at that precise moment. Well she could, but she didn't want to think about Jet and Tiffany walking hand in hand along the beach, sharing long, slow kisses, or making mad passionate love in Jet's bed at Little Pond Farm.

'There's a fortune-teller?' Ella queried, grinning at Mia. 'Bloody Nora, yes! I'm definitely up for that. Let's go.'

Before she knew what was happening, Mia was being led towards the fortune-teller's tent.

When Tiffany went in, Mia wanted to ask Jet then and there how long they had been dating, but she stopped herself from doing so and instead, he and Garrick discussed the weather. Surely someone else would ask? But no one did. She tried in vain, to catch Ella's eye and to ask if she knew who Tiffany was, but Ella and Justin were staring into one another's eyes and Lori and Franklin were just as bad.

Once or twice, she stole a glance at Jet and each time she did, he was looking at her with a strange glint in his eyes. Garrick must have noticed because he tightened his arm about Mia's waist.

'Tiffany seems nice,' Garrick finally said.

'She is,' Jet replied, with a grin.

'Have you known her long?'

Before Jet had time to answer Garrick's question, Tiffany came bursting out and screamed at the top of her lungs.

'Jet! Jet! You'll never believe this. The woman said I'll soon be getting engaged! Isn't that wonderful? Can it be true?'

He smiled and shrugged his shoulders. 'If that's what she said, who am I to disagree?'

Tiffany threw her arms around him and hugged him as she screamed with joy, but for someone who was going to propose to his new girlfriend outside a fortune-teller's tent, he didn't seem quite as euphoric about it as Tiffany clearly was.

'You go next,' Ella said, pushing Mia forward.

Mia was grateful to her friend. At least in the tent, no one would see her cry. Or perhaps that was being overly dramatic. At least she wouldn't see Jet propose. She bit back the tears and took a seat.

'I see great fortune for you,' the woman said, peering into a cloudy-looking crystal ball the moment Mia sat down. 'I also see great sadness and a cold wind from the north.'

So the woman gave weather forecasts as well as telling people's fortunes? How bizarre.

'I see love that's black and white and surprising too. I see a man you can't forget, and a woman you want to remember. I see happiness and joy beyond your wildest dreams. I see water and fear and overcoming things that have held you back for so long. But I also see someone who you think you can trust. You can't. Beware! Feelings may not be genuine. Love may not be where you are looking for it. And someone you love will soon walk out of your life. You can't hold them back. Some things are meant to be and some are not. That is all I see. That will be fifteen pounds.'

'Thanks,' Mia said, utterly bewildered. What on earth had that all been about? She paid the woman and got up to leave.

'Wait!' The woman stood up. 'A bell is tolling. It's a beautiful sound but it brings a warning. Never fear. An angel is on your shoulder. Choose love wisely. You could so easily make a mistake. And autumn will bring many changes and many opportunities.'

'Thank you,' Mia said. 'Will that bit cost me extra?'

The woman smiled, but it wasn't an altogether friendly one. 'No. That bit was free. You're a disbeliever, I can tell. But the spirits don't lie. And there's a very powerful spirit surrounding you. A very powerful spirit indeed.'

Mia smiled, pushed open the tent curtain and walked into the blinding sunlight.

'What did she say?' Ella and Lori asked in unison.

'Yes, what did she say?' Jet repeated. Tiffany was nowhere to be seen.

'Well, I'm not getting engaged,' Mia said.

Everyone turned to Garrick as he made a choking sound and his face was as crimson as the tent curtain. He swallowed and fiddled in his pocket.

Jet narrowed his eyes and looked Garrick up and down. 'I wouldn't be so sure,' he said. And he turned and walked away.

Mia stood and watched him go and a cold shiver ran down her spine, despite the searing heat of the day. Her heart wanted her to call his name, but her head wouldn't let her. It seemed the fortune-teller's prophecy was already coming true. And she wished she hadn't stepped over the threshold of the fortune-teller's tent. Because right now, she'd give anything not to know that Jet Cross wasn't simply walking away. He was walking out of her life.

End of Part Two: Summer secrets

Will Jet walk out of Mia's life forever?
And will the rest of the fortune-teller's predictions for Mia come true?
What did the fortune-teller have to say for Ella, Garrick and Lori?

Find out in Book Two, containing:
Part Three: Autumn leaves and
Part Four: Trick or Treat
Coming soon.

Coming soon

The Cottage on Lily Pond Lane –
Book Two
Part Three: Autumn leaves.
Part Four: Trick or treat

A Note from Emily

Thank you for reading this book. A little piece of my heart goes into all of my books and when I send them on their way, I really hope they bring a smile to someone's face. If this book made you smile, or gave you a few pleasant hours of relaxation, I'd love it if you would tell your friends.

I'd be really happy if you have a minute or two to post a review. Just a line will do, and a kind review makes such a difference to my day – to any author's day. Huge thanks to those of you who do so, and for your lovely comments and support on social media. Thank you.

A writer's life can be lonely at times. Sharing a virtual cup of coffee or a glass of wine, or exchanging a few friendly words on Facebook, Twitter or Instagram is so much fun.

You might like to join my Readers' Club by signing up for my newsletter. It's absolutely free, your email address is safe and won't be shared and I won't bombard you, I promise. You can enter competitions and enjoy some giveaways. In addition to that, there's my author page on Facebook and there's also a new Facebook group. You can chat with me and with other fans and get access to my book news, snippets from my daily life, early extracts from my books and lots more besides. Details are on the 'For You' page of my website. You'll find all my contact links in the Contact section following this.

I'm working on my next book right now. Let's see where my characters take us this time. Hope to chat with you soon.

To see details of my other books, please go to the books page on my website, or scan the QR code below to see all my books on Amazon.

Contact

If you want to be the first to hear Emily's news, find out about book releases, enter competitions and gain automatic entry into her Readers' Club, go to: https://www.emilyharvale.com and subscribe to her newsletter via the 'Sign me up' box. If you love Emily's books and want to chat with her and other fans, ask to join the exclusive Emily Harvale's Readers' Club Facebook group.

Or come and say 'Hello' on Facebook, Twitter and Instagram.

Contact Emily via social media:
www.twitter.com/emilyharvale
www.facebook.com/emilyharvalewriter
www.facebook.com/emilyharvale
www.instagram.com/emilyharvale

Or by email via the website:
www.emilyharvale.com